SPINNING-WHEEL STORIES

"THAT'S THE SORT I LIKE," SAID JEOFF AS AUNT ELINOR ENDED
THE STORY.

Spinning Wheel Stories   *Frontispiece (Page 99)*

Spinning-Wheel Stories

By
LOUISA M. ALCOTT

AUTHOR OF "SILVER PITCHERS," "PROVERB STORIES," "A GARLAND
FOR GIRLS," "LITTLE WOMEN," "AN OLD-FASHIONED
GIRL," "WORK, A STORY OF EXPERIENCE,"
"MOODS, A NOVEL," ETC.

ILLUSTRATED BY
WILLIAM A. McCULLOUGH

GROSSET & DUNLAP
Publishers   New York

CONTENTS

SPINNING-WHEEL STORIES

SPINNING-WHEEL
STORIES

———◆———

GRANDMA'S STORY

" IT is too bad to have our jolly vacation
spoiled by this provoking storm. Did n't
mind it yesterday, because we could eat
all the time; but here we are cooped up for a
week, perhaps, and I 'd like to know what we are
to do," growled Geoff, as he stood at the window looking gloomily at the bleak scene without.
It certainly was discouraging; for the north
wind howled, the air was dark with falling snow,
and drifts were rising over fences, roads, and
fields, as if to barricade the Christmas party in
the great country house.

" We can bear it pleasantly, since it can't be
helped," said gentle sister Mary, with a kind
hand on his shoulder, and a face full of sympathy for his disappointment. " I 'm sorry for
the coasting, skating, and sleighing frolics we
have lost; but if we must be shut up, I 'm sure
we could n't have a pleasanter prison or a kinder

jailer. Don't let grandma hear us complain, for she has made great exertions to have our visit a merry one, and it will trouble her if we are not gay and contented."

"That's easy for a parcel of girls, who only want to mull over the fire, and chatter, and drink tea; but it's rough on us fellows, who come for the outside fun. House is well enough; but when you've seen it once, there's an end. Eating is jolly, but you can't stuff forever. We might dig, or snowball, if it did n't blow a gale. Never saw such a beast of a storm!" — and Geoff flattened his nose against the window-pane and scowled at the elements.

A laugh made him turn around, and forget his woes to stare at the quaint little figure that stood curtseying in the door-way of the keeping-room, where a dozen young people were penned while the maids cleared up the remains of yesterday's feast in the kitchen, the mothers were busy with the babies upstairs, and the fathers read papers in the best parlor; for this was a family gathering under the roof of the old homestead.

A rosy, dark-eyed face looked out from the faded green calash, a gayly flowered gown was looped up over a blue quilted petticoat, and a red camlet cloak hung down behind. A big reticule and a funny umbrella were held in either hand, and red hose and very high-heeled, pointed shoes covered a trim pair of feet.

"God bless you, merry gentlemen !
May nothing you dismay;
Here's your ancient granny come
To call, this Christmas day,"

sang Minnie, the lively member of the flock, as
she bobbed little curtseys and smiled so infec-
tiously that even cross Geoff cheered up.

"Where did you get that rigging?" "Isn't
it becoming?" "What queer stuff!" "Did
grandma ever look so, I wonder?"

These and many other questions rained upon
the wearer of the old costume, and she answered
them as fast as she could.

"I went rummaging up garret for something
to read, and found two chests of old duds.
Thought I'd dress up and see how you liked me.
Grandma said I might, and told me I looked
like her when she was young. She was a beauty,
you know; so I feel as proud as a peacock."
And Min danced away to stand before the portrait of a blooming girl in a short-waisted white-
satin gown and a pearl necklace, which hung
opposite the companion portrait of an officer in
an old-fashioned uniform.

"So you do. Wonder if I should look like
grandpa if I got into his old toggery!" said
Geoff, looking up at the handsome man with the
queue and the high coat-collar.

"Go and try; the uniform is in the chest, and

not much moth-eaten. Let's have a jolly rummage, and see what we can find. *We* did n't eat ourselves sick, so we will amuse these lazy invalids;" and Min glanced pityingly at several cousins who lay about on sofas or in easy chairs, pretending to read, but evidently suffering from too great devotion to the bountiful dinner and evening feast of yesterday.

Away went Min and Lotty, Geoff and Walt, glad of anything to beguile the stormy afternoon. Grandma smiled as she heard the tramp of feet overhead, the peals of laughter, and the bang of chest-lids, well knowing that a scene of dire confusion awaited her when the noisy frolic was done, but thankful for the stores of ancient finery which would keep the restless children happy for a day.

It was truly a noble garret, for it extended the whole length of the great square house, with windows at either end, and divided in the middle by a solid chimney. All around stood rows of chests, dilapidated furniture, and wardrobes full of old relics, while the walls were hung with many things for which modern tongues can find no names. In one corner was a bookcase full of musty books and papers; in another, kitchen utensils and rusty weapons; the third was devoted to quilts hung on lines, and in the fourth stood a loom with a spinning-wheel beside it, both seemingly well cared for, as the dust lay lightly on them, and flax was still upon the distaff.

A glorious rummage followed the irruption of the Goths and Vandals into this quiet spot, and soon Geoff quite forgot the storm as he pranced about in the buff-and-blue coat, with a cocked hat on his head, and grandfather's sword at his side. Lotty arrayed herself in a pumpkin hood and quilted cloak for warmth, while Walt, the book-worm, went straight to the ancient library, and became absorbed in faded souvenirs, yellow newspapers, and almanacs of a century ago.

Having displayed themselves below and romped all over the house, the masqueraders grew tired at last, and early twilight warned them to leave before ghostly shadows began to haunt the garret.

"I mean to take this down and ask grandma to show me how it's done. I've heard her tell about spinning and weaving when she was a girl, and I know I can learn," said Minnie, who had fallen in love with the little wheel, and vainly tried to twist the flax into as smooth a thread as the one hanging from the distaff, as if shadowy fingers had lately spun it.

"Queen Victoria set the fashion in England, and we might do it here. Would n't it be fun to have a wheel in the parlor at home, and really use it; not keep it tied up with blue ribbons, as the other girls do!" cried Lotty, charmed with the new idea.

"Come, Geoff, take it down for us. You ought to do it out of gratitude for my cheering you up so nicely," said Min, leading the way.

"So I will. Here, Walt, give it a hoist, and come behind to pick up the pieces, for the old machine must be about a hundred, I guess."

Shouldering the wheel, Geoff carried it down; but no bits fell by the way, for the stout little wheel was all in order, kept so by loving hands that for more than eighty years had been spinning the mingled thread of a long and useful life.

Glorious fires were roaring up the wide chimneys in parlor and keeping-room, and old and young were gathering around them, while the storm beat on the window-panes, and the wintry wind howled as if angry at being shut out.

"See what we 've stolen, grandma," cried Min, as the procession came in, rosy, dusty, gay, and eager.

"Bless the child! What possessed you to lug that old thing down?" asked Madam Shirley, much amused as the prize was placed before her, where she sat in her high-backed chair, — a right splendid old lady in her stately cap, black silk gown, and muslin apron, with a bunch of keys at her side, like a model housekeeper, as she was.

"You don't mind our playing with it, do you? And will you teach me to spin? I think it 's such a pretty little thing, and I want to be like you in

all ways, grandma dear," answered Min, sitting
on the arm of the great chair, with her fresh
cheek close to the wrinkled one where winter
roses still bloomed.

"You wheedling gipsy! I'll teach you with
all my heart, for it is pretty work, and I often
wonder ladies don't keep it up. I did till I was
too busy, and now I often take a turn at it when
I'm tired of knitting. The hum is very soothing, and the thread much stronger than any we
get nowadays."

As she spoke, the old lady dusted the wheel,
and gave it a skilful turn or two, till the soft
whir made pleasant music in the room.

"Is it really a hundred years old?" asked
Geoff, drawing nearer with the others to watch
the new work.

"Just about. It was one of my mother's wedding presents, and she gave it to me when I was
fifteen. Deary me, how well I remember that
day!" and grandma seemed to fall a-dreaming
as her eyes rested on the letters E. R. M. rudely
cut in the wood, and below these were three
others with something meant for a true lover's
knot between.

"Whose initials are these?" asked Min,
scenting a romance with girlish quickness, for
grandma was smiling as if her eyes read the title
to some little story in those worn letters.

"Elizabeth Rachel Morgan, and Joel Manlius
Shirley. Your blessed grandfather cut our names

there the day I was sixteen, and put the flourish
between to show what he wanted," added the
old lady, laughing as she made the wheel hum
again.

"Tell about it, please do," begged Min, remembering that grandma had been a beauty and
a belle.

"It's a long tale, my darling, and I couldn't
tell it now. Sometime when I'm teaching you
to spin I'll do it, maybe."

But the girl was determined to have her story;
and after tea, when the little ones were in bed,
the elders playing whist in the parlor, and the
young folks deciding what game to begin, Minnie sat down and tried to spin, sure that the
familiar sound would lure grandma to give the
lesson and tell the tale.

She was right, for the wheel had not gone
around many times, when the tap of the cane
was heard, and the old lady came rustling in,
quite ready for a chat, now that three cups of
her own good tea and a nap in the chimney
corner had refreshed her.

"No, dear, that's not the way; you need a
dish of water to wet your fingers in, and you
must draw the flax out slow and steady, else
it runs to waste, and makes a poor thread.
Fetch me that chair, and I'll show you how,
since you are bent on learning."

Establishing herself in the straight-back seat,

a skilful tap of the foot set the wheel in swift
and easy motion, and the gray thread twisted
fine and evenly from the distaff.

"Isn't it a pretty picture?" said Min to
Lotty, as they watched the old lady work.

"Not so pretty as the one I used to see when
my dear mother sat here, and I, a little child, at
her knee. Ah, my dears, she could have told
you stories all night long, and well worth hearing. I was never tired of them."

"Please tell me now, grandma. We don't
know what to play, and it would be so nice to
sit around the fire and hear it this stormy night,"
suggested Min, artfully seizing the hint.

"Do! Do! We all love stories, and we'll
be as still as mice," added Geoff, beckoning to
the others as he took the big arm-chair, being
the oldest grandson and leader of the flock.

Camping on the rug, or nestling in the sofa
corner, the boys and girls all turned expectant
faces toward grandma, who settled her cap-
strings and smoothed her spotless apron, with an
indulgent smile at her little audience.

"I don't know which one to tell first."

"The ghost story; that's a splendid one, and
most of the children never heard it," said Walt.

"Have Indians and fighting in it. I like that
kind," added Geoff.

"No; tell a love story. They are *so* interesting," said Lotty.

"I want the story about the initials first. I know it is very sentimental. So do begin with that, grandma," begged Min.

"Well, dears, perhaps I'd better choose that one, for it has the battle of New Orleans, and wolves, and spinning, and sweethearts in it; so it will suit you all, I hope."

"Oh, lovely! Do begin right away," cried Minnie, as the clapping of hands showed how satisfactory the prospect was.

Grandma gave a loud "hem!" and began at once, while the little wheel hummed a soft accompaniment to her words.

GRANDMA'S STORY

"When I was fifteen, my mother gave me this wheel, and said: 'Now, daughter Betsey, it is time for you to begin your wedding outfit, for I mistrust you'll marry young.' In those days girls spun and wove webs of fine linen and laid 'em up in chests, with lavender and rosemary, for sheets and table-linen after they married. So I spun away, making all manner of fine plans in my silly head, for I was a pretty piece, they all said, and young as I was, two or three fine lads used to come evenings and sit staring at me while I worked.

"Among these, was my neighbor Joel Manlius Shirley, and I was fond of him; but he had n't much money, so I put on airs, and tried his patience very much.   One day he came in and said: 'Betsey, I'm going a-soldiering; they need men, and I'm off.   Will you think of poor Joe when I'm gone?'

" I don't know how I looked, but I felt as if I could n't bear it.   Only I was too proud to show my trouble; so I laughed, and gave my wheel a twist, and said I was glad of it, since anything was better than hanging round at home.

" That hurt him; but he was always gentle to saucy Betsey, and taking out his knife, he cut those letters under mine, saying, with a look I never could forget: —

" 'That will remind you of me if you are likely to forget.   Good-by; I'm going right away and may never come back.'

" He kissed me, and was off before I could say a word, and then I cried till my flax was wet and my thread tangled, and my heart 'most broken.   Deary me, how well I remember that heavy day!"

Grandma smiled, but something shone in her old eyes very like a tear, and sentimental Lotty felt deeply interested at this point.

" Where does the fighting come in?" asked Geoff, who was of a military turn, as became the descendant of a soldier.

" I did n't know or care much about the War of 1812, except as far as the safety of one man was concerned.   Joe got on without any harm till the battle of New Orleans, when he was nearly killed behind the cotton-bale breastworks General Jackson built."

"Yes, I know all about it. Jackson fought against twelve thousand, and lost only seven men. That was the last battle of the war, January 8, 1815. Three cheers for grandpa!" shouted Geoff, waving a tidy, as no hat was at hand.

The others echoed the hurrah, and grandma beamed with pride as she went on: "We could n't get news from the army very often in those troublous times, and Joe was gone two years before the war ended. After the great battle we had no news for a long spell, and we feared he was one of the seven men killed. Those were dreadful days for all of us. My honored mother was a pious soul, and so was Mrs. Shirley; and they kept up their hearts with hope and prayer; but I, poor thing, was young and weak, and I cried myself half blind, remembering how naughty I had been. I would spin no more, but set the wheel away, saying I should have no need of wedding gear, as I should never marry; and I wore black ribbon on my caps, and one of Joe's buttons strung about my neck, mourning dismally for my lost dear.

"So the winter ended, and the summer went, and no news came of Joe. All said he was dead, and we had prayers at church, and talked of setting up a stone in the grave-yard, and I thought my life was done; for I pined sadly, and felt as

if I could never laugh again. But I did; for the
Lord was very good to us, and out of danger
and captivity delivered that dear boy."

Grandma spoke solemnly, and folded her
hands in thanksgiving as she looked up at the
picture of the handsome officer hanging on the
wall before her. The elder children could just
remember grandpa as a very old and feeble man,
and it struck them as funny to speak of him as
a " dear boy; " but they never smiled, and duti-
fully lifted their eyes to the queue and the high-
collared coat, wondering if Joe was as rosy in
real life as in the portrait.

" Well, that's the sentimental part; now
comes the merry part, and that will suit the
boys," said the old lady, briskly, as she spun
away, — and went on in a lively tone: —

" One December day, as I sat by that very
window, dreaming sorrowfully at my sewing
work, while old Sally nodded over her knitting
by the fire, I saw a man come creeping along by
the fence and dodge behind the wood-pile.
There were many bad folks 'round in those
times; for war always leaves a sight of lazy
rascals afloat as well as poor fellows maimed and
homeless.

" Mother had gone over to the sewing society
at Mrs. Shirley's, and I was all alone; for Sally
was so stiff with rheumatics she could scarce stir,
and that was why I stayed to take care of her.
The old musket always hung over the kitchen

chimney-piece, loaded, and I knew how to fire it,
for Joe had taught me. So away I went and
got it down; for I saw the man popping up his
head now and then to spy the land, and I felt
sure he meant mischief. I knew Sally would
only scream like a scared hen, so I let her sleep;
and getting behind the shutter I pointed my gun,
and waited to blaze away as soon as the enemy
showed signs of attacking.

"Presently he came creeping up to the back
door, and I heard him try the latch. All was
fast, so I just slipped into the kitchen and stood
behind the settle, for I was surer than ever he
was a rascal since I'd seen him nearer. He was
a tall man, dreadful shabby in an old coat and
boots, a ragged hat over his eyes, and a great
beard hiding the lower part of his face. He had
a little bundle and a big stick in his hands, and
limped as if foot-sore or lame.

"I was much afeard; but those were times
that made heroes of men, and taught women to
be brave for love of home and country. So I kept
steady, with my eye on the window, and my
finger on the trigger of the old gun, that had n't
been fired for years. Presently the man looked
in, and I saw what a strange roll his great eyes
had, for he was thin-faced and looked half-
starved. If mother had been there, she 'd have
called him in and fed him well, but I dared not,
and when he tried the window I aimed, but did
not fire; for finding the button down he went

away, and I dropped on the settle, shaking like a leaf. All was still, and in a minute I plucked up courage to go to look out a bit; but just as I reached the middle of the kitchen, the buttery door opened, and there stood the robber, with a carving knife in one hand and my best loaf of spice bread in the other. He said something, and made a rush at me; but I pulled the trigger, saw a flash, felt a blow, and fell somewhere, thinking, 'Now I'm dead!'"

Here grandma paused for breath, having spoken rapidly and acted out the scene dramatically, to the intense delight of the children, who sat like images of interest, staring at her with round eyes.

"But you weren't dead? What next?" cried Walt, eagerly.

"Bless you, no! I only fell into Joe's arms, and when I came to, there the dear fellow was, crying over me like a baby, while old Sally danced round us like a bedlamite, in spite of her rheumatics, shouting: 'Hosanna! Thanks and praise! He's come, he's come!'"

"Was he shot?" asked Geoff, anxious for a little bloodshed.

"No, dear; the old gun burst and hurt my hands, but not a mite of harm was done to Joe. I don't think I could tell all that happened for a spell, being quite dazed with joy and surprise; but by the time mother came home I was as peart as a wren, and Joe was at the table eating and drinking every mortal thing I could find in the house.

"He'd been kept a prisoner till exchanged, and had had a hard time getting home, with little money and a bad wound in the leg, besides being feeble with jail fever. But we did n't fret over past troubles, being so glad to get him back. How my blessed mother did laugh, when we told her the reception I gave the poor lad! But I said it served him right, since he came sneaking home like a thief, instead of marching in like a hero. Then he owned that he came there to get something to eat, being ashamed to go in upon his mother with all her company about her. So we fed and comforted him; and when we'd got our wits about us, I whipped away to Mrs. Shirley's and told my news, and every one of those twenty-five women went straight over to our house and burst in upon poor Joe, as he lay resting on the settle. That was my revenge for the scare he gave me, and a fine one it was; for the women chattered over him like a flock of magpies, and I sat in the corner and laughed at him. Ah, I was a sad puss in those days!"

The old lady's black eyes twinkled with fun, and the children laughed with her, till Walt caused a lull by asking: —

"Where do the wolves come in, grandma?"

"Right along, dear; I 'm not likely to forget 'em, for they most cost me my life, to say nothing of my new slippers. There was great re-

joicing over Joe, and every one wanted to do
something to honor our hero; for he had done
well, we found out, when the General heard his
story. We had a great dinner, and Judge Mulli-
kin gave a supper; but Major Belknap was
bound to outshine the rest, so he invited all the
young folks over to his house, nigh ten miles
away, to a ball, and we all went. I made myself
fine, you may believe, and wore a pair of blue
kid slippers, with mother's best buckles to set
'em off. Joe had a new uniform, and was an
elegant figure of a man, I do assure you. He
could n't dance, poor dear, being still very lame:
but I was a proud girl when I marched into that
ballroom on the arm of my limping beau. The
men cheered, and the ladies stood up in chairs
to see him, and he was as red as my ribbons,
and I could hardly keep from crying, as I held
him up, — the floor being slippery as glass with
the extra waxing it had got.

"I declared I would n't dance, because Joe
could n't; but he made me, saying he could see
me better; so I footed it till two o'clock, soon
forgetting all my sorrow and my good resolu-
tions as well. I wanted to show Joe that I was
as much a favorite as ever, though I'd lived
like a widow for a year. Young folks will be
giddy, and I hope these girls will take warning
by me and behave better when their time comes.
There may n't be any wolves to sober 'em, but
trouble of some sort always follows foolish ac-

tions; so be careful, my dears, and behave with propriety when you 'come out,' as you call it nowadays."

Grandma held up a warning forefinger at the girls, and shook her head impressively, feeling that the moral of her tale must be made clear before she went on. But the lassies blushed a little, and the lads looked all impatience, so the dear old lady introduced the wolves as quickly as she could.

" About half-past two, Joe and I drove off home with four fine hams in the bottom of the sleigh, sent by the Major to our mothers. It was a bitter-cold February night, with just light enough to see the road, and splendid sleighing; so we went along at a good pace, till we came to the great woods. They are all gone now, and the woollen mills stand there, but then they were a thick forest of pines, and for more than three miles the road led through them. In former days Indians had lurked there; bears and foxes were still shot, and occasionally wolves were seen, when cold weather drove them to seek food near the sheep-folds and barn-yards.

" Well, we were skimming along pleasantly enough, I rather sleepy, and Joe very careful of me, when, just as I was beginning to doze a bit with my head on his arm I felt him start. Old Buck, the horse, gave a jump that woke me up, and in a minute I knew what the trouble was, for from behind us came the howl of a wolf.

"'Just the night to bring 'em out,' muttered Joe, using the whip till Buck went at his quickest trot, with his ears down and every sign of hurry and worry about him.

"'Are you afraid of them?' I asked, for I'd never had a scare of this sort, though I'd heard other people tell of the fierceness of the brutes when hunger made them bold.

"'Not a bit, only I wish I had my gun along,' said Joe, looking over his shoulder anxiously.

"'Pity I had n't brought mine — I do so well with it,' I said, and I laughed as I remembered how I aimed at Joe and hurt myself.

"'Are they chasing us?' I asked, standing up to look back along the white road, for we were just on the edge of the woods now.

"'Should n't wonder. If I had a better horse it would be a lively race; but Buck can't keep this pace long, and if he founders we are in a fix, for I can't run, and you can't fight. Betsey, there 's more than one; hold tight and try to count 'em.'

"Something in Joe's voice told me plainer than words that we were in danger, and I wished we 'd waited till the rest of our party came; but I was tired, and so we had started alone.

"Straining my eyes, I could see *three* black spots on the snow, and hear three howls as the wolves came galloping after us. I was a brave girl, but I 'd never tried this kind of thing before, and in a minute all the wolf stories I 'd ever heard came flying through my mind. I *was* mortally afeard, but I would n't show it, and turned to Joe, trying to laugh as I said: ' Only three as yet. Tell me just what to do, and I 'll do it.'

" ' Brave lass! I must see to Buck or he 'll be down, for he 's badly scared. You wait till the rascals are pretty close, then heave over one of these confounded hams to amuse 'em, while we make the most of their halt. They smell this meat, and that 's what they are after,' said Joe, driving his best, for the poor old horse began to pant, and limp on his stiff legs.

" ' Lucky for us we 've got 'em,' says I, bound to be cool and gay; ' if we had n't, they 'd get fresh meat instead of smoked.'

" Joe laughed, but a long howl close by made me dive for a ham; for in the darkness of the woods the beasts had got closer, and now all I could see were several balls of fire not many yards away. Out went the ham, and a snarl-ing sound showed that the wolves were busy eating it.

" ' All right!' said Joe. ' Rest a bit, and have another ready. They 'll soon finish that and want more. We must go easy, for Buck is nearly blown.'

" I prepared my ammunition, and, in what seemed five minutes, I heard the patter of feet behind us, and the fiery eyes were close by. Over went the second mouthful, and then the third, and the fourth; but they seemed more ravenous than ever, and each time were back sooner in greater numbers.

"We were nearly out of the woods when the last was gone, and if Buck had only had strength we should have been safe. But it was plain to see that he could n't keep up much longer, for he was very old, though he 'd been a fine horse in his prime.

" ' This looks bad, little Betsey. Cover up in the robes, and hold fast to me. The beasts will begin to snatch presently, and I 'll have to fight 'em off. Thank the powers, I 've my arms left.'

"As he spoke, Joe pulled me close, and wrapped me up, then took the whip, ready to rap the first wolf that dared come near enough to be hit. We did n't wait long; up they raced, and began to leap and snarl in a way that made my heart stand still, at first. Then my temper rose, and catching up the hot brick I had for my feet, I fired it with such good aim that one sharp, black nose disappeared with a yelp of pain.

" ' Hit 'em again, Betsey! Take the demijohn and bang 'em well. We are nearing Beaman's, and the brutes will soon drop off.'

"It was a lively scrimmage for a few minutes, as we both warmed to our work, Joe thrashing away with his whip on one side, and I on the other flourishing the demijohn in which we had carried some cider for the supper.

"But it was soon over, for in the fury of the

fight Joe forgot the horse; poor Buck made a sudden bolt, upset the sleigh down a bank, and, breaking loose, tore back along the road with the wolves after him.

" ' Run, Betsey! run for your life, and send Beaman's folks back! I 'm done for — my leg 's broken. Never mind. I 'll crawl under the sleigh, and be all right till you come. The wolves will take a good while to pick poor Buck's bones.'

" Just waiting to see Joe safe, I ran as I never ran before, — and I was always light of foot. How I did it I don't know, for I 'd forgot to put on my moccasins (we did n't have snow-boots, you know, in my young days), and there I was, tearing along that snowy road in my blue kid slippers like a crazy thing. It was nigh a mile, and my heart was 'most broke before I got there; but I kept my eye on the light in Hetty's winder and tugged along, blessing her for the guide and comfort that candle was. The last bit was down hill, or I could n't have done it; for when I fell on the doorstep my voice was clean gone, and I could only lie and rap, rap, rap! till they came flying. I just got breath enough to gasp out and point: —

" ' Joe — wolves — the   big   woods — go! ' when my senses failed me, and I was carried in."

Here Madam Shirley leaned back in her chair quite used up, for she had been acting the scene to a breathless audience, and laying about her

with her handkerchief so vigorously that her
eyes snapped, her cheeks were red, and her dear
old cap all awry.

"But Joe — did they eat him?" cried the
boys in great excitement, while the girls held to
one another, and the poor little wheel lay flat, upset by the blows of the imaginary demijohn,
dealt to an equally imaginary wolf.

"Hardly, — since he lived to be your grandfather," laughed the old lady, in high feather at
the success of her story.

"No, no, — we mean the horse;" shouted
Geoff, while the others roared at the mistake.

"Yes, they did. Poor old Buck saved us, at
the cost of his own life. His troubles were over,
but mine were not; for when I came to, I saw
Mr. Beaman, and my first thought and word was
'Joe?'"

"'Too late — they'd got him, so we turned
back to tell you,' said that stupid man.

"I gave one cry and was going off again,
when his wife shook me, and says, laughing:
'You little goose! He means the folks from
the Major's. A lot came along and found Joe,
and took him home, and soon's ever you're fit
we'll send you along, too.'

"'I'm ready now,' says I, jumping up in a
hurry. But I had to sit down again, for my feet
were all cut and bleeding and my slippers just
rags. They fixed me up and off I went, to find
mother in a sad taking. But Joe was all right;

he hadn't broken his leg, but only sprained it badly, and being the wounded one he was laid up longer than I. We both got well, however, and the first time Joe went out he hobbled over to our house. I was spinning again then, and thought I might need my wedding outfit, after all — On the whole, I guess we'll end the story here; young folks wouldn't care for that part."

As grandma paused, the girls cried out with one voice: "Yes, we do! we like it best. You said you would. Tell about the wedding and all."

"Well, well, it isn't much. Joe came and sat by me, and, as we talked over our adventure, he cut that true lover's knot between the letters. I didn't seem to mind and spun away till he pointed to it, saying, with the look that always made me meek as a lamb, 'May it stand so, my little Betsey?'

"I said 'Yes, Joe,' and then — well, never mind that bit; — we were married in June, and I spun and wove my wedding things afterward. Dreadful slack, my mother thought, but I didn't care. My wedding gown was white lutestring, full trimmed with old lace. Hair over a cushion with white roses, and the pearl necklace, just as you see up there. Joe wore his uniform, and I tied up his hair with a white satin ribbon. He looked beautiful, — and so did I."

At this artless bit of vanity, the girls smiled,

but all agreed that grandma was right, as they looked at the portraits with fresh interest.

"I call that a pretty good story," said Walt, with the air of an accomplished critic.

"'Specially the wolf part. I wanted that longer," added Geoff.

"It was quite long enough for me, my dear, and I did n't hear the last of it for years. Why, one of my wedding presents was four hams done up elegantly in white paper, with posies on 'em, from the Major. He loved a joke, and never forgot how well we fought with the pigs' legs that night. Joe gave me a new sleigh, the next Christmas, with two wolf-skin robes for it, — shot the beasts himself, and I kept those rugs till the moths ate the last bit. He kept the leavings of my slippers, and I have them still. Fetch 'em, Minnie — you know where they are."

Grandma pointed to the tall secretary that stood in a corner, and Minnie quickly took a box from one of the many drawers. All the heads clustered around grandma, and the faded, ragged shoes went from hand to hand, while questions rained upon the story-teller till she bade them go to bed.

Nothing but the promise of more tales would appease them; then, with thanks and kisses, the young folks trooped away, leaving the old lady to put the little wheel to rights, and sit thinking over her girlhood, in the fire-light.

THE storm kept on all night, and next morning the drifts were higher, the wind stronger, and the snow falling faster than ever. Through the day the children roved about the great house, amusing themselves as best they could; and, when evening came, they gathered around the fire again, eager for the promised story from grandmamma.

"I 've a little cold," said the old lady, "and am too hoarse for talking, my dears; but Aunt Elinor has looked up a parcel of old tales that I 've told her at different times and which she has written down. You will like to hear her reading better than my dull way of telling them, and I can help Minnie and Lotty with their work, for I see they are bent on learning to spin."

The young folk were well pleased with grandma's proposal; for Aunt Nell was a favorite with all, being lively and kind and fond of children, and the only maiden aunt in the family. Now, she smilingly produced a faded old portfolio, and, turning over a little pile of manuscripts, said in her pleasant way: —

"Here are all sorts, picked up in my travels at home and abroad; and in order to suit all of you, I have put the names on slips of paper into this basket, and each can draw one in turn. Does that please my distinguished audience?"

"Yes, yes. Geoff's the oldest, let him draw first," cried the flock, fluttering like a flight of birds before they settle.

"Girls come first," answered the boy, with a nod toward the eldest girl cousin.

Lotty put in her hand and, after some fumbling, drew out a paper on which was written, "*Tabby's Table-cloth.*" "Is that a good one?" she asked, for Geoff looked disappointed.

"More fighting, though a girl is still the heroine," answered Aunt Nell, searching for the manuscript.

"I think two revolutions will be enough for you, General," added grandmamma, laughing.

"Do we beat in both?" asked the boy, brightening up at once.

"Yes."

"All right, then. I vote for 'Dolly's Dishcloth,' or whatever it is; though I don't see what it can possibly have to do with war," he added.

"Ah, my dear, women have their part to play as well as men at such times, and do it bravely, though one does not hear so much about their courage. I've often wished some one would collect all that can be found about these neglected heroines, and put it in a book for us to read, admire, and emulate when our turn comes."

Grandma looked thoughtfully at the fire as she spoke, and Lotty said, with her eye on the portfolio: "Perhaps Aunt Nell will do it for us. Then history won't be so dry, and we can glorify our fore-mothers as well as fathers."

"I'll see what I can find. Now spin away, Minnie, and sit still, boys, — if you can."

Then, having settled grandma's foot-stool, and turned up the lamp, Aunt Nell read the tale of

TABBY'S TABLE - CLOTH

On the 20th day of March, 1775, a little girl was trudging along a country road, with a basket of eggs on her arm. She seemed in a great hurry, and looked anxiously about her as she went; for those were stirring times, and Tabitha Tarbell lived in a town that took a famous part in the Revolution. She was a rosy-faced, bright-eyed lass of fourteen, full of vigor, courage, and patriotism, and just then much excited by the frequent rumors which reached Concord that the British were coming to destroy the stores sent there for safe keeping while the enemy occupied Boston. Tabby glowed with wrath at the idea, and (metaphorically speaking) shook her fist at august King George, being a stanch little Rebel, ready to fight and die for her country rather than submit to tyranny of any kind.

In nearly every house something valuable was hidden. Colonel Barrett had six barrels of powder; Ebenezer Hubbard, sixty-eight barrels of flour; axes, tents, and spades were at Daniel Cray's; and Captain David Brown had guns, cartridges, and musket balls. Cannon were hidden in the woods; fire-arms were being manufactured at Barrett's Mills; cartouch-boxes, belts, and holsters, at Reuben Brown's; saltpetre at Josiah Melvin's; and much oatmeal was prepared at Captain Timothy Wheeler's. A morning gun was fired, a guard of ten men patrolled the town at night, and the brave farmers were making ready for what they felt must come.

There were Tories in the town who gave the enemy all the information they could gather; therefore much caution was necessary in making plans, lest these enemies should betray them. Pass-words were adopted, secret signals used, and messages sent from house to house in all sorts of queer ways. Such a message lay hidden under the eggs in Tabby's basket, and the brave little girl was going on an important errand from her uncle, Captain David Brown, to Deacon Cyrus Hosmer, who lived at the other end of the town, by the South Bridge. She had been employed several times before in the same way, and had proved herself quick-witted, stout-hearted, and light-footed. Now, as she trotted along in her scarlet cloak and hood, she was wishing she

could still further distinguish herself by some
great act of heroism; for good Parson Emerson
had patted her on the head and said, "Well
done, child!" when he heard how she ran all the
way to Captain Barrett's, in the night, to warn
him that Doctor Lee, the Tory, had been detected
sending information of certain secret plans to the
enemy.

"I would do more than that, though it was
a fearsome run through the dark woods.
Would n't those two like to know all I know
about the stores? But I would n't tell 'em, not
if they drove a bayonet through me. I 'm not
afeard of 'em;" and Tabby tossed her head de-
fiantly, as she paused to shift her basket from
one arm to the other.

But she evidently was "afeard" of something,
for her ruddy cheeks turned pale and her heart
gave a thump, as two men came in sight, and
stopped suddenly on seeing her. They were
strangers; and though nothing in their dress
indicated it, the girl's quick eye saw that they
were soldiers; step and carriage betrayed it, and
the rapidity with which these martial gentlemen
changed into quiet travellers roused her suspicions at once. They exchanged a few whispered words; then they came on, swinging their
stout sticks, one whistling, the other keeping a
keen lookout along the lonely road before and
behind them.

"My pretty lass, can you tell me where **Mr.** Daniel Bliss lives?" asked the younger, with a smile and a salute.

Tabby was sure now that they were British; for the voice was deep and full, the face a ruddy English face, and the man they wanted was a well-known Tory. But she showed no sign of alarm, beyond the modest color in her cheeks, and answered civilly: "Yes, sir, over yonder a piece."

"Thanks and a kiss for that," said the young man, stooping to bestow his gift. But he got a smart box on the ear, and Tabby ran off in a fury of indignation.

With a laugh they went on, never dreaming that the little Rebel was going to turn spy herself, and get the better of them. She hurried away to Deacon Hosmer's, and did her errand, adding thereto the news that strangers were in town. "We must know more of them," said the Deacon. "Clap a different suit on her, wife, and send her with the eggs to Mrs. Bliss. We have all we want of them, and Tabby can look well about her, while she rests and gossips over there. Bliss must be looked after smartly, for he is a knave, and will do us harm."

Away went Tabby in a blue cloak and hood, much pleased with her mission; and, coming to the Tory's house about noon, smelt afar off a savory odor of roasting meat and baking pies.

Stepping softly to the back-door, she peeped

through a small window, and saw Mrs. Bliss and
her handmaid cooking away in the big kitchen,
too busy to heed the little spy, who slipped around
to the front of the house, to take a general survey before she went in. All she saw confirmed
her suspicions; for in the keeping-room a table
was set forth in great style, with the silver tank-
ards, best china, and the fine damask table-cloth,
which the housewife kept for holidays. Still another peep through the lilac bushes before the
parlor windows showed her the two strangers
closeted with Mr. Bliss, all talking earnestly, but
in too low a tone for a word to reach even her
sharp ears.

"I *will* know what they are at. I'm sure it
is mischief, and I won't go back with only my
walk for my pains," thought Tabby; and marching into the kitchen, she presented her eggs with
a civil message from Madam Hosmer.

"They are mighty welcome, child. I've used
a sight for my custards, and need more for the
flip. We've company to dinner unexpected, and
I'm much put about," said Mrs. Bliss, who
seemed to be concerned about something besides
the dinner, and in her flurry forgot to be surprised at the unusual gift; for the neighbors
shunned them, and the poor woman had many
anxieties on her husband's account, the family
being divided, — one brother a Tory, and one a
Rebel.

"Can I help, ma'am? I'm a master hand at

beating eggs, Aunt Hitty says. I'm tired, and would n't mind sitting a bit if I'm not in the way," said Tabby, bound to discover something more before she left.

"But you be in the way. We don't want any help, so you 'd better be steppin' along home, else suthin' besides eggs may git whipped. Tale-bearers ain't welcome here," said old Puah, the maid, a sour spinster, who sympathized with her master, and openly declared she hoped the British would put down the Yankee Rebels soon and sharply.

Mrs. Bliss was in the pantry, and heard nothing of this little passage of arms; for Tabby hotly resented the epithet of "tale-bearer," though she knew that the men in the parlor were not the only spies on the premises.

"When you are all drummed out of town and this house burnt to the ground, you may be glad of my help, and I wish you may get it. Good-day, old crab-apple," answered saucy Tabby; and catching up her basket, she marched out of the kitchen with her nose in the air.

But as she passed the front of the house, she could not resist another look at the fine dinner-table; for in those days few had time or heart for feasting, and the best napery and china seldom appeared. One window stood open, and as the girl leaned in, something moved under the long cloth that swept the floor. It was not the wind, for the March day was still and sunny, and in a minute out popped a gray cat's head, and puss came purring to meet the new-comer whose step had roused her from a nap.

"Where one tabby hides, another can. Can I dare to do it? What would become of me if found out? How wonderful it would be if I could hear what these men are plotting. I will!"

A sound in the next room decided her; and, thrusting the basket among the bushes, she leaped lightly in and vanished under the table, leaving puss calmly washing her face on the window-sill.

As soon as it was done Tabby's heart began to flutter; but it was too late to retreat, for at that moment in bustled Mrs. Bliss, and the poor girl could only make herself as small as possible, quite hidden under the long folds that fell on all sides from the wide, old-fashioned table. She discovered nothing from the women's chat, for it ran on sage-cheese, egg-nog, roast pork, and lamentations over a burnt pie. By the time dinner was served, and the guests called in to eat it, Tabby was calm enough to have all her wits about her, and pride gave her courage to be ready for the consequences, whatever they might be.

For a time the hungry gentlemen were too busy eating to talk much; but when Mrs. Bliss went out, and the flip came in, they were ready for business. The window was shut, whereat Tabby exulted that she was inside; the talkers drew closer together, and spoke so low that she could only catch a sentence now and then, which caused her to pull her hair with vexation; and they

swore a good deal, to the great horror of the
pious little maiden curled up at their feet. But
she heard enough to prove that she was right;
for these men were Captain Brown and Ensign
De Bernicre, of the British army, come to learn
where the supplies were stored and how well the
town was defended. She heard Mr. Bliss tell
them that some of the " Rebels," as he called his
neighbors, had sent him word that he should not
leave the town alive, and he was in much fear for
his life and property. She heard the Englishmen
tell him that if he came with them they would
protect him; for they were armed, and three of
them together could surely get safely off, as no
one knew the strangers had arrived but the slip
of a girl who showed them the way. Here " the
slip of a girl " nodded her head savagely, and
hoped the speaker's ear still tingled with the
buffet she gave it.

Mr. Bliss gladly consented to this plan, and
told them he would show them the road to Lexington, which was a shorter way to Boston than
through Weston and Sudbury, the road they
came.

" These people won't fight, will they? " asked
Ensign De Bernicre.

" There goes a man who will fight you to the
death," answered Mr. Bliss, pointing to his
brother Tom, busy in a distant field.

The Ensign swore again, and gave a stamp
that brought his heavy heel down on poor

Tabby's hand, as she leaned forward to catch every word. The cruel blow nearly forced a cry from her; but she bit her lips and never stirred, though faint with pain. When she could listen again, Mr. Bliss was telling all he knew about the hiding places of the powder, grain, and cannon the enemy wished to capture and destroy. He could not tell much, for the secrets had been well kept; but if he had known that our young Rebel was taking notes of his words under his own table, he might have been less ready to betray his neighbors. No one suspected a listener, however, and all Tabby could do was to scowl at three pairs of muddy boots, and wish she were a man that she might fight the wearers of them.

She very nearly had a chance to fight or fly; for just as they were preparing to leave the table, a sudden sneeze nearly undid her. She thought she was lost, and hid her face, expecting to be dragged out — to instant death, perhaps — by the wrathful men of war.

" What 's that? " exclaimed the Ensign, as a sudden pause followed that fatal sound.

" It came from under the table," added Captain Brown, and a hand lifted a corner of the cloth.

A shiver went through Tabby, and she held her breath, with her eye upon that big, brown hand; but the next moment she could have laughed with joy, for pussy saved her. The cat had come to doze on her warm skirts, and when the cloth was raised, fancying she was to be fed

by her master, puss rose and walked out purring
loudly, tail erect, with its white tip waving like
a flag of truce.

" 'T is but the old cat, gentlemen. A good
beast, and, fortunately for us, unable to report
our conference," said Mr. Bliss, with an air of
relief, for he had started guiltily at the bare idea
of an eavesdropper.

" She sneezed as if she were as great a snuff-
taker as an old woman of whom we asked our
way above here," laughed the Ensign, as they all
rose.

" And there she is now, coming along as if our
grenadiers were after her!" exclaimed the Captain, as the sound of steps and a wailing voice
came nearer and nearer.

Tabby took a long breath, and vowed that she
would beg or buy the dear old cat that had saved
her from destruction. Then she forgot her own
danger in listening to the poor woman, who came
in crying that her neighbors said she must leave
town at once, or they would tar and feather her
for showing spies the road to a Tory's house.

" Well for me I came and heard their plots,
or I might be sent off in like case," thought the
girl, feeling that the more perils she encountered,
the greater heroine she would be.

Mr. Bliss comforted the old soul, bidding her
stay there till the neighbors forgot her, and the
officers gave her some money to pay for the costly
service she had done them. Then they left the

room, and after some delay the three men set off; but Tabby was compelled to stay in her hiding-place till the table was cleared, and the women deep in gossip, as they washed dishes in the kitchen. Then the little spy crept out softly, and raising the window with great care, ran away as fast as her stiff limbs would carry her.

By the time she reached the Deacon's, however, and told her tale, the Tories were well on their way, Mr. Bliss having provided them with horses that his own flight might be the speedier.

So they escaped; but the warning was given, and Tabby received great praise for her hour under the table. The town's-people hastened their preparations, and had time to remove the most valuable stores to neighboring towns; to mount their cannon and drill their minute-men; for these resolute farmers meant to resist oppression, and the world knows how well they did it when the hour came.

Such an early spring had not been known for years; and by the 19th of April fruit trees were in bloom, winter grain was up, and the stately elms that fringed the river and overarched the village streets were budding fast. It seemed a pity that such a lovely world should be disturbed by strife; but liberty was dearer than prosperity or peace, and the people leaped from their beds when young Dr. Prescott came, riding for his life, with the message Paul Revere brought from Boston in the night: —

"Arm! arm! the British are coming!"

Like an electric spark the news ran from house to house, and men made ready to fight, while the brave women bade them go, and did their best to guard the treasure confided to their keeping. A little later, word came that the British were at Lexington, and blood had been shed. Then the farmers shouldered their guns, with few words but stern faces, and by sunrise a hundred men stood ready, with good Parson Emerson at their head. More men were coming in from the neighboring towns, and all felt that the hour had arrived when patience ceased to be a virtue and rebellion was just.

Great was the excitement everywhere; but at Captain David Brown's one little heart beat high with hope and fear, as Tabby stood at the door, looking across the river to the town, where drums were beating, bells ringing, and people hurrying to and fro.

"I can't fight, but I *must* see," she said; and catching up her cloak, she ran over the North Bridge, promising her aunt to return and bring her word as soon as the enemy appeared.

"What news? Are they coming?" called the people, from the Manse and the few houses that then stood along that road. But Tabby could only shake her head and run the faster, in her eagerness to see what was happening on that memorable day. When she reached the middle of the town she found that the little company had gone along the Lexington road to meet the enemy. Nothing daunted, she hurried in that direction and, climbing a high bank, waited to catch a glimpse of the British grenadiers, of whom she had heard so much.

About seven o'clock they came, the sun glittering on the arms of eight hundred English soldiers marching toward the hundred stout-hearted farmers, who waited till they were within a few rods of them.

"Let us stand our ground; and if we die, let us die here," said brave Parson Emerson, still among his people, ready for anything but surrender.

"Nay," said a cautious Lincoln man, "it will not do for us to *begin* the war."

So they reluctantly fell back to the town, the British following slowly, being weary with their seven-mile march over the hills from Lexington. Coming to a little brown house perched on the hillside, one of the thirsty officers spied a well, with the bucket swinging at the end of the long pole. Running up the bank, he was about to drink, when a girl, who was crouching behind the well, sprang up, and with an energetic gesture, flung the water in his face, crying: —

"That's the way we serve spies!"

Before Ensign De Bernicre — for it was he, acting as guide to the enemy — could clear his eyes and dry his drenched face, Tabby was gone over the hill with a laugh and a defiant gesture toward the red-coats below.

In high feather at this exploit, she darted about the town, watching the British at their work of destruction. They cut down and burnt the liberty pole, broke open sixty barrels of flour, flung five hundred pounds of balls into the mill-pond and wells, and set the court-house on fire. Other parties were ordered to different quarters of the town to ransack houses and destroy all the stores they found. Captain Parsons was sent to take possession of the North Bridge, and De Bernicre led the way, for he had taken notes on his former visit, and was a good guide. As they marched, a little scarlet figure went flying on before them, and vanished at the turn of the road. It was Tabby hastening home to warn her aunt.

"Quick child, whip on this gown and cap and hurry into bed. These prying fellows will surely have pity on a sick girl, and respect this room if no other," said Mrs. Brown, briskly helping Tabby into a short night-gown and round cap, and tucking her well up when she was laid down, for between the plump feather-beds were hidden many muskets, the most precious of their stores. This had been planned beforehand, and Tabby was glad to rest and tell her tale while Aunty Brown put physic bottles and glasses on the table, set some evil-smelling herbs to simmer on the hearth, and, compromising with her conscience, concocted a nice little story to tell the invaders.

Presently they came, and it was well for

Tabby that the ensign remained below to guard the doors while the men ransacked the house from garret to cellar; for he might have recognized the saucy girl who had twice maltreated him.

"These are feathers; lift the covers carefully or you'll be half smothered, they fly about so," said Mrs. Brown, as the men came to some casks of cartridges and flints, which she had artfully ripped up several pillows to conceal.

Quite deceived, the men gladly passed on, leaving the very things they most wanted to destroy. Coming to the bed-room, where more treasures of the same valuable sort were hidden in various nooks and corners, the dame held up her finger, saying, with an anxious glance toward Tabby: —

"Step softly, please. You wouldn't harm a poor, sick girl. The doctor thinks it is small-pox, and a fright might kill her. I keep the chamber as fresh as I can with yarbs, so I guess there isn't much danger of catching it."

The men reluctantly looked in, saw a flushed face on the pillow (for Tabby was red with running, and her black eyes wild with excitement), took a sniff at the wormwood and motherwort, and with a hasty glance into a closet or two where sundry clothes concealed hidden doors, hastily retired to report the danger and get away as soon as possible.

They would have been much disgusted at the

trick played upon them if they had seen the sick
girl fly out of bed and dance a jig of joy as they
tramped away to Barrett's Mills. But soon
Tabby had no heart for merriment, as she
watched the minute-men gather by the bridge,
saw the British march down on the other side,
and when their first volley killed brave Isaac
Davis and Abner Hosmer, of Acton, she heard
Major Buttrick give the order, " Fire, fellow-
soldiers; for God's sake, fire!"

For a little while shots rang, smoke rose,
shouts were heard, and red and blue coats mingled in the struggle on the bridge. Then the
British fell back, leaving two dead soldiers behind them. These were buried where they fell;
and the bodies of the Acton men were sent home
to their poor wives, Concord's first martyrs for
liberty.

No need to tell more of the story of that day;
all children know it, and many have made a pilgrimage to see the old monument set up where
the English fell, and the bronze Minute-Man,
standing on his granite pedestal to mark the spot
where the brave Concord farmers fired the shot
that made the old North Bridge immortal.

We must follow Tabby, and tell how she got
her table-cloth. When the fight was over, the
dead buried, the wounded cared for, and the
prisoners exchanged, the Tories were punished.
Dr. Lee was confined to his own farm, on penalty
of being shot if he left it, and the property of

Daniel Bliss was confiscated by government. Some things were sold at auction, and Captain Brown bought the fine cloth and gave it to Tabby, saying heartily: —

" There, my girl, that belongs to you, and you may well be proud of it; for, thanks to your quick wits and eyes and ears, we were not taken unawares, but sent the red-coats back faster than they came."

And Tabby *was* proud of it, keeping it carefully, displaying it with immense satisfaction whenever she told the story, and spinning busily to make a set of napkins to go with it. It covered the table when her wedding supper was spread, was used at the christening of her first boy, and for many a Thanksgiving and Christmas dinner through the happy years of her married life.

Then it was preserved by her daughters, as a relic of their mother's youth, and long after the old woman was gone, the well-worn cloth still appeared on great occasions, till it grew too thin for anything but careful keeping, to illustrate the story so proudly told by the grandchildren, who found it hard to believe that the feeble old lady of ninety could be the lively lass who played her little part in the Revolution with such spirit.

In 1861, Tabby's table-cloth saw another war, and made an honorable end. When men were called for, Concord responded " Here! " and sent a goodly number, led by another brave Colonel

Prescott.   Barretts, Hosmers, Melvins, Browns,
and Wheelers stood shoulder to shoulder, as
their grandfathers stood that day to meet the
British by the bridge.   Mothers said, " Go my
son," as bravely as before, and sisters and sweethearts smiled with wet eyes as the boys in blue
marched away again, cheered on by another
noble Emerson.   More than one of Tabby's de-
scendants went, some to fight, some to nurse;
and for four long years the old town worked and
waited, hoped and prayed, burying the dear dead
boys sent home, nursing those who brought back
honorable wounds, and sending more to man the
breaches made by the awful battles that filled
both North and South with a wilderness of
graves.

The women knit and sewed Sundays as well
as week-days, to supply the call for clothes; the
men emptied their pockets freely, glad to give;
and the minister, after preaching like a Christian
soldier, took off his coat and packed boxes of
comforts like a tender father.

" More lint and bandages called for, and I do
believe we 've torn and picked up every old rag
in the town," said one busy lady to another, as
several sat together making comfort-bags in the
third year of the long struggle.

" I have cleared my garret of nearly everything in it, and only wish I had more to give,"
answered one of the patriotic Barrett mothers.

" We can't buy anything so soft and good as

worn-out sheets and table-cloths. New ones won't do, or I'd cut up every one of mine," said a newly married Wheeler, sewing for dear life, as she remembered the many cousins gone to the war.

" I think I shall have to give our Revolutionary table-cloth. It's old enough, and soft as silk, and I'm sure my blessed grandmother would think that it could n't make a better end," spoke up white-headed Madam Hubbard; for Tabby Tarbell had married one of that numerous and worthy race.

" Oh, you would n't cut up that famous cloth, would you?" cried the younger woman.

" Yes, I will. It's in rags, and when I'm gone no one will care for it. Folks don't seem to remember what the women did in those days, so it's no use keeping relics of 'em," answered the old lady, who would have owned herself mistaken if she could have looked forward to 1876, when the town celebrated its centennial, and proudly exhibited the little scissors with which Mrs. Barrett cut paper for cartridges, among other ancient trophies of that earlier day.

So the ancient cloth was carefully made into a boxful of the finest lint and softest squares to lay on wounds, and sent to one of the Concord women who had gone as a nurse.

" Here's a treasure!" she said, as she came to it among other comforts newly arrived from home. " Just what I want for my brave Rebel and poor little Johnny Bullard."

The " brave Rebel " was a Southern man who had fought well and was badly wounded in many ways, yet never complained; and in the midst of great suffering was always so courteous, patient, and courageous, that the men called him " our gentleman," and tried to show how much they respected so gallant a foe. John Bullard was an English drummer-boy, who had been through several battles, stoutly drumming away in spite of bullets and cannon-balls; cheering many a camp-fire with his voice, for he sang like a blackbird, and was always merry, always plucky, and so great a favorite in his regiment, that all mourned for " little Johnny " when his right arm was shot off at Gettysburg. It was thought he would die; but he pulled through the worst of it, and was slowly struggling back to health, still trying to be gay, and beginning to chirp feebly now and then, like a convalescent bird.

" Here, Johnny, is some splendid lint for this poor arm, and some of the softest compresses for Carrol's wound. He is asleep, so I 'll begin with you, and while I work I 'll amuse you with the story of the old table-cloth this lint came from," said Nurse Hunt, as she stood by the bed where the thin, white face smiled at her, though the boy dreaded the hard quarter of an hour he had to endure every day.

" Thanky, mum. We 'ave n't 'ad a story for a good bit. I 'm 'arty this mornin', and think I 'll be hup by this day week, won't I? "

"I hope so. Now shut your eyes and listen; then you won't mind the twinges I give you, gentle as I try to be," answered the nurse, beginning her painful task.

Then she told the story of Tabby's table-cloth, and the boy enjoyed it immensely, laughing out at the slapping and the throwing water in the ensign's face, and openly rejoicing when the red-coats got the worst of it.

"As we've beaten all the rest of the world, I don't mind our 'aving bad luck that time. We har' friends now, and I'll fight for you, mum, like a British bull-dog, if I hever get the chance," said Johnny, when the tale and dressing were ended.

"So you shall. I like to turn a brave enemy into a faithful friend, as I hope we shall yet be able to do with our Southern brothers. I admire their courage and their loyalty to what they believe to be right, and we are all suffering the punishment we deserve for waiting till this sad war came, instead of settling the trouble years ago, as we might have done if we had loved honesty and honor more than money and power."

As she spoke, Miss Hunt turned to her other patient, and saw by the expression of his face that he had heard both the tale and the talk. He smiled, and said, "Good morning," as usual, but when she stooped to lay a compress of the soft, wet damask on the angry wound in his breast, he whispered, with a grateful look: —

"You *have* changed one 'Southern brother' from an enemy into a friend. Whether I live or die, I never can forget how generous and kind you have all been to me."

"Thank you! It is worth months of anxiety and care to hear such words. Let us shake hands, and do our best to make North and South as good friends as England and America now are," said the nurse, offering her hand.

"Me, too! I've got one 'and left, and I give it ye with all me 'art. God bless ye, sir, and a lively getting hup for the two of us!" cried Johnny, stretching across the narrow space that divided the beds, with a beaming face and true English readiness to forgive a fallen foe when he had proved a brave one.

The three hands met in a warm shake, and the act was a little lesson more eloquent than words to the lookers-on; for the spirit of brotherhood that should bind us all together worked the miracle of linking these three by the frail threads spun a century ago.

So Tabby's table-cloth did make a beautiful and useful end at last.

ELI'S EDUCATION

"MY turn now," said Walt, as they assembled again, after a busy day spent in snow-balling, statue-making, and tumbling in the drifts that still continued to rise on all sides.

"Here is just the story for you and Geoff. You are getting ready for college, after years of the best schooling, and it will do you good to hear how hard some boys have had to work to get a little learning," said Grandma, glancing at the slip that Walt drew from the basket which Aunt Elinor held out to him, and from which Lotty had drawn the story of "Tabby's Table Cloth."

"This is a true tale, and the man became famous for his wisdom, as well as much loved and honored for his virtue, and interest in all good things," added Aunt Elinor, as she began to read the story of

ELI'S EDUCATION

MANY years ago, a boy of sixteen sat in a little room in an old farm-house up among the Connecticut hills, writing busily in a book made

of odd bits of paper stitched together, with a
cover formed of two thin boards. The lid of a
blue chest was his desk, the end of a tallow candle stuck into a potato was his lamp, a mixture
of soot and vinegar his ink, and a quill from the
gray goose his pen. A "Webster's Spelling-
book," "Dilworth's New Guide to the English Tongue," "Daboll's Arithmetic," and the
"American Preceptor," stood on the chimney-
piece over his head, with the "Assembly Cate-
chism," and New Testament, in the place of
honor. This was his library; and now and then
a borrowed "Pilgrim's Progress," "Fox's Book
of Martyrs," or some stray volume, gladdened
his heart; for he passionately loved books, and
scoured the neighborhood for miles around to
feed this steadily increasing hunger. Every
penny he could earn or save went to buy a song
or a story from the peddlers who occasionally
climbed the hill to the solitary farm-house.
When others took a noon-spell, he read under
the trees or by the fire. He carried a book in his
pocket, and studied as he went with the cows to
and from the pasture, and sat late in his little
room, ciphering on an old slate, or puzzling his
young brain over some question which no one
could answer for him.

His father had no patience with him, called
him a shiftless dreamer, and threatened to burn
the beloved books. But his mother defended
him, for he was her youngest and the pride of

her heart; so she let him scribble all over her
floors before she scrubbed them up, dipped extra
thick candles for his use, saved every scrap of
paper to swell his little store, and firmly believed
that he would turn out the great man of the
family. His brothers joked about his queer
ways, but in his sisters he found firm friends and
tender comforters for all his woes. So he strug-
gled along, working on the farm in summer and
in a clock shop during the winter, with such
brief spells of schooling as he could get between
whiles, improving even these poor opportunities
so well that he was letter-writer for all the young
people in the neighborhood.

Now, he was writing in his journal very
slowly, but very well, shaping his letters with
unusual grace and freedom; for the wide snow-
banks were his copy-books in winter, and on
their white pages he had learned to sweep splendid capitals or link syllables handsomely together. This is what he wrote that night, with
a sparkle in the blue eyes and a firm folding of
the lips that made the boyish face resolute and
manly.

" I am set in my own mind that I get learning.
I see not how, but my will is strong, and mother
hopes for to make a scholar of me. So, please
God, we shall do it."

Then he shut the little book and put it carefully away in the blue chest, with pen and ink,

as if they were very precious things; piously said
his prayers, and was soon asleep under the home-
spun coverlet, dreaming splendid dreams, while
a great bright star looked in at the low window,
as if waiting to show him the road to fortune.

And God did please to help the patient lad;
only the next evening came an opportunity he
had never imagined. As he sat playing "Over
the Hills and Far Away" on the fiddle that he
had himself made out of maple-wood, with a
bow strung from the tail of the old farm horse,
a neighbor came in to talk over the fall pork
and cider, and tell the news.

"Ef you want ter go over the hills and far
away, Eli, here 's the chance. I see a man down
to Woodtick who was askin' ef I knew any likely
young chap who 'd like to git 'scribers for a pious
book he wants to sell. He 'd pay for the job
when the names is got and the books give out.
That 's ruther in your line, boy, so I calk'lated
your daddy would spare you, as you ain't much
of a hand at shuckin' corn nor cartin' pummace."

"Haw! haw!" laughed the big brothers, Ambrose Vitruvius and Junius Solomon, as neighbor Terry spoke with a sly twinkle in his eye.

But the sisters, Miranda and Pamela, smiled
for joy, while the good mother stopped her busy
wheel to listen eagerly. Eli laid down his fiddle
and came to the hearth where the others sat, with
such a wide-awake expression on his usually
thoughtful face that it was plain that he liked the
idea.

"I 'll do it, if father 'll let me," he said, looking wistfully at the industrious man, who was
shaving axe-handles for the winter wood-chop-
ping, after his day's work was over.

"Wal, I can spare you for a week, mebby.
It 's not time for the clock shop yet, and sence
you 've heerd o' this, you won't do your chores
right, so you may as wal see what you can make
of peddlin'."

"Thank you, sir; I 'll give you all I get, to
pay for my time," began Eli, glowing with pleasure at the prospect of seeing a little of the world;
for one of his most cherished dreams was to cross
the blue hills that hemmed him in, and find what
lay beyond.

"Guess I can afford to give you all you 'll
make this trip," answered his father, in a tone
that made the brothers laugh again.

"Boys, don't pester Eli. Every one has n't a
call to farmin', and it 's wal to foller the leadin's
of Providence when they come along," said the
mother, stroking the smooth, brown head at her
knee; for Eli always went to her footstool with
his sorrows and his joys.

So it was settled, and next day the boy, in his
home-spun and home-made Sunday best, set off
to see his employer and secure the job. He got
it, and for three days trudged up and down the
steep roads, calling at every house with a sample
of his book, the Rev. John Flavel's treatise on
"Keeping the Heart." Eli's winning face, mod-

est manner, and earnest voice served him well, and he got many names; for books were scarce in those days, and a pious work was a treasure to many a good soul who found it difficult to keep the heart strong and cheerful in troublous times.

Then the books were to be delivered, and, anxious to save his small earnings, Eli hired no horse to transport his load, but borrowed a stout, green shawl from his mother, and, with his pack on his back, marched bravely away to finish his task. His wages were spent in a new prayer-book for his mother, smart handkerchief-pins for the faithful sisters, and a good store of paper for himself.

This trip was so successful that he was seized with a strong desire to try a more ambitious and extended one; for these glimpses of the world showed him how much he had to learn, and how pleasantly he could pick up knowledge in these flights.

"What be you a-brewdin' over now, boy? Gettin' ready for the clock shop? It's 'most time for winter work, and Terry says you do pretty wal at puttin' together," said the farmer, a day or two after the boy's return, as they sat at dinner, all helping themselves from the large pewter platter heaped with pork and vegetables.

"I was wishin' I could go South with Gad Upson. He's been twice with clocks and notions, and wants a mate. Hoadley fits him out and pays him a good share if he does well. Could n't I go along? I hate that old shop, and I know I can do something better than put together the insides of cheap clocks."

Eli spoke eagerly, and gave his mother an imploring look which brought her to second the motion at once, her consent having been already won.

The brothers stared as if Eli had proposed to go up in a balloon, for to them the South seemed farther off than Africa does nowadays. The father had evidently been secretly prepared, for he showed no surprise, and merely paused a moment to look at his ambitious son with a glance in which amusement and reproach were mingled.

"When a hen finds she 's hatched a duck's egg, it 's no use for her to cackle; that ducklin' will take to the water in spite on her, and paddle off, nobody knows where. Go ahead, boy, and when you get enough of junketin' 'round the world, come home and fall to work."

"Then I *may* go?" cried Eli, upsetting his mug of cider in his excitement.

His father nodded, being too busy eating cabbage with a wide-bladed green-handled knife to speak just then. Eli, red and speechless with delight and gratitude, could only sit and beam at his family till a sob drew his attention to sister Pamela, whose pet he was.

"Don't, Pam, don't! I 'll come back all right, and bring you news and all the pretty things I can. I *must* go; I feel as if I could n't breathe, shut up here winters. I s'pose it 's wicked, but I can't help it," whispered Eli, with his arm around his buxom eighteen-year old sister, who laid her head on his shoulder and held him tight.

" Daughter, it 's sinful to repine at the ways of Providence. I see a leadin' plain in this, and ef *I* can be chirk when my dear boy is goin', 'pears to me you ought to keep a taut rein on your feelin's, and not spile his pleasure."

The good mother's eyes were full of tears as she spoke, but she caught up the end of her short gown and wiped them quickly away to smile on Eli, who thanked her with a loving look.

" It 's so lonesome when he 's not here. What will we do evenings without the fiddle, or Eli to read a piece in some of his books while we spin ? " said poor Pam, ashamed of her grief, yet glad to hide her tears by affecting to settle the long wooden bodkin that held up her coils of brown hair.

" Obed Finch will be comin' along, I guess likely, and he 'll read to you out uv Eli's book about keepin' the heart, and you 'll find your 'n gone 'fore you know it," said Junius Solomon, in a tone that made pretty Pam blush and run away, while the rest laughed at her confusion.

So it was settled, and when all was ready, the boy came home to show his equipment before he started. A very modest outfit, — only two tin trunks slung across the shoulders, filled with jewelry, combs, lace, essences, and small wares.

" I hate to have ye go, son, but it 's better than to be mopin' to hum, gettin' desperut for books and rilin' father. We 'll all be workin' for ye, so be chipper and do wal. Keep steddy, and don't disgrace your folks. The Lord bless ye, my dear boy, and hold ye in the holler of his hand! "

Her own rough hand was on his head as his mother spoke, with wet eyes, and the tall lad kissed her tenderly, whispering, with a choke in his throat : —

" Good-by, mammy dear; I 'll remember."

Then he tramped away to join his mate, turning now and then to nod and smile and show a ruddy face full of happiness, while the family watched him out of sight with mingled hopes and doubts and fears.

Mails were slow in those days, but at length a letter came; and here it is, — a true copy of one written by a boy in 1820 : —

" NORFOLK, VA., December 4th.

" HONORED PARENTS : I write to inform you I am safe here and to work. Our business is profitable, and I am fast learning the Quirks and Turns of trade. We are going to the eastern shore of Va., calculating to be gone six weeks. The inhabitants are sociable and hospitable, and you need not fear I shall suffer, for I find many almost fathers and mothers among these good folks.

"Taking our trunks, we travel through the country, entering the houses of the rich and poor, offering our goods, and earning our wages by the sweat of our brows. How do you think we look? Like two Awkward, Homespun, Tugging Yankee peddlers? No, that is not the case. By people of breeding we are treated with politeness and gentility, and the low and vulgar we do not seek. For my part, I enjoy travelling more than I expected. Conversation with new folks, observing manners and customs, and seeing the world, does me great good.

"I never met a real gentleman till I came here. Their hospitality allows me to see and copy their fine ways of acting and speaking, and they put the most Bashful at ease. Gad likes the maids and stays in the kitchen most times. I get into the libraries and read when we put up nights, and the ladies are most kind to me everywhere.

"I'm so tall they can't believe I'm only sixteen. They aren't as pretty as our rosy-faced girls, but their ways are elegant, and so are their clothes, tell Pam.

"When I think how kind you were to let me come, I am full of gratitude. I made some verses, one day, as I waited in a hovel for the rain to hold up.

> "To conduce to my own and parents' good,
>   Was why I left my home;
> To make their cares and burdens less,
>   And try to help them some.

'T was my own choice to earn them cash,
  And get them free from debt;
Before that I am twenty-one
  It shall be done, I bet.
My parents they have done for me
  What I for them can never do,
So if I serve them all I may,
  Sure God will help me through.
My chief delight, therefore, shall be
  To earn them all I can,
Not only now, but when that I
  At last am my own man.

"These are the genuine Sentiments of your son, who returns thanks for the many favors you have heaped upon him, and hopes to repay you by his best Endeavors. Accept this letter and the inclosed small sum as a token of his love and respect.

"Your dutiful son,

"Tell the girls to write.   ELI."

In reply to this, came a letter from the anxious mother, which shows not only the tender, pious nature of the good woman, but also how much need of education the boy had, and how well he was doing for himself: —

"AFFECTIONATE SON: We was very glad to receave your letter. I feal very anctious about you this winter, and how you are a doing. You cannot know a mother's concern for her boy wen he is fur away. Do not git into bad habbits.

Take the Bible for your rule and guide to vartue.
I pray for your prosperity in all spiritall and
temporrall things, and leave you in the care of
Him who gave you breath and will keep you
safe.

"We are all well, and your father enjoys his
helth better than last year. I visited Uncle
Medad a spell last week. I am provided with
a horse and shay to ride to meatin. Mr. Eben
Welton took our cow and give us his old horse.
Captain Stephen Harrington was excommuni-
cated last Sabbath. Pamely goes away to learn
dressmakin soon. I mistrust Mirandy will take
up with Pennel Haskell; he is likely, and comes
frequent. I wish you had been here a Christmas.
We had a large company to dinner, and I got
some wheat flower and made a fine chicken pye.
Eli, I hope you attend meatin when you can. Do
not trifle away the holy day in vane pleasures,
but live to the glory of God, and in the fear of
your parents. Father sold the white colt. He
was too spirity, and upsat Ambrose and nigh
broke his head. His nose is still black. Dear
son: I miss you every time I set a platter in
your place. Is your close warm and suffitient?
Put your stockin round your throat if sore. Do
you git good cyder to drink? Take the Penny-
ryal if you feal wimbly after a long spell of travil.
The girls send love. No more now. Wright
soon.

"Your mother.   HANNAH GARDENER."

" P. S. — Liddy Finch is married. Our pigs give us nine hundred pound of prime pork."

Many such letters went to and fro that winter, and Eli faithfully reported all his adventures. For he had many, and once or twice was in danger of losing his life.

On one occasion, having parted from his mate for a day or two, wishing to try his luck alone, our young peddler found himself, late in the afternoon, approaching the Dismal Swamp. A tempest arose, adding to the loneliness and terror of the hour. The cypresses uprooted by the blast fell now and then across the road, endangering the poor boy's head. A sluggish stream rolled through tangled junipers and beds of reeds, and the fen on either side was full of ugly creatures, lizards, snakes, and toads; while owls, scared by the storm, flew wildly about and hooted dismally. Just at the height of the tumult, Eli saw three men coming toward him, and gladly hastened to meet them, hoping to have their company or learn of them where he could find a shelter. But their bad faces daunted him, and he would have hurried by without speaking if they had not stopped him, roughly demanding his name and business.

The tall stripling was brave, but his youthful face showed him to be but a boy, and the consciousness of a well-filled purse in his pocket made him anxious to escape. So he answered briefly, and tried to go on. But two men held him, in spite of his struggles, while the third rifled his pockets, broke open his trunks, and took all that was of any value in the way of watches and jewelry. Then they left him, with a cruel joke about a good journey, and made off with their booty. It was the first time poor Eli had met with such a mishap, and as he stood in the rain looking at his wares scattered about the road, he felt inclined to throw himself into the creek, and forget his woes there among the frogs and snakes. But he had a stout heart, and soon decided to make the best of it, since nothing could be done to mend the matter. Gathering up his bedraggled laces, scattered scent-bottles, and dirty buttons, pins, and needles, he trudged sadly on, feeling that for him this was indeed a Dismal Swamp.

"I told you we'd better stick together, but you wanted to be so dre'dful smart, and go travellin' off alone in them out 'n the way places. Might 'a' known you'd get overhauled somers. I always did think you was a gump, Eli, and now I'm sure on 't," was all the comfort Gad gave him when they met, and the direful tale was told.

"What shall I do now?" asked the poor lad. "My notions are n't worth selling, and my money's gone. I'll have to pay Hoadley somehow."

"You'd better foot it home and go to choppin' punkins for the cows, or help your marm spin. I vow I never did see such a chap for gettin' into a mess," scolded Gad, who was a true Yankee, and made a successful trader, even in a small way.

" We 'll sleep on it," said Eli, gently, and went to bed very low in his mind.

Perhaps a few tears wet his pillow as he lay awake, and the prayers his mother taught him were whispered in the silence of the night; for hope revived, comfort came, and in the morning his serene face and sensible plan proved to his irate friend that the " gump " had a wise head and a manly heart, after all.

" Gad, it is just the time for the new almanacs, and Allen wants men to sell 'em. I thought it was small business before, but beggars must n't be choosers, so I 'm going right off to offer for the job 'round here. It will do for a start, and if I 'm smart, Allen will give me a better chance maybe."

" That 's a fust-rate plan. Go ahead, and I 'll say a good word for you. Allen knows me, and books is in your line, so I guess you 'll do wal if you keep out 'n the mashes," answered Gad, with great good will, having slept off his vexation.

The plan did go well, and for weeks the rosy-faced, gentle-voiced youth might have been seen mildly offering the new almanacs at doors and shops, and at street corners, with a wistful look in his blue eyes, and a courtesy of manner that attracted many customers and earned many a dollar. Several mates, envying his fine hand-writing and pitying his hard luck, took lessons in penmanship of him and paid him fairly, whereat he rejoiced over the hours spent at home, flat on the kitchen floor, or flourishing splendid capitals on the snow-banks, when his nose was blue with cold and his hands half-frozen.

When the season for the yellow-covered almanacs was over, Eli, having won the confidence of his employer, was fitted out with more notions, and again set forth on his travels, armed, this time, and in company with his townsman. He prospered well, and all winter trudged to and fro, seemingly a common peddler, but really a student, making the world his book, and bent on learning all he could. Travel taught him geography and history, for he soon knew every corner of Virginia; looked longingly at the ancient walls of William and Mary College, where Jefferson and Monroe studied; where young George Washington received his surveyor's commission, and in his later years served as Chancellor. In Yorktown, he heard all about the siege of 1781; saw Lord Cornwallis's lodgings and the cave named for him; met pleasant people, whose fine speech and manners he carefully copied; read excellent books wherever he could find them, and observed, remembered, and stored away all that he saw, heard, and learned, to help and adorn his later life.

By spring he set out for home, having slowly

saved enough to repay Hoadley for the lost
goods. But as if Providence meant to teach him
another lesson, and make him still more prudent,
humble, and manly, a sad adventure befell him
on his way.

While waiting for the coaster that was to take
them home, he one day went in swimming with
Gad; for this was one of the favorite pastimes
of the Connecticut boys, who on Saturday nights
congregated by the score at a pond called Ben-
son's Pot, and leaped from the spring-board like
circus tumblers, turning somersaults into the
deep water below.

It was too early for such sport now; the water
was very cold, and poor Gad, taken with cramp,
nearly drowned Eli by clinging to his legs as he
went down. Freeing himself with difficulty, Eli
tried to save his friend; but the current swept the
helpless man away, and he was lost. Hurriedly
dressing, Eli ran for aid, but found himself regarded with suspicion by those to whom he told
his story; for he was a stranger in the place and
certain peddlers who had gone before had left
a bad name behind them.

To his horror, he was arrested, accused of
murder, and would have been tried for his life,
if Mr. Allen of Norfolk had not come to testify
to his good character, and set him free. Poor
Gad's body was found and buried, and after a
month's delay, Eli set out again, alone, heavy-
hearted, and very poor, for all his own little

savings had been consumed by various expenses.
Mr. Hoadley's money was untouched, but not
increased, as he hoped to have it; and rather
than borrow a penny of it, Eli landed barefooted.
His boots were so old he threw them overboard,
and spent his last dollar for a cheap pair of shoes
to wear when he appeared at home, for they
were not stout enough to stand travel. So, like
Franklin with his rolls, the lad ate crackers and
cheese as he trudged through the city, and set
out for the far-away farm-house among the hills.

A long journey, but a pleasant one, in spite of
his troubles; for spring made the world lovely,
habit made walking no hardship, and all he had
seen in his wanderings passed before him at will,
like a panorama full of color and variety.

Letters had gone before, but it was a sad
home-coming, and when all was told, Eli said: —

"Now, father, I'll go to work. I've had my
wish and enjoyed it a sight; and would go again,
but I feel as if I ought to work, as long as I
can't pay for my time."

"That's hearty, son, and I'm obleeged to ye.
Hear what mother's got to say, and then do
whichever you prefer," answered the farmer,
with a nod toward his wife, who, with the girls,
seemed full of some pleasant news which they
longed to tell.

"I've sold all the cloth we made last winter
for a good sum, and father says you may hev
the spendin' on 't. It will be enough to pay your

board down to Uncle Tillotson's while you study with him, so 's 't you kin be gettin' ready for college next year. I 've sot my heart on 't, and you mus n't disapp'int me and the girls," said the good woman, with a face full of faith and pride in her boy, in spite of all mishaps.

" Oh, mammy, how good you be! It don't seem as if I ought to take it. But I *do* want to go!" cried Eli, catching her round the neck in an ecstasy of boyish delight and gratitude.

Here Miranda and Pamela appeared, bringing their homely gifts of warm hose, and new shirts made from wool and flax grown by the father, and spun and woven by the accomplished house-wife.

A very happy youth was Eli when he again set off to the city, with his humble outfit and slender purse, though father still looked doubt-ful, and the brothers were more sure than ever that Eli was a fool to prefer dry books to country work and fun.

A busy year followed, Eli studying, as never boy studied before, with the excellent minister, who soon grew proud of his best pupil. Less preparation was needed in those days, and per-haps more love and industry went to the work; for necessity is a stern master, and poor boys often work wonders if the spark of greatness is there.

Eli had his wish in time, and went to college, mother and sisters making it possible by the sale

of their handiwork; for the girls were famous
spinners, and the mother the best weaver in the
country around.   How willingly they toiled for
Eli! — rising early and sitting late, cheering
their labor with loving talk of the dear lad's
progress, and an unfailing faith in his future
success.   Many a long ride did that good mother
take to the city, miles away, with a great roll of
cloth on the pillion behind her to sell, that she
might pay her son's college bills.   Many a coveted pleasure did the faithful sisters give up
that they might keep Eli well clothed, or send
him some country dainty to cheer the studies
which seemed to them painfully hard and mys-
teriously precious.   Father began to take pride
in the ugly duckling now, and brothers to brag
of his great learning.   Neighbors came in to
hear his letters, and when vacation brought him
home, the lads and lasses regarded him with a
certain awe; for his manners were better, his
language purer, than theirs, and the new life he
led refined the country boy till he seemed a
gentleman.

The second year he yielded to temptation, and
got into debt.   Being anxious to do credit to his
family, of whom he was secretly a little ashamed
about this time, he spent money on his clothes,
conscious that he was a comely youth with a
great love of beauty, and a longing for all that
cultivates and embellishes character and life.   An
elegant gentleman astonished the hill folk that

season, by appearing at the little church in a suit such as the greatest rustic dandy never imagined in his wildest dreams, — the tall white hat with rolling brim, Marseilles vest with watch-chain and seals festooned across it, the fine blue coat with its brass buttons, and the nankeen trousers strapped over boots so tight that it was torture to walk in them. Armed with a cane in the well-gloved hand, an imposing brooch in the frills of the linen shirt, Eli sauntered across the green, the observed of all observers, proudly hoping that the blue eyes of a certain sweet Lucinda were fixed admiringly upon him.

The boys were the first to recover from the shock, and promptly resented the transformation of their former butt into a city beau, by jeering openly and affecting great scorn of the envied splendor. The poor jackdaw, somewhat abashed at the effect of his plumes, tried to prove that he felt no superiority, by being very affable, which won the lasses, but failed to soften the hearts of the boys; and when he secured the belle of the village for the Thanksgiving drive and dance, the young men resolved that pride should have a fall.

Arrayed in all his finery, Eli drove pretty Lucinda in a smart borrowed wagon to the tavern where the dance was held. Full of the airs and graces he had learned at college, the once bashful, awkward Eli was the admired of all eyes, as he pranced down the long contra-

dance in the agonizing boots, or played "thread-
ing the needle" without the least reluctance on
the part of the blushing girls to pay the fine of
a kiss when the players sung the old rhyme: —

> "The needle's eye no one can pass;
> The thread that runs so true —
> It has caught many a pretty lass,
> And now it has caught you."

But his glory was short-lived; for some enemy
maliciously drew out the linchpin from the smart
wagon, and as they were gayly driving homeward over the hills, the downfall came, and out
they both went, to the great damage of Eli's city
suit, and poor Lucinda's simple finery.

Fortunately, no bones were broken, and picking themselves up, they sadly footed it home,
hoping the mishap would remain unknown. But
the rogues took care that Eli should not escape,
and the whole neighborhood laughed over the
joke; for the fine hat was ruined, and the costly
coat split down the back, in the ignominious
tumble.

Great was the humiliation of the poor student;
for not only was he ridiculed, but Lucinda would
not forgive him, and the blue eyes smiled upon
another; worst of all, he had to confess his debts
and borrow money of his father to pay them.
He meekly bore the stern rebuke that came with
the hard-earned dollars, but the sight of the tears

his mother shed, even while she comforted him, filled him with remorse. He went back to his books, in a homespun suit, a sadder and a wiser boy, and fell to work as if resolved to wash out past errors and regain the confidence he had lost.

All that winter the wheels turned and the loom jangled, that the rolls of cloth might be increased; and never was the day too cold, the way too long, for the good mother's pious pilgrimage.

That summer, a man came home to them, shabby enough as to his clothes, but so wonderfully improved in other ways, that not only did the women folk glow with tender pride, but father and brothers looked at him with respect, and owned at last there was something in Eli. "No vacation for me," he said; "I must work to pay my debts; and as I am not of much use here, I 'll try my old plan, and peddle some money into my empty pockets."

It was both comic and pathetic to see the shoulders that had worn the fine broadcloth burdened with a yoke, the hands that had worn kid gloves grasping the tin trunks, and the dapper feet trudging through dust and dew in cow-hide boots. But the face under the old straw hat was a manlier one than that which the tall beaver crowned, and the heart under the rough vest was far happier than when the gold chain glittered above it. He did so well that when he returned to college his debts were paid, and the family faith in Eli restored.

That was an eventful year; for one brother married, and one went off to seek his fortune, the father mortgaging his farm to give these sons a fair start in life. Eli was to be a minister, and the farmer left his fortunes in the hands of his wife, who, like many another good mother, was the making of the great man of the family, and was content with that knowledge, leaving him the glory.

The next year, Eli graduated with honor, and went home, to be received with great rejoicing, just twenty-one, and a free man. He had longed for this time, and planned a happy, studious life, preparing to preach the gospel in a little parsonage of his own. But suddenly all was changed; joy turned to sorrow, hope to doubt, and Eli was called to relinquish liberty for duty, — to give up his own dreams of a home, to keep a roof over the heads of the dear mother and the faithful sisters. His father died suddenly, leaving very little for the women folk besides the independence that lay in the skill of their own thrifty hands. The elder brothers could not offer much help, and Eli was the one to whom the poor souls turned in their hour of sorrow and anxiety.

" Go on, dear, and don't pester yourself about us. We can find food and firin' here as long as the old farm is ours. I guess we can manage to pay off the mortgage by-and-by. It don't seem as if I *could* turn out, after livin' here ever

sense I was married, and poor father so fond
on 't."

The widow covered her face with her apron,
and Eli put his arms about her, saying manfully,
as he gave up all his fondest hopes for her dearer
sake: —

"Cheer up, mother, and trust to me. I should
be a poor fellow if I allowed you and the girls
to want, after all you 've done for me. I can
get a school, and earn instead of spend. Teaching and studying can go on together. I 'm sure
I should n't prosper if I shirked my duty, and
I won't." The three sad women clung to him,
and the brothers, looking at his brave, bright
face, felt that Eli was indeed a man to lean on
and to love in times like this.

"Well," thought the young philosopher, "the
Lord knows what is best for me, and perhaps
this is a part of my education. I 'll try to think
so, and hope to get some good out of a hard
job."

In this spirit he set about teaching, and prospered wonderfully, for his own great love of
learning made it an easy and delightful task to
help others as he had longed to be helped. His
innocent and tender nature made all children love
him, and gave him a remarkable power over
them; so when the first hard months were past,
and his efforts began to bear fruit, he found that
what had seemed an affliction was a blessing,
and that teaching was his special gift. Filial

duty sweetened the task, a submissive heart found
happiness in self-sacrifice, and a wise soul showed
him what a noble and lovely work it was to minister to little children, — for of such is the kingdom of heaven.

For years Eli taught, and his school grew
famous; for he copied the fashions of other
countries, invented new methods, and gave himself so entirely to his profession that he could
not fail of success. The mortgage was paid off,
and Eli made frequent pilgrimages to the dear
old mother, whose staff and comfort he still was.
The sisters married well, the brothers prospered,
and at thirty, the schoolmaster found a nobler
mate than pretty Lucinda, and soon had some
little pupils of his very own to love and teach.

There his youth ends; but after the years of
teaching he began to preach at last, not in one
pulpit, but in many all over the land, diffusing
good thoughts now as he had peddled small wares
when a boy; still learning as he went, still loving
books and studying mankind, still patient, pious,
dutiful, and tender, a wise and beautiful old man,
till, at eighty, Eli's education ended.

ONAWANDAH

"WHAT in the world have *I* chosen?" exclaimed Geoff, as he drew out a manuscript in his turn and read the queer name.

"A story that will just suit you, I think. The hero is an Indian, and a brave one, as you will see. I learned the little tale from an old woman who lived in the valley of the Connecticut, which the Indians called the Long River of Pines."

With this very short preface, Aunt Elinor began to read, in her best manner, the story of

ONAWANDAH

Long ago, — when hostile Indians haunted the great forests, and every settlement had its fort for the protection of the inhabitants, — in one of the towns on the Connecticut River, lived Parson Bain and his little son and daughter. The wife and mother was dead; but an old servant took care of them, and did her best to make Reuben and Eunice good children. Her direst threat, when they were naughty, was, "The Indians will come and fetch you, if you don't

behave." So they grew up in great fear of the
red men. Even the friendly Indians, who sometimes came for food or powder, were regarded
with suspicion by the people. No man went to
work without his gun near by. On Sundays,
when they trudged to the rude meeting-house,
all carried the trusty rifle on the shoulder; and
while the pastor preached, a sentinel mounted
guard at the door, to give warning if canoes
came down the river or a dark face peered from
the wood.

One autumn night, when the first heavy rains
were falling and a cold wind whistled through
the valley, a knock came at the minister's door,
and, opening it, he found an Indian boy, ragged,
hungry, and foot-sore, who begged for food and
shelter. In his broken way, he told how he had
fallen ill, and been left to die by enemies who
had taken him from his own people, months before; how he had wandered for days till almost
sinking; and that he had come now to ask for
help, led by the hospitable light in the parsonage
window.

" Send him away, master, or harm will come
of it. He is a spy, and we shall all be scalped
by the murdering Injuns who are waiting in the
wood," said old Becky, harshly; while little
Eunice hid in the old servant's ample skirts, and
twelve-year-old Reuben laid his hand on his
cross-bow, ready to defend his sister if need be.

But the good man drew the poor lad in, saying, with his friendly smile: " Shall not a Christian be as hospitable as a godless savage? Come in, child, and be fed; you sorely need rest and shelter."

Leaving his face to express the gratitude he had no words to tell, the boy sat by the comfortable fire and ate like a famished wolf, while Becky muttered her forebodings and the children eyed the dark youth at a safe distance. Something in his pinched face, wounded foot, and eyes full of dumb pain and patience, touched the little girl's tender heart, and, yielding to a pitiful impulse, she brought her own basin of new milk and, setting it beside the stranger, ran to hide behind her father, suddenly remembering that this was one of the dreaded Indians.

" That was well done, little daughter. Thou shalt love thine enemies, and share thy bread with the needy. See, he is smiling; that pleased him, and he wishes us to be his friends."

But Eunice ventured no more that night, and quaked in her little bed at the thought of the strange boy sleeping on a blanket before the fire below. Reuben hid his fears better, and resolved to watch while others slept; but was off as soon as his curly head touched the pillow, and dreamed of tomahawks and war-whoops till morning.

Next day, neighbors came to see the waif, and one and all advised sending him away as soon as possible, since he was doubtless a spy, as Becky said, and would bring trouble of some sort.

"When he is well, he may go whithersoever he will; but while he is too lame to walk, weak with hunger, and worn out with weariness, I will harbor him. He cannot feign suffering and starvation like this. I shall do my duty, and leave the consequences to the Lord," answered the parson, with such pious firmness that the neighbors said no more.

But they kept a close watch upon Onawandah, when he went among them, silent and submissive, but with the proud air of a captive prince, and sometimes a fierce flash in his black eyes when the other lads taunted him with his red skin. He was very lame for weeks, and could only sit in the sun, weaving pretty baskets for Eunice, and shaping bows and arrows for Reuben. The children were soon his friends, for with them he was always gentle, trying in his soft language and expressive gestures to show his good-will and gratitude; for they defended him against their ruder playmates, and, following their father's example, trusted and cherished the homeless youth.

When he was able to walk, he taught the boy to shoot and trap the wild creatures of the wood, to find fish where others failed, and to guide himself in the wilderness by star and sun, wind and water. To Eunice he brought little offerings of bark and feathers; taught her to make moccasins of skin, belts of shells, or pouches gay with porcupine quills and colored grass. He would not work for old Becky, — who plainly showed her distrust, — saying: "A brave does not grind corn and bring wood; that is squaw's work. Onawandah will hunt and fish and fight for you, but no more." And even the request of the parson could not win obedience in this, though the boy would have died for the good man.

"We can not tame an eagle as we can a barnyard fowl. Let him remember only kindness of us, and so we turn a foe into a friend," said Parson Bain, stroking the sleek, dark head, that always bowed before him, with a docile reverence shown to no other living creature.

Winter came, and the settlers fared hardly through the long months, when the drifts rose to the eaves of their low cabins, and the stores, carefully harvested, failed to supply even their simple wants. But the minister's family never lacked wild meat, for Onawandah proved himself a better hunter than any man in the town; and the boy of sixteen led the way on his snow-shoes when they went to track a bear to its den, chase the deer for miles, or shoot the wolves that howled about their homes in the winter nights.

But he never joined in their games, and sat apart when the young folk made merry, as if he scorned such childish pastimes and longed to be a man in all things. Why he stayed when he was well again, no one could tell, unless he waited for spring to make his way to his own people. But Reuben and Eunice rejoiced to keep him; for while he taught them many things, he was their pupil also, learning English rapidly, and proving himself a very affectionate and devoted friend and servant, in his own quiet way.

" Be of good cheer, little daughter; I shall be gone but three days, and our brave Onawandah will guard you well," said the parson, one April morning, as he mounted his horse to visit a distant settlement, where the bitter winter had brought sickness and death to more than one household.

The boy showed his white teeth in a bright smile as he stood beside the children, while Becky croaked, with a shake of the head: —

" I hope you may n't find you 've warmed a viper in your bosom, master."

Two days later, it seemed as if Becky was a true prophet, and that the confiding minister *had* been terribly deceived; for Onawandah went away to hunt, and that night the awful war-whoop woke the sleeping villagers, to find their houses burning, while the hidden Indians shot at them by the light of the fires kindled by dusky scouts. In terror and confusion the whites flew to the fort; and, while the men fought bravely, the women held blankets to catch arrows and bullets, or bound up the hurts of their defenders.

It was all over by daylight, and the red men sped away up the river, with several prisoners, and such booty as they could plunder from the

deserted houses. Not till all fear of a return of
their enemies was over, did the poor people venture to leave the fort and seek their ruined homes.
Then it was discovered that Becky and the parson's children were gone, and great was the be-
wailing, for the good man was much beloved by
all his flock.

Suddenly the smothered voice of Becky was
heard by a party of visitors, calling dolefully: —

"I am here, betwixt the beds. Pull me out,
neighbors, for I am half dead with fright and
smothering."

The old woman was quickly extricated from
her hiding-place, and with much energy declared
that she had seen Onawandah, disguised with
war-paint, among the Indians, and that he had
torn away the children from her arms before she
could fly from the house.

"He chose his time well, when they were
defenceless, dear lambs! Spite of all my warn-
ings, master trusted him, and this is the thanks
we get. Oh, my poor master! How can I tell
him this heavy news?"

There was no need to tell it; for, as Becky
sat moaning and beating her breast on the fire-
less hearth, and the sympathizing neighbors stood
about her, the sound of a horse's hoofs was
heard, and the parson came down the hilly road
like one riding for his life. He had seen the
smoke afar off, guessed the sad truth, and hurried on, to find his home in ruins, and to learn

by his first glance at the faces around him that his children were gone.

When he had heard all there was to tell, he sat down upon his door-stone with his head in his hands, praying for strength to bear a grief too deep for words. The wounded and weary men tried to comfort him with hope, and the women wept with him as they hugged their own babies closer to the hearts that ached for the lost children. Suddenly a stir went through the mournful group, as Onawandah came from the wood with a young deer upon his shoulders, and amazement in his face as he saw the desolation before him. Dropping his burden, he stood an instant looking with eyes that kindled fiercely; then he came bounding toward them, undaunted by the hatred, suspicion, and surprise plainly written on the countenances before him. He missed his playmates, and asked but one question : —

" The boy, the little squaw, — where gone? "

His answer was a rough one, for the men seized him and poured forth the tale, heaping reproaches upon him for such treachery and ingratitude. He bore it all in proud silence till they pointed to the poor father, whose dumb sorrow was more eloquent than all their wrath. Onawandah looked at him, and the fire died out of his eyes as if quenched by the tears he would not shed. Shaking off the hands that held him, he went to his good friend, saying with passionate earnestness : —

"Onawandah is *not* traitor! Onawandah remembers! Onawandah grateful! You believe?"

The poor parson looked up at him, and could not doubt his truth; for genuine love and sorrow ennobled the dark face, and he had never known the boy to lie.

"I believe and trust you still, but others will not. Go, you are no longer safe here, and I have no home to offer you," said the parson, sadly, feeling that he cared for none, unless his children were restored to him.

"Onawandah has no fear. He goes; but he comes again to bring the boy, the little squaw."

Few words, but they were so solemnly spoken that the most unbelieving were impressed; for the youth laid one hand on the gray head bowed before him, and lifted the other toward heaven, as if calling the Great Spirit to hear his vow.

A relenting murmur went through the crowd, but the boy paid no heed, as he turned away, and with no arms but his hunting knife and bow, no food but such as he could find, no guide but the sun by day, the stars by night, plunged into the pathless forest and was gone.

Then the people drew a long breath, and muttered to one another: —

"He will never do it, yet he is a brave lad for his years."

"Only a shift to get off with a whole skin, I warrant you. These varlets are as cunning as foxes," added Becky, sourly.

The parson alone believed and hoped, though weeks and months went by, and his children did not come.

Meantime, Reuben and Eunice were far away in an Indian camp, resting as best they could, after the long journey that followed that dreadful night. Their captors were not cruel to them, for Reuben was a stout fellow, and, thanks to Onawandah, could hold his own with the boys who would have tormented him if he had been feeble or cowardly. Eunice also was a hardy creature for her years, and when her first fright and fatigue were over, made herself useful in many ways among the squaws, who did not let the pretty child suffer greatly; though she was neglected, because they knew no better.

Life in a wigwam was not a life of ease, and fortunately the children were accustomed to simple habits and the hardships that all endured in those early times. But they mourned for home till their young faces were pathetic with the longing, and their pillows of dry leaves were often wet with tears in the night. Their clothes grew ragged, their hair unkempt, their faces tanned by sun and wind. Scanty food and exposure to all weathers tried the strength of their bodies, and uncertainty as to their fate saddened their spirits; yet they bore up bravely, and said their prayers faithfully, feeling sure that God would bring them home to father in His own good time.

One day, when Reuben was snaring birds in the wood, — for the Indians had no fear of such young children venturing to escape, — he heard the cry of a quail, and followed it deeper and deeper into the forest, till it ceased, and, with a sudden rustle, Onawandah rose up from the brakes, his finger on his lips to prevent any exclamation that might betray him to other ears and eyes.

"I come for you and little Laroka" (the name he gave Eunice, meaning " Wild Rose "). " I take you home. Not know me yet. Go and wait."

He spoke low and fast; but the joy in his face told how glad he was to find the boy after his long search, and Reuben clung to him, trying not to disgrace himself by crying like a girl, in his surprise and delight.

Lying hidden in the tall brakes they talked in whispers, while one told of the capture, and the other of a plan of escape; for, though a friendly tribe, these Indians were not Onawandah's people, and they must not suspect that he knew the children, else they might be separated at once.

"Little squaw betray me. You watch her. Tell her not to cry out, not speak me any time. When I say come, we go — fast — in the night. Not ready yet."

These were the orders Reuben received, and, when he could compose himself, he went back to the wigwams, leaving his friend in the wood, while he told the good news to Eunice, and prepared her for the part she must play.

Fear had taught her self-control, and the poor child stood the test well, working off her relief and rapture by pounding corn on the stone mortar till her little hands were blistered, and her arms ached for hours afterward.

Not till the next day did Onawandah make his appearance, and then he came limping into the village, weary, lame, and half starved, after his long wandering in the wilderness. He was kindly welcomed, and his story believed; for he told only the first part, and said nothing of his life among the white men. He hardly glanced at the children when they were pointed out to him by their captors, and scowled at poor Eunice, who forgot her part in her joy, and smiled as she met the dark eyes that till now had always looked kindly at her. A touch from Reuben warned her, and she was glad to hide her confusion by shaking her long hair over her face, as if afraid of the stranger.

Onawandah took no further notice of them, but seemed to be very lame with the old wound in his foot, which prevented his being obliged to hunt with the men. He was resting and slowly gathering strength for the hard task he had set himself, while he waited for a safe time to save the children. They understood, but the suspense proved too much for little Eunice, and she pined with impatience to be gone. She lost appetite

and color, and cast such appealing glances at
Onawandah, that he could not seem quite in-
different, and gave her a soft word now and
then, or did such acts of kindness as he could
perform unsuspected. When she lay awake at
night thinking of home, a cricket would chirp
outside the wigwam, and a hand slip in a leaf
full of berries, or a bark-cup of fresh water for
the feverish little mouth. Sometimes it was only
a caress or a whisper of encouragement, that re-
assured the childish heart, and sent her to sleep
with a comfortable sense of love and protection,
like a sheltering wing over a motherless bird.

Reuben stood it better, and entered heartily
into the excitement of the plot; for he had grown
tall and strong in these trying months, and felt
that he must prove himself a man to sustain and
defend his sister. Quietly he put away each day
a bit of dried meat, a handful of parched corn,
or a well-sharpened arrowhead, as provision for
the journey; while Onawandah seemed to be
amusing himself with making moccasins and a
little vest of deer-skin for an Indian child about
the age of Eunice.

At last, in the early autumn, all the men went
off on the war-path, leaving only boys and
women behind. Then Onawandah's eyes began
to kindle, and Reuben's heart to beat fast, for
both felt that their time for escape had come.

All was ready, and one moonless night the
signal was given. A cricket chirped shrilly out-

side the tent where the children slept with one
old squaw. A strong hand cut the skin beside
their bed of fir-boughs, and two trembling creatures crept out to follow the tall shadow that
flitted noiselessly before them into the darkness
of the wood. Not a broken twig, a careless step,
or a whispered word betrayed them, and they
vanished as swiftly and silently as hunted deer
flying for their lives.

Till dawn they hurried on, Onawandah carrying Eunice, whose strength soon failed, and
Reuben manfully shouldering the hatchet and the
pouch of food. At sunrise they hid in a thicket
by a spring and rested, while waiting for the
friendly night to come again. Then they pushed
on, and fear gave wings to their feet, so that
by another morning they were far enough away
to venture to travel more slowly and sleep at
night.

If the children had learned to love and trust
the Indian boy in happier times, they adored him
now, and came to regard him as an earthly
Providence; so faithful, brave, and tender was
he, — so forgetful of himself, so bent on saving
them. He never seemed to sleep, ate the poorest
morsels, or went without any food when provision failed; let no danger daunt him, no hardship wring complaint from him, but went on
through the wild forest, led by guides invisible
to them, till they began to hope that home was
near.

Twice he saved their lives. Once, when he went in search of food, leaving Reuben to guard his sister, the children, being very hungry, ignorantly ate some poisonous berries which looked like wild cherries, and were deliciously sweet. The boy generously gave most of them to Eunice, and soon was terror-stricken to see her grow pale, and cold, and deathly ill. Not knowing what to do, he could only rub her hands and call wildly for Onawandah.

The name echoed through the silent wood, and, though far away, the keen ear of the Indian heard it, his fleet feet brought him back in time, and his knowledge of wild roots and herbs made it possible to save the child when no other help was at hand.

"Make fire. Keep warm. I soon come," he said, after hearing the story and examining Eunice, who could only lift her eyes to him, full of childish confidence and patience.

Then he was off again, scouring the woods like a hound on the scent, searching everywhere for the precious little herb that would counteract the poison. Any one watching him would have thought him crazy, as he rushed hither and thither, tearing up the leaves, creeping on his hands and knees that it might not escape him, and when he found it, springing up with a cry that startled the birds, and carried hope to poor Reuben, who was trying to forget his own pain in his anxiety for Eunice, whom he thought dying.

"Eat, eat, while I make drink. All safe now," cried Onawandah, as he came leaping toward them with his hands full of green leaves, and his dark face shining with joy.

The boy was soon relieved, but for hours they hung over the girl, who suffered sadly, till she grew unconscious and lay as if dead. Reuben's courage failed then, and he cried bitterly, thinking how hard it would be to leave the dear little creature under the pines and go home alone to father. Even Onawandah lost hope for a while, and sat like a bronze statue of despair, with his eyes fixed on his Wild Rose, who seemed fading away too soon.

Suddenly he rose, stretched his arms to the west, where the sun was setting splendidly, and in his own musical language prayed to the Great Spirit. The Christian boy fell upon his knees, feeling that the only help was in the Father who saw and heard them even in the wilderness. Both were comforted, and when they turned to Eunice there was a faint tinge of color on the pale cheeks, as if the evening red kissed her; the look of pain was gone, and she slept quietly, without the moans that had made their hearts ache before.

"He hears! he hears!" cried Onawandah, and for the first time Reuben saw tears in his keen eyes, as the Indian boy turned his face to the sky, full of a gratitude that no words were sweet enough to tell.

All night Eunice lay peacefully sleeping, and the moon lighted Onawandah's lonely watch, for Reuben was worn out with suspense, and slept beside his sister.

In the morning she was safe, and great was the rejoicing; but for two days the little invalid was not allowed to continue the journey, much as they longed to hurry on. It was a pretty sight, the bed of hemlock boughs spread under a green tent of woven branches, and on the pillow of moss the pale child watching the flicker of sunshine through the leaves, listening to the babble of a brook close by, or sleeping tranquilly, lulled by the murmur of the pines. Patient, loving, and grateful, it was a pleasure to serve her, and both the lads were faithful nurses. Onawandah cooked birds for her to eat, and made a pleasant drink of the wild-raspberry leaves to quench her thirst. Reuben snared rabbits, that she might have nourishing food, and longed to shoot a deer for provision, that she might not suffer hunger again on their journey. This boyish desire led him deeper into the wood than it was wise for him to go alone, for it was near nightfall, and wild creatures haunted the forest in those days. The fire, which Onawandah kept constantly burning, guarded their little camp where Eunice lay; but Reuben, with no weapon but his bow and hunting knife, was beyond this protection when he at last gave up his vain hunt and turned homeward. Suddenly, the sound of

stealthy steps startled him, but he could see
nothing through the dusk at first, and hurried
on, fearing that some treacherous Indian was
following him. Then he remembered his sister,
and resolved not to betray her resting-place if
he could help it, for he had learned courage of
Onawandah, and longed to be as brave and generous as his dusky hero.

So he paused to watch and wait, and soon saw
the gleam of two fiery eyes, not behind, but
above him, in a tree. Then he knew that it was
an "Indian devil," as they called a species of
fierce animal that lurked in the thickets and
sprang on its prey like a small tiger.

"If I could only kill it alone, how proud
Onawandah would be of me," thought Reuben,
burning for the good opinion of his friend.

It would have been wiser to hurry on and give
the beast no time to spring; but the boy was over
bold, and, fitting an arrow to the string, aimed
at the bright eye-ball and let fly. A sharp snarl
showed that some harm was done, and, rather
daunted by the savage sound, Reuben raced
away, meaning to come back next day for the
prize he hoped he had secured.

But soon he heard the creature bounding after
him, and he uttered one ringing shout for help,
feeling too late that he had been foolhardy. Fortunately, he was nearer camp than he thought.
Onawandah heard him, and was there in time
to receive the beast, as, mad with the pain of the

wound, it sprung at Reuben. There was no time for words, and the boy could only watch in breathless interest and anxiety the fight which went on between the brute and the Indian.

It was sharp but short; for Onawandah had his knife, and as soon as he could get the snarling, struggling creature down, he killed it with a skilful stroke. But not before it had torn and bitten him more dangerously than he knew; for the dusk hid the wounds, and excitement kept him from feeling them at first. Reuben thanked him heartily, and accepted his few words of warning with grateful docility; then both hurried back to Eunice, who till next day knew nothing of her brother's danger.

Onawandah made light of his scratches, as he called them, got their supper, and sent Reuben early to bed, for to-morrow they were to start again.

Excited by his adventure, the boy slept lightly, and waking in the night, saw by the flicker of the fire Onawandah binding up a deep wound in his breast with wet moss and his own belt. A stifled groan betrayed how much he suffered; but when Reuben went to him, he would accept no help, said it was nothing, and sent him back to bed, preferring to endure the pain in stern silence, with true Indian pride and courage.

Next morning, they set out and pushed on as fast as Eunice's strength allowed. But it was evident that Onawandah suffered much, though

he would not rest, forbade the children to speak
of his wounds, and pressed on with feverish
haste, as if he feared that his strength might
not hold out.   Reuben watched him anxiously,
for there was a look in his face that troubled the
boy and filled him with alarm, as well as with
remorse and love.   Eunice would not let him
carry her as before, but trudged bravely behind
him, though her feet ached and her breath often
failed as she tried to keep up; and both children
did all they could to comfort and sustain their
friend, who seemed glad to give his life for
them.

In three days they reached the river, and, as
if Heaven helped them in their greatest need,
found a canoe, left by some hunter, near the
shore.   In they sprang, and let the swift current
bear them along, Eunice kneeling in the bow
like a little figure-head of Hope, Reuben steering
with his paddle, and Onawandah sitting with
arms tightly folded over his breast, as if to control the sharp anguish of the neglected wound.
He knew that it was past help now, and only
cared to see the children safe; then, worn out
but happy, he was proud to die, having paid his
debt to the good parson, and proved that he was
not a liar nor a traitor.

Hour after hour they floated down the great
river, looking eagerly for signs of home, and
when at last they entered the familiar valley,
while the little girl cried for joy, and the boy

paddled as he had never done before, Onawandah sat erect, with his haggard eyes fixed on the dim distance, and sang his death-song in a clear, strong voice, — though every breath was pain, — bent on dying like a brave, without complaint or fear.

At last they saw the smoke from the cabins on the hillside, and, hastily mooring the canoe, all sprang out, eager to be at home after their long and perilous wandering. But as his foot touched the land, Onawandah felt that he could do no more, and stretching his arms toward the parsonage, the windows of which glimmered as hospitably as they had done when he first saw them, he said, with a pathetic sort of triumph in his broken voice: " Go. I cannot. Tell the good father, Onawandah not lie, not forget. He keep his promise."

Then he dropped upon the grass and lay as if dead, while Reuben, bidding Eunice keep watch, ran as fast as his tired legs could carry him to tell the tale and bring help.

The little girl did her part tenderly, carrying water in her hands to wet the white lips, tearing up her ragged skirt to lay fresh bandages on the wound that had been bleeding the brave boy's life away, and, sitting by him, gathered his head into her arms, begging him to wait till father came.

But poor Onawandah had waited too long; now he could only look up into the dear, loving,

little face bent over him, and whisper wistfully:
" Wild Rose will remember Onawandah? " as
the light went out of his eyes, and his last breath
was a smile for her.

When the parson and his people came hurrying up full of wonder, joy, and good-will, they
found Eunice weeping bitterly, and the Indian
boy lying like a young warrior smiling at death.

" Ah, my neighbors, the savage has taught us
a lesson we never can forget. Let us imitate his
virtues, and do honor to his memory," said the
pastor, as he held his little daughter close and
looked down at the pathetic figure at his feet,
whose silence was more eloquent than any words.

All felt it, and even old Becky had a remorse-
ful sigh for the boy who had kept his word so
well and given back her darlings safe.

They buried him where he lay; and for years
the lonely mound under the great oak was kept
green by loving hands. Wild roses bloomed
there, and the murmur of the Long River of
Pines was a fit lullaby for faithful Onawandah.

LITTLE THINGS

"THAT'S the sort I like," said Geoff, as the story ended; "Onawandah was a trump, and I'd give a good deal to know such a fellow, and go hunting with him. Got any more like it, aunty?"

"Perhaps; but it is the girls' turn now, and here is a quiet little story that teaches the same lesson in a different way. It contains a hint which some of you would better take;" and Aunt Elinor glanced around the circle with a smile that set her hearers on the alert to see who was to be hit.

"Hope it isn't *very* moral," said Geoff, with a boyish dislike of being preached at.

"It won't harm you to listen, and take the moral to heart, my lad. Wild horses, gold mines, and sea scrapes, are not the only things worth reading about. If you ever do half so much good in the world as the people in this story did, I shall be proud of you," answered Aunt Elinor, so soberly that Geoff folded his hands, and tried to look meekly impressed.

"Is it true?" asked Min.

"Yes. I heard 'Abby' tell it herself, and saw the silk stocking, and the scar."

"That sounds *very* interesting. I do like to hear about good clothes and awful accidents," cried the girl, forgetting to spin, in her eagerness to listen.

They all laughed at her odd mixture of tastes, and then heard the story of

LITTLE THINGS

ABIGAIL sat reading "Rasselas" aloud to her father while he shaved, pausing now and then to explain a word or correct the girl's pronunciation; for this was a lesson, as well as a pleasure. The handsome man, in his nankin dressing-gown, ruffled shirt, black small-clothes, and silk stockings, stood before the tall, old-fashioned bureau, looking often from the reflection of his own ruddy face to the pale one beside him, with an expression of tender pride, which plainly showed how dear his young daughter was to him.

Abby was a slender girl of fifteen, in a short-waisted gingham gown, with a muslin tucker, dimity apron, and morocco shoes on a pair of small feet demurely crossed before her. A blue-eyed, brown-haired little creature, with a broad brow, and a sweet mouth, evidently both intelligent and affectionate; for she heartily enjoyed the story, and answered her father's approving glances with a face full of the loving reverence so beautiful to see.

Schools were not abundant in 1815; and, after learning to read, spell, sew, and cipher a little at some dame school, girls were left to pick up knowledge as they could; while the brothers went to college, or were apprenticed to some trade. But the few things they did study were well learned; so that Abby's reading was a pleasure to hear. She wrote a fine, clear hand, seldom misspelled a word, kept her own little account-book in good order, and already made her father's shirts, hemstitching the linen cambric ruffles with the daintiest skill, and turning out button-holes any one might be proud of. These accomplishments did not satisfy her, however, and she longed to know much more, — to do and be something great and good, — with the sincere longing of an earnest, thoughtful girl.

These morning talks with her father were precious half-hours to her; for they not only read and discussed well-chosen books, but Abby opened her heart freely, and received his wise counsels with a grateful docility which helped to make her after-life as benevolent and blessed as his.

" I don't wonder that Rasselas wanted to get out of the Happy Valley and see the world for himself. I often feel so, and long to go and have adventures, like the people I read about; to do something very splendid, and be brave and great and loved and honored," said Abby, as she closed the book, and looked out of the open window with wistful eyes; for the chestnut trees were rustling in the May sunshine, and spring was stirring in the girl's heart, as well as in the budding boughs and early flowers on the green bank below.

"Do not be in a hurry to leave your Happy Valley, my dear; but help to keep it so by doing your part well. The happiness of life depends very much on little things; and one can be brave and great and good while making small sacrifices and doing small duties faithfully and cheerfully," answered Mr. Lyon, with the look of one who practised what he preached.

"But *my* little things are so stupid and easy. Sewing, and learning to pickle and preserve, and going out to tea when I don't want to, and helping mother, are none of them romantic or exciting duties and sacrifices. If I could take care of poor people, or be a colonel in a splendid uniform, and march with drums and trumpets, — or even a fire-warden, and run to save lives and property, and be loved and thanked and trusted, as you are, I should be contented," continued Abby, kindling at the thought; for she considered her father the noblest of men, and glowed with pride when she saw him in his regimentals on great occasions, or when she helped him into the leathern cap and coat, and gave him the lantern, staff, and canvas bags he used, as fire-warden, long before steam-engines, hook and ladder companies, and electric alarms were dreamed of.

Mr. Lyon laughed as he washed his face at the queer, three-cornered stand, and then sat down to have his hair tied in a queue by his daughter, who prided herself on doing this as well as a barber.

"Ah, my girl, it's not the things that make the most noise and show that are the bravest and the best; but the everlasting patience, charity, and courage needed to bear our daily trials like good Christians." And the smile changed to a sigh, for the excellent man knew the value of these virtues, and their rarity.

"Yes, I know, sir; but it is so splendid to be a hero, and have the world ringing with one's glory, like Washington and Lafayette, or Perry, Hull, and Lawrence," said Abby, winding the black ribbon so energetically that it nearly broke; for her head was full of the brave deeds performed in the wars of 1775 and 1812, the latter of which she well remembered.

"Easy, my dear, easy! — remember that it was the faithful doing of small things which fitted these men to do the grand deeds well, when the time came. Heroes are not made in a minute, and we never know what we may be called upon to live through. Train yourself now to be skilful, prompt, courageous, and kind; then when the duty or the danger comes, you will be prepared for it. 'Keep your spindle ready, and the Lord will send the flax,' as the old proverb says."

"I will, father, and remember the other saying that you like and live up to, 'Do right and leave the consequences to God,'" answered Abby, with her arm about his neck, and a soft cheek against his, feeling that with such an example before her she ought not to fail.

"That's my good girl! Come, now, begin at once. Here's a little thing to do, a very homely one, but useful, and some honor may be gained by doing it nicely; for, if you'll darn this bad rent in my new stocking, I'll give you five dollars."

As he spoke, Mr. Lyon handed her a heavy silk stocking with a great "barn-door" tear in the calf. He was rather proud of his handsome legs, and dressed them with care, importing hose of unusual fineness for state occasions; being one of the old-time gentlemen whose stately elegance added dignity to any scene.

Abby groaned as she examined the hole torn by a nail, for it was a very bad one, and she knew that if not well done, the costly stocking would be ruined. She hated to darn, infinitely preferring to read, or study Latin with her brother, instead of repairing old damask, muslin gowns, and the family hose. But she did it well, excelling her elder sister in this branch of needle-work; so she could not refuse, though the sacrifice of time and taste would have been almost impossible for any one but father.

"I'll try, sir, and you shall pay me with a kiss; five dollars is too much for such a little thing," she said, smiling at him as she put the stocking into the capacious pocket where girls kept housewife, scissors, thimble, pin-ball, and a bit of lovage or flag-root in those days.

"I'm not so sure that you'll find it an easy job; but remember Bruce and his spider, and don't be conquered by the 'little thing.' Now I must be off. Good-by, my darling," and Mr. Lyon's dark eyes twinkled as he thought of the task he had set her; for it seemed as if nothing short of a miracle could restore his damaged stocking.

Abby forgot her heroics and ran to get his hat and cane, to receive his morning kiss, and answer the salute he always paused at the street corner to give her before he went away to the many cares and labors of his own busy day. But while she put her little room in order, dusted the parlor, and clapped laces for her mother, who, like most ladies long ago, did up her own caps and turbans, Abby was thinking over the late conversation, and wondering if strict attention to small affairs would really lead to something good or glorious in the end.

When her other duties were done, she resolutely sat down to the detested darn, although it would have been much pleasanter to help her sister cut out green satin leaves and quill up pink ribbon into roses for a garland to festoon the skirt of a new white dress.

Hour after hour she worked, slowly and carefully weaving the torn edges together, stitch by stitch, till her eyes ached and the delicate needle grew rusty in her warm hand. Her mother begged her to stop and rest, sister Catharine called her to come and see how well the garland looked, and a friend came to take her to drive. But she refused to stir, and kept at her weaving, as patiently as King Robert's spider, picking out a bit that puckered, turning the corner with breathless care, and rapping it with her thimble on the wooden egg till it lay flat. Then she waited till an iron was heated, and pressed it nicely, finishing in time to put it on her father's bureau, where he would see it when he dressed for dinner.

"Nearly four hours over that dreadful darn! But it's done now, and hardly shows, so I do think I've earned my money. I shall buy that work-box I have wanted so long. The inlaid one, with nice velvet beds for the thimble, scissors, and bodkin, and a glass in the cover, and a little drawer for my silk-reels. Father will like that, and I shall be proud to show it."

These agreeable thoughts were passing through Abby's mind as she went into the front yard for a breath of air, after her long task was over. Tulips and hyacinths were blooming there, and, peeping through the bars of the gate, stood a little girl wistfully watching the gay blossoms and enjoying their perfume. Now, Abby was fond of her garden, and had been hurrying the early flowers, that they might be ready for her father's birthday nosegay; so her first impulse was to feign that she did not see the child, for she did not want to give away a single tulip. But the morning talk was fresh in her memory, and presently she thought : —

"Here is a little thing I can do;" and ashamed of the selfish impulse, she gathered several of her finest flowers and offered them, saying cordially : —

"I think you would like these. Please take them, and by and by when there are more, you shall have prettier ones."

"Oh, thank you! I did want some for mamma. She is ill, and will be so pleased," was the grateful answer, given with a little courtesy, and a smile that made the wistful face a very happy one.

"Do you live near by?" asked Abby, seeing at once from the child's speech and manner that she was both well-bred and grateful.

"Just around the corner. We are English, and papa is dead. Mamma kept school in another place till she was too ill, and now I take care of her and the children as well as I can."

The little girl of twelve, in her black frock, with a face far too old and anxious for her years, was so innocently pathetic as she told the sad story, that Abby's tender heart was touched, and an impetuous desire to do something at once made her exclaim : —

"Wait a minute, and I'll send something better than flowers. Would n't your mother like some wine jelly? I helped make it, and have a glassful all my own."

"Indeed she would!" began the child, blushing with pleasure; for the poor lady needed just such delicacies, but thought only of the children's wants.

Waiting to hear no more, Abby ran in to get her offering, and came back beaming with benevolent good-will.

"As it is not far and you have that big basket, I'll go with you and help carry the things, if I may? My mother will let me, and my father will come and see you, I'm sure, if you'd like to have him. He takes care of everybody, and is the best and wisest man in all the world."

Lucy Mayhew accepted these kind offers with childish confidence, thinking the young lady a sort of angel in a coal-scuttle bonnet, and the two went chatting along, good friends at once; for Abby had most engaging manners, and her cheerful face won its way everywhere.

She found the English family a very interesting one, for the mother was a gentlewoman, and in sore straits now, — being unable to use her accomplishments any longer, and failing fast, with no friends to protect the four little children she must soon leave alone in a strange land.

"If *they* were only cared for, I could go in peace; but it breaks my heart to think of them in an asylum, when they need a home," said the poor lady, telling her greatest anxiety to this sympathetic young visitor; while Lucy regaled the noses of the eager little ones with delicious sniffs of the pink and blue hyacinths.

"Tell father all about it, and he'll know just what to do. He always does, and every one goes to him. May he come and see you, ma'am?" said Abby, longing to take them all home at once.

"He will be as welcome as an angel from Heaven, my child. I am failing very fast, and help and comfort are sorely needed," answered the grateful woman, with wet eyes and a heart too full for many thanks.

Abby's eyes were full also, and promising to "send father soon," she went away, little dreaming that the handful of flowers and a few kind words were the first links in a chain of events that brought a blessing into her own home.

She waited anxiously for her father's return, and blushed with pleasure as he said, after examining her morning's work:—

"Wonderfully well done, my dear! Your mother says she could n't have done it better herself."

"I 'm sorry that it shows at all; but it was impossible to hide that corner, and if you wear it on the inside of the leg, it won't be seen much," explained Abby, anxiously.

"It shows just enough for me to know where to point when I boast of my girl's patience and skill. People say I'm making a blue-stocking of you, because we read Johnson; but my black stocking will prove that I haven't spoiled you yet," said Mr. Lyon, pinching her cheek, as they went down to dinner arm in arm.

Literary ladies were looked upon with awe, and by many with disapproval, in those days; so Abby's studious tastes were criticised by the good cousins and aunts, who feared she might do something peculiar; though, years later, they were very proud of the fine letters she wrote, and the intellectual society which she had unconsciously fitted herself to enjoy and adorn.

Abby laughed at her father's joke, but said no more just then; for young people sat silent at table while their elders talked. She longed to tell about Lucy; and when dessert came, she drew her chair near to her father's, that she might pick the kernels from his walnuts and drop them into his wine, waiting till he said, as usual: "Now, little girl, let's take comfort." For both enjoyed the hour of rest he allowed himself in the middle of the day.

On this occasion he varied the remark by adding, as he took a bill from his pocket-book and gave it to her with a kiss: "Well-earned money, my dear, and most cheerfully paid."

"Thank you, sir! It seems a great deal for such a small job. But I *do* want it very much. May I tell you how I'd like to spend it, father?" cried Abby, beaming with the sweet delight of helping others.

"Yes, child; come and tell me. Something for sister, I suspect; or a new book, perhaps." And, drawing her to his knee, Mr. Lyon waited with a face full of benignant interest in her little confidences.

She told her story eagerly and well, exclaiming as she ended: "And now, I'm so glad, so very glad, I have this money, all my own, to spend for those dear little things! I know you'll help them; but it's so nice to be able to do my part, and giving away is such a pleasure."

"You are your father's own daughter in that, child. I must go and get my contribution ready, or I shall be left out," said Mrs. Lyon, hastening away to add one more charity to the many which made her quiet life so beautiful.

"I will go and see our neighbor this evening, and you shall come with me. You see, my girl, that the homely 'little job' is likely to be a large and pleasant one, and you have earned your part in it. Do the duty that comes first, and one never knows what beautiful experience it may blossom into. Use your earnings as you like, and God bless you, my dear."

So Abby had her part in the happy days that came to the Mayhews, and enjoyed it more than a dozen work-boxes; while her father was never tired of showing the handsome darn and telling the story of it.

Help and comfort were much needed around the corner; for very soon the poor lady died.

But her confidence in the new friends raised up
to her was not misplaced; and when all was over,
and people asked, " What will become of the children?" Mr. Lyon answered the sad question by
leading the four little orphans to his own house,
and keeping them till good homes were found for
the three youngest.

Lucy was heart-broken, and clung to Abby in
her sorrow, as if nothing else could console her
for all she had lost. No one had the heart to
speak of sending her away at present; and, before long, the grateful little creature had won
a place for herself which she never forfeited.

It was good for Abby to have a care of this
sort, and her generous nature enjoyed it thor-
oughly, as she played elder sister in the sweetest
way. It was her first real lesson in the charity
that made her after-life so rich and beautiful;
but then she little dreamed how well she was to
be repaid for her small share in the good work
which proved to be a blessing to them all.

Soon, preparations for sister Catharine's wedding produced a pleasant bustle in the house, and
both the younger girls were as busy as bees,
helping everywhere. Dressmakers ripped and
stitched upstairs, visitors gossiped in the parlor,
and cooks simmered and scolded in the kitchen;
while notable Madam Lyon presided over the
household, keeping the peace and gently bringing
order out of chaos.

Abby had a new sprigged muslin frock, with

a white sash, and her first pair of silk stockings, a present from her father. A bunch of pink roses gave the finishing touch, and she turned up her hair with a tortoise-shell comb in honor of the occasion.

All the relations — and there were many of them — came to the wedding, and the hospitable mansion was crowded with old and young. A fine breakfast was prepared, a line of carriages filled the quiet street, and troops of stately ladies and gentlemen came marching in; for the Lyons were a much-honored family.

The interesting moment arrived at last, the minister opened his book, the lovely bride entered with her groom, and a solemn silence fell upon the rustling crowd. Abby was much excited, and felt that she was about to disgrace herself by crying. Fortunately she stood near the door, and finding that a sob *would* come at thought of her dear sister going away forever, she slipped out and ran upstairs to hide her tears in the back bedroom, where she was put to accommodate guests.

As she opened the door, a puff of smoke made her catch her breath, then run to throw open the window before she turned to look for the fallen brand. A fire had been kindled in this room a short time before, and, to Abby's dismay, the sudden draught fanned the smouldering sparks which had crept from a fallen log to the mop-board and thence around the wooden mantelpiece. A suspicious crackling was heard, little tongues of flame darted from the cracks, and the air was full of smoke.

Abby's first impulse was to fly downstairs, screaming "Fire!" at the top of her voice; her second was to stand still and think what to do, — for an instant's recollection showed her what terror and confusion such a cry would produce in the crowded house, and how unseemly a panic would be at such a time.

"If I could only get at father! But I can't without scaring every one. What would he do? I've heard him tell about fires, and how to put them out; I know, — stop the draught first," and Abby shut the window. "Now water and wet blankets," and away she ran to the bath-room, and filling a pail, dashed the water over the burning wood. Then, pulling the blankets from off the bed, she wet them as well as she could, and hung them up before the fire-place, going to and fro for more water till the smoke ceased to pour out and the crackling stopped.

Those energetic measures were taken just in time to prevent a serious fire, and when Abby dared to rest a moment, with her eyes on the chimney, fearing the treacherous blaze might burst out in a new place, she discovered that her clothes were wet, her face blackened, her hands blistered, and her breath gone.

"No matter," she thought, still too much elated with her success to feel the pain. "Father will be pleased, I know; for this is what he would call an emergency, and I 've had my wits about me. I wish mother would come. Oh, dear! how queerly I feel — " and in the midst of her self-congratulation, poor little Abby fainted away, — slipping to the floor and lying there, like a new sort of Casabianca, faithful at her post.

Lucy found her very soon, having missed her and come to look for her the minute the service was over. Much frightened, she ran down again and tried to tell Mr. and Mrs. Lyon quietly. But her pale face alarmed every one, and when Abby came to herself, she was in her father's arms, being carried from the scene of devastation to her mother's room, where a crowd of anxious relatives received her like a conquering hero.

" Well done, my brave little fire-warden! I 'm proud of you! " were the first words she heard; and they were more reviving than the burnt feathers under her nose, or the lavender-water plentifully sprinkled over her by her mother and sister.

With that hearty commendation, her father left her, to see that all was safe, and Abby found that another sort of courage was needed to support her through the next half-hour of trial; for her hands were badly burned, and each of the excellent relatives suggested a different remedy.

" Flour them! " cried Aunt Sally, fanning her violently.

" Goose-oil and cotton-batting," suggested Aunt Patty.

"Nothing so good as lard," pronounced Aunt Nabby.

"I always use dry starch or a piece of salt pork," added cousin Lucretia.

"Butter them!" commanded grandma. "That's what I did when my Joseph fell into the boiler and came out with his blessed little legs the color of lobsters. Butter them, Dolly."

That settled the vexed question, and Abby's hands were well buttered, while a hearty laugh composed the spirits of the agitated party; for the contrast between grandma's words and her splendid appearance, as she sat erect in the big arm-chair issuing commands like a general, in silver-gray satin and an imposing turban, was very funny.

Then Abby was left to repose, with Lucy and old Nurse beside her, while the rest went down to eat the wedding feast and see the happy pair off in a chaise, with the portmanteau slung underneath, on their quiet honey-moon trip to Pomfret.

When the bustle was all over, Abby found herself a heroine in her small circle of admiring friends and neighbors, who praised and petted her as if she had saved the city from destruction. She needed comfort very much; for one hand was so seriously injured that it never entirely recovered from the deep burn, which contracted two of her finger-tips. This was a great sorrow to the poor girl; for she could no longer play on her piano, and was forced to content herself with singing like a lark when all joined in the sweet old ballads forgotten now.

It was a misfortune, but it had its happy side; for, during the long months when she was partially helpless, books were her solace, and she studied many things which other duties or pleasures would have crowded out, if "Abby's poor hand" had not been an excuse for such liberty and indulgence. It did not make her selfish, however, for while regretting her uselessness, she unexpectedly found work to do that made her own life happy by cheering that of another.

Lucy proved to be a most intelligent child; and when Abby asked what return she could make for all the little girl's loving service during her trouble, she discovered that help about lessons would be the favor most desired. Lucy's too early cares had kept her from learning much, and now that she had leisure, weak eyes forbade study, and she longed vainly to get on as her new friend did; for Abby was her model in all things, — looked up to with admiration, love, and wonder.

"Father, I've been thinking that I might read Lucy's lessons to her and hear her recite. Then she would n't grieve about being backward, and I can be eyes to her as she is hands to me. I can't sew or work now, but I can teach the little I know. May I, sir?" asked Abby, one morning, after reading a paper in the *Spectator,* and having a pleasant talk about it during the happy half-hour.

"A capital plan, daughter, if you are sure you can keep on. To begin and then fail would leave the child worse off for the hope and disappointment. It will be tiresome to go on day after day, so think well before you propose it," answered her father, much pleased with the idea.

"I *can* do it, and I *will!* If I get tired, I'll look at you and mother, — always so faithful to what you undertake — and remember my motto," cried Abby, anxious to follow the example set her in the daily life of these good parents.

A hearty hand-shake rewarded her, and she set about the new task with a resolute purpose to succeed. It was hard at first to go back to her early lessons and read them over and over again to eager Lucy, who did her best to understand, remember, and recite. But good-will and gratitude worked wonders; and day after day, week after week, month after month, the teaching went on, to the great surprise and satisfaction of those who watched this labor of love. Both learned much, and a very strong, sweet friendship grew up, which lasted till the young girls became old women.

For nearly two years the daily lessons were continued; then Lucy was ready and able to go to school, and Abby free from the duty that had grown a pleasure. Sister Catharine being gone, she was the young lady of the house now, and began to go to a few parties, where she distinguished herself by her graceful dancing, and

sprightly though modest manners. She had
grown strong and rosy with the exercise her
sensible mother prescribed and her energetic
father encouraged, taking long walks with her
to Roxbury and Dorchester on holidays, over
bridges and around the common before breakfast
each morning, till the pale little girl was a tall
and blooming creature, full of life and spirit, —
not exactly beautiful, but with a sweet, intelligent
face, and the frank, cordial ways that are so
charming. Her brother Sam was very proud of
her, and liked to see her surrounded by his
friends at the merry-makings to which he escorted her; for she talked as well as she danced,
and the older gentlemen enjoyed a good chat with
Miss Abby as much as the younger ones did the
elaborate pigeon-wings and pirouettes then in
vogue.

Among the older men was one whom Abby
much admired; for he had fought, travelled, and
studied more than most men of his age, and
earned the honors he wore so modestly. She
was never tired of asking him questions when
they met, and he never seemed tired of giving
long, interesting replies; so they often sat and
talked while others danced, and Abby never
guessed that he was studying her bright face and
innocent heart as eagerly as she listened to his
agreeable conversation and stirring adventures.

Presently he came to the house with brother
Sam, who shared Abby's regard for him; and

there, while the young men amused themselves, or paid their respects to the elders, one of them was still watching the tall girl with the crown of brown hair, as she sat by her father, poured the tea for Madam, laughed with her brother, or made bashful Lucy share their pleasures; always so busy, dutiful, and winning, that the visitor pronounced Mr. Lyon's the most delightful house in Boston. He heard all the little tales of Abby's youth from Sam, and Lucy added her tribute with the eloquence of a grateful heart; he saw how loved and trusted she was, and he soon longed to know how she would answer the question he desired to ask her. Having received permission from Papa, in the decorous old style, he only waited for an opportunity to discover if charming Abigail would consent to change her name from Lyon to Lamb; and, as if her lesson was to be quite complete, a little thing decided her fate and made a very happy woman of the good girl.

On Abby's seventeenth birthday, there was to be a party in her honor, at the hospitable family mansion, to which all her friends were invited; and, when she came down early to see that all was in order, she found one impatient guest had already arrived.

It was not alone the consciousness that the new pink taffeta gown and the wreath of white roses were very becoming which made her blush so prettily as she thanked her friend for the fine nosegay he brought her, but something in his face, though he only wished her many happy returns in a hearty way, and then added, laughing, as the last button flew off the glove he was awkwardly trying to fasten, —

"It is evident that you did n't sew on these buttons, Miss Abby. I 've observed that Sam's never come off, and he says you always keep them in order."

"Let me put one on for you. It will take but a moment, and you 'll be so uncomfortable without it," said Abby, glad to find employment for her eyes.

A minute afterward she was sorry she had offered; for he accepted the little service with thanks, and stood watching while she sat down at her work-table and began to sew. She was very sensitive about her hand, yet ashamed of being so; for the scar was inside and the drawn fingers showed very little, as it is natural to half close them. She hoped he had never seen it, and tried to hide it as she worked. But this, or some new consciousness, made her usually nimble fingers lose their skill, and she knotted the silk, split the button, and dropped her thimble, growing angry with herself for being so silly and getting so red and flurried.

"I 'm afraid I 'm giving you a deal of trouble," said the gentleman, who was watching the white hand with great interest.

"No; it is I who am foolish about my burnt

hands," answered Abby, in her frank, impetuous way. "See how ugly it is!" And she held it out, as if to punish herself for the girlish feeling she despised.

The answer to this little outburst made her forget everything but the sweetest pleasure and surprise; for, kissing the scarred palm with tender respect, her lover said: —

"To me it is the finest and the dearest hand in the world. I know the brave story, and I 've seen the good this generous hand is never tired of doing. I want it for my own. Will you give it to me, dear?"

Abby must have answered, "Yes;" for she wore a new ring under her glove that night, and danced as if there were wings on the heels of her pink shoes.

Whether the button ever got sewed on or not, no one knows; but that bit of needlework was even more successful than the other small job; for in due time there was a second wedding, without a fire, and Abby went away to a happy home of her own, leaving sister Lucy to fill her place and be the most loving and faithful of daughters to her benefactors while they lived.

Long years afterward, when she had children and grandchildren about her, listening to the true old stories that are the best, Abby used to say, with her own cheerful laugh: —

"My father and mother taught me many useful lessons, but none more valuable than those

me like a boy, with the old tales your mother used
to tell, when we watched the fagots blaze in the
winter nights. It is long since I have heard one,
and I am never tired hearing of the deeds I mean
to match, if not outdo, some day."

"Let me think a bit till I remember your
favorites, and do you listen to the bees above
there in the willow, setting you a good example,
idle boy," said Yvonne, spreading a coarse apron
for his head, while she sat beside him racking
her brain for tales to beguile this truant hour.

Her father was the count's forester, and when
the countess had died some sixteen years before,
leaving a month-old boy, good dame Gillian had
taken the motherless baby, and nursed and reared
him with her little girl, so faithfully and tenderly
that the count never could forget the loyal service. As babies, the two slept in one cradle; as
children they played and quarrelled together; and
as boy and girl they defended, comforted, and
amused each other. But time brought inevitable
changes, and both felt that the hour of separation
was near; for, while Yvonne went on leading the
peasant life to which she was born, Gaston was
receiving the education befitting a young count.
The chaplain taught him to read and write, with
lessons in sacred history, and a little Latin; of
the forester he learned woodcraft; and his father
taught him horsemanship and the use of arms,
accomplishments considered all-important in those
days.

Gaston cared nothing for books, except such as told tales of chivalry; but dearly loved athletic sports, and at sixteen rode the most fiery horse without a fall, handled a sword admirably, could kill a boar at the first shot, and longed ardently for war, that he might prove himself a man. A brave, high-spirited, generous boy, with a very tender spot in his heart for the good woman who had been a mother to him, and his little foster-sister, whose idol he was. For days he seemed to forget these humble friends, and led the gay, active life of his age and rank; but if wounded in the chase, worried by the chaplain, disappointed in any plan, or in disgrace for any prank, he turned instinctively to Dame Gillian and Yvonne, sure of help and comfort for mind and body.

Companionship with him had refined the girl, and given her glimpses of a world into which she could never enter, yet where she could follow with eager eyes and high hopes the fortunes of this dear Gaston, who was both her prince and brother. Her influence over him was great, for she was of a calm and patient nature, as well as brave and prudent beyond her years. His will was law; yet in seeming to obey, she often led him, and he thanked her for the courage with which she helped him to control his fiery temper and strong will. Now, as she glanced at him she saw that he was already growing more tranquil, under the soothing influences of the murmuring river, the soft flicker of the sunshine, and a blessed sense of freedom.

So, while she twisted her distaff, she told the stirring tales of warriors, saints, and fairies, whom all Breton peasants honor, love, and fear. But best of all was the tale of Gaston's own ancestor, Jean de Beaumanoir, "the hero of Ploërmel, where, when sorely wounded and parched with thirst, he cried for water, and Geoffrey du Bois answered, like a grim old warrior as he was, 'Drink thy blood, Beaumanoir, and the thirst will pass;' and he drank, and the battle madness seized him, and he slew ten men, winning the fight against great odds, to his everlasting glory."

"Ah, those were the times to live in! If they could only come again, I would be a second Jean!"

Gaston sprung to his feet as he spoke, all aglow with the warlike ardor of his race, and Yvonne looked up at him, sure that he would prove himself a worthy descendant of the great baron and his wife, the daughter of the brave Du Guesclin.

"But you shall not be treacherously killed, as he was; for I will save you, as the peasant woman saved poor Giles de Bretagne when starving in the tower, or fight for you, as Jeanne d'Arc fought for her lord," answered Yvonne, dropping her distaff to stretch out her hand to him; for she, too, was on her feet.

Gaston took the faithful hand, and pointing to the white banner floating over the ruins of the old castle, said heartily: "We will always stand by one another, and be true to the motto of our house till death."

"We will!" answered the girl, and both kept the promise loyally, as we shall see.

Just at that moment the sound of hoofs made the young enthusiasts start and look toward the road that wound through the valley to the hill. An old man on a slowly pacing mule was all they saw, but the change that came over both was comical in its suddenness; for the gallant knight turned to a truant school-boy, daunted by the sight of his tutor, while the rival of the Maid of Orleans grew pale with dismay.

"I am lost if he spy me, for my father vowed I should not hunt again unless I did my task. He will see me if I run, and where can I hide till he has past?" whispered Gaston, ashamed of his panic, yet unwilling to pay the penalty of his prank.

But quick-witted Yvonne saved him; for lifting one end of the long web of linen, she showed a hollow whence some great stone had been removed, and Gaston slipped into the green nest, over which the linen lay smoothly when replaced.

On came the chaplain, glancing sharply about him, being of an austere and suspicious nature. He saw nothing, however, but the peasant girl in her quaint cap and wooden sabots, singing to herself as she leaned against a tree, with her earthen jug in her hand. The mule paused in the light shadow of the willows, to crop a mouthful of grass before climbing the hill, and the chaplain seemed glad to rest a moment, for the day was warm and the road dusty.

"Come hither, child, and give me a draught of water," he called, and the girl ran to fill her pitcher, offering it with a low reverence.

"Thanks, daughter! A fine day for the bleaching, but over warm for much travel. Go to your work child; I will tarry a moment in the shade before I return to my hard task of sharpening a dull youth's wit," said the old man when he had drunk; and with a frowning glance at the room where he had left his prisoner, he drew a breviary from his pocket and began to read, while the mule browsed along the road-side.

Yvonne went to sprinkling the neglected linen, wondering with mingled anxiety and girlish merriment how Gaston fared. The sun shone hotly on the dry cloth, and as she approached the boy's hiding-place, a stir would have betrayed him had the chaplain's eyes been lifted.

"Sprinkle me quickly; I am stifling in this hole," whispered an imploring voice.

"Drink thy blood, Beaumanoir, and the thirst will pass," quoted Yvonne, taking a naughty satisfaction in the ignominious captivity of the wilful boy. A long sigh was the only answer he gave, and taking pity on him, she made a

little hollow in the linen where she knew his head
lay, and poured in water till a choking sound
assured her Gaston had enough. The chaplain
looked up, but the girl coughed loudly, as she
went to refill her jug, with such a demure face
that he suspected nothing, and presently ambled
away to seek his refractory pupil.

The moment he disappeared, a small earthquake seemed to take place under the linen, for
it flew up violently, and a pair of long legs waved
joyfully in the air as Gaston burst into a ringing
laugh, which Yvonne echoed heartily. Then,
springing up, he said, throwing back his wet hair
and shaking his finger at her: " You dared not
betray me, but you nearly drowned me, wicked
girl. I cannot stop for vengeance now; but I 'll
toss you into the river some day, and leave you
to get out as you can."

Then he was off as quickly as he came, eager
to reach his prison again before the chaplain
came to hear the unlearned lesson. Yvonne
watched him till he climbed safely in at the high
window and disappeared with a wave of the
hand, when she, too, went back to her work, little
dreaming what brave parts both were to play in
dangers and captivities of which these youthful
pranks and perils were but a fore-shadowing.

Two years later, in the month of March, 1793,
the insurrection broke out in Vendée, and Gaston
had his wish; for the old count had been an officer of the king's household, and hastened to

prove his loyalty. Yvonne's heart beat high with pride as she saw her foster-brother ride gallantly away beside his father, with a hundred armed vassals behind them, and the white banner fluttering above their heads in the fresh wind.

She longed to go with him; but her part was to watch and wait, to hope and pray, till the hour came when she, like many another woman in those days, could prove herself as brave as a man, and freely risk her life for those she loved.

Four months later the heavy tidings reached them that the old count was killed and Gaston taken prisoner. Great was the lamentation among the old men, women, and children left behind; but they had little time for sorrow, for a band of the marauding Vendeans burned the chateau, and laid waste the Abbey.

" Now, mother, I must up and away to find and rescue Gaston. I promised, and if he lives, it shall be done. Let me go; you are safe now, and there is no rest for me till I know how he fares," said Yvonne, when the raid was over, and the frightened peasants ventured to return from the neighboring forests, whither they had hastily fled for protection.

" Go, my girl, and bring me news of our young lord. May you lead him safely home again to rule over us," answered Dame Gillian, devoted still, — for her husband was reported dead with his master, yet she let her daughter go without a murmur, feeling that no sacrifice was too great.

So Yvonne set out, taking with her Gaston's pet dove and the little sum of money carefully hoarded for her marriage portion. The pretty winged creature, frightened by the destruction of its home, had flown to her for refuge, and she had cherished it for its master's sake. Now, when it would not leave her, but came circling around her head a league away from Dinan, she accepted the good omen, and made the bird the companion of her perilous journey.

There is no room to tell all the dangers, disappointments, and fatigues endured before she found Gaston; but after being often misled by false rumors, she at last discovered that he was a prisoner in Fort Penthièvre. His own reckless courage had brought him there; for in one of the many skirmishes in which he had taken part, he ventured too far away from his men, and was captured after fighting desperately to cut his way out. Now, alone in his cell, he raged like a caged eagle, feeling that there was no hope of escape; for the fort stood on a plateau of precipitous rock washed on two sides by the sea. He had heard of the massacre of the royalist emigrants who landed there, and tried to prepare himself for a like fate, hoping to die as bravely as young Sombreuil, who was shot with twenty others on what was afterward named the *"Champ des Martyrs."* [1] His last words, when ordered by the executioner to kneel, were, " I do

[1] The Field of Martyrs.

it; but one knee I bend for my God, the other for my king."

Day after day Gaston looked down from his narrow window, past which the gulls flew screaming, and watched the fishers at their work, the women gathering sea-weed on the shore, and the white sails flitting across the bay of Quiberon. Bitterly did he regret the wilfulness which brought him there, well knowing that if he had obeyed orders he would now be free to find his father's body and avenge his death.

"Oh, for one day of liberty, one hope of escape, one friend to cheer this dreadful solitude!" he cried, when weeks had passed and he seemed utterly forgotten.

As he spoke, he shook the heavy bars with impotent strength, then bent his head as if to hide even from himself the few hot tears wrung from him by captivity and despair.

Standing so, with eyes too dim for seeing, something brushed against his hair, and a bird lit on the narrow ledge. He thought it was a gull, and paid no heed; but in a moment a soft coo started him, and looking up, he saw a white dove struggling to get in.

"Blanchette!" he cried, and the pretty creature flew to his hand, pecking at his lips in the old caressing way he knew so well.

"My faithful bird, God bless thee!" exclaimed the poor lad, holding the dove close against his cheek to hide the trembling of his lip, — so touched, so glad was he to find in his dreary prison even a dumb friend and comforter.

But Blanchette had her part to play, and presently fluttered back to the window ledge, cooing loudly as she pecked at something underneath her wing.

Then Gaston remembered how he used to send messages to Yvonne by this carrier-dove, and with a thrill of joy looked for the token, hardly daring to hope that any would be found. Yes! there, tied carefully among the white feathers, was a tiny roll of paper, with these words rudely written on it : —

" Be ready; help will come. Y."

" The brave girl! the loyal heart! I might have known she would keep her promise, and come to save me;" and Gaston dropped on his knees in gratitude.

Blanchette meantime tripped about the cell on her little rosy feet, ate a few crumbs of the hard bread, dipped her beak in the jug of water, dressed her feathers daintily, then flew to the bars and called him. He had nothing to send back by this sure messenger but a lock of hair, and this he tied with the same thread, in place of the note. Then kissing the bird he bade it go, watching the silver wings flash in the sunshine as it flew away, carrying joy with it and leaving hope behind.

After that the little courier came often unperceived, carrying letters to and fro; for Yvonne sent bits of paper, and Gaston wrote his answers with his blood and a quill from Blanchette's wing. He thus learned how Yvonne was living in a fisher's hut on the beach, and working for his rescue as well as she dared. Every day she might be seen gathering sea-weed on the rocks or twirling her distaff at the door of the dilapidated hut, not as a young girl, but as an old woman; for she had stained her fair skin, put on ragged clothes, and hidden her fresh face under the pent-house cap worn by the women of Quiberon. Her neighbors thought her a poor soul left desolate by the war, and let her live unmolested. So she worked on secretly and steadily, playing her part well, and biding her time till the long hempen rope was made, the sharp file procured unsuspected, and a boat ready to receive the fugitives.

Her plan was perilously simple, but the only one possible; for Gaston was well guarded, and out of that lofty cell it seemed that no prisoner could escape without wings. A bird and a woman lent him those wings, and his daring flight was a nine days' wonder at the fort. Only a youth accustomed to feats of agility and strength could have safely made that dangerous escape along the face of the cliff that rose straight up from the shore. But Gaston was well trained, and the boyish pranks that used to bring him into dire disgrace now helped to save his life.

Thus, when the order came, written in the rude hand he had taught Yvonne long ago, " Pull up the thread which Blanchette will bring at midnight. Watch for a light in the bay. Then come down, and St. Barbe protect you," he was ready; for the tiny file of watch-spring, brought by the bird, had secretly done its work, and several bars were loose. He knew that the attempt might cost him his life, but was willing to gain liberty even at that price; for imprisonment seemed worse than death to his impatient spirit. The jailer went his last round, the great bell struck the appointed hour, and Gaston stood at the window, straining his eyes to catch the first ray of the promised light, when the soft whir of wings gladdened his ear, and Blanchette arrived, looking scared and wet and weary, for rain fell, the wind blew fitfully, and the poor bird was unused to such wild work as this. But obedient to its training, it flew to its master; and no angel could have been more welcome than the storm-beaten little creature as it nestled in his bosom, while he untangled the lengths of strong thread wound about one of its feet.

He knew what to do, and tying a bit of the broken bar to one end, as a weight, he let it down, praying that no cruel gust would break or blow it away. In a moment a quick jerk at the thread bade him pull again. A cord came up, and when that was firmly secured, a second jerk was the signal for the last and most important haul. Up came the stout rope, knotted here and there to add safety and strength to the hands and feet that were to climb down that frail ladder, unless some cruel fate dashed the poor boy dead upon the rocks below. The rope was made fast to an iron staple inside, the bars were torn away, and Gaston crept through the narrow opening to perch on the ledge without, while Blanchette flew down to tell Yvonne he was coming.

The moment the distant spark appeared, he bestirred himself, set his teeth, and boldly began the dangerous descent. Rain blinded him, the wind beat him against the rock, bruising hands and knees, and the way seemed endless, as he climbed slowly down, clinging with the clutch of a drowning man, and blessing Yvonne for the knots that kept him from slipping when the gusts blew him to and fro. More than once he thought it was all over; but the good rope held fast, and strength and courage nerved heart and limbs. One greater than St. Barbe upheld him, and he dropped at last, breathless and bleeding, beside the faithful Yvonne.

There was no time for words, only a grasp of the hand, a sigh of gratitude, and they were away to the boat that tossed on the wild water with a single rower in his place.

"It is our Hoël. I found him looking for you. He is true as steel. In, in, and off, or you are lost!" whispered Yvonne, flinging a cloak about

Gaston, thrusting a purse, a sword, and a flask into his hand, and holding the boat while he leaped in.

"But you?" he cried; "I cannot leave you in peril, after all you have dared and done for me."

"No one suspects me; I am safe. Go to my mother; she will hide you, and I will follow soon."

Waiting for no further speech, she pushed the boat off, and watched it vanish in the darkness; then went away to give thanks, and rest after her long work and excitement.

Gaston reached home safely, and Dame Gillian concealed him in the ruins of the Abbey, till anxiety for Yvonne drove him out to seek and rescue in his turn. For she did not come, and when a returning soldier brought word that she had been arrested in her flight, and sent to Nantes, Gaston could not rest, but disguising himself as a peasant, went to find her, accompanied by faithful Hoël, who loved Yvonne, and would gladly die for her and his young master. Their hearts sunk when they discovered that she was in the Boufflay, an old fortress, once a royal residence, and now a prison, crowded with unfortunate and innocent creatures, arrested on the slightest pretexts, and guillotined or drowned by the infamous Carrier. Hundreds of men and women were there, suffering terribly, and among them was Yvonne, brave still, but with no hope of escape; for few were saved, and then only by some lucky accident. Like a sister of mercy she went among the poor souls crowded together in the great halls, hungry, cold, sick, and despairing, and they clung to her as if she were some strong, sweet saint who could deliver them or teach them how to die.

After some weeks of this terrible life, her name was called one morning, on the list for that day's execution, and she rose to join the sad procession setting forth.

" Which is it to be? " she asked, as she passed one of the men who guarded them, a rough fellow, whose face was half hidden by a shaggy beard.

" You will be drowned; we have no time to waste on women; " was the brutal answer; but as the words passed his lips, a slip of paper was pressed into her hand, and these words breathed into her ear by a familiar voice: " I am here! "

It was Gaston, in the midst of enemies, bent on saving her at the risk of his life, remembering all he owed her, and the motto of his race. The shock of this discovery nearly betrayed them both, and turned her so white that the woman next her put her arm about her, saying sweetly: —

" Courage, my sister; it is soon over."

" I fear nothing now! " cried Yvonne, and went on to take her place in the cart, looking so serene and happy that those about her thought her already fit for heaven.

No need to repeat the dreadful history of the Noyades; it is enough to say that in the confusion of the moment Yvonne found opportunity to read and destroy the little paper, which said briefly: —

"When you are flung into the river, call my name and float. I shall be near."

She understood, and being placed with a crowd of wretched women on the old vessel which lay in the river Loire, she employed every moment in loosening the rope that tied her hands, and keeping her eye on the tall, bearded man who moved about seeming to do his work, while his blood boiled with suppressed wrath, and his heart ached with unavailing pity. It was dusk before the end came for Yvonne, and she was all unnerved by the sad sights she had been forced to see; but when rude hands seized her, she made ready for the plunge, sure that Gaston would "be near." He was, for in the darkness and uproar, he could leap after her unseen, and while she floated, he cut the rope, then swam down the river with her hand upon his shoulder till they dared to land. Both were nearly spent with the excitement and exertion of that dreadful hour; but Hoël waited for them on the shore and helped Gaston carry poor Yvonne into a deserted house, where they gave her fire, food, dry garments, and the gladdest welcome one human creature ever gave to another.

Being a robust peasant, the girl came safely

through hardships that would have killed or crazed a frailer creature; and she was soon able to rejoice with the brave fellows over this escape, so audaciously planned and so boldly carried out. They dared stay but a few hours, and before dawn were hastening through the least frequented ways toward home, finding safety in the distracted state of the country, which made fugitives no unusual sight, and refugees plentiful. One more adventure, and that a happy one, completed their joy, and turned their flight into a triumphant march.

Pausing in the depths of the great forest of Hunaudaye to rest, the two young men went to find food, leaving Yvonne to tend the fire and make ready to cook the venison they hoped to bring. It was nightfall, and another day would see them in Dinan, they hoped; but the lads had consented to pause for the girl's sake, for she was worn out with their rapid flight. They were talking of their adventures in high spirits, when Gaston laid his hand on Hoël's mouth and pointed to a green slope before them. An early moon gave light enough to show them a dark form moving quickly into the coppice, and something like the antlers of a stag showed above the tall brakes before they vanished. " Slip around and drive him this way. I never miss my aim, and we will sup royally to-night," whispered Gaston, glad to use the arms with which they had provided themselves.

Hoël slipped away, and presently a rustle in the wood betrayed the cautious approach of the deer. But he was off before a shot could be fired, and the disappointed hunters followed long and far, resolved not to go back empty-handed. They had to give it up, however, and were partially consoled by a rabbit, which Hoël flung over his shoulder, while Gaston, forgetting caution, began to sing an old song the women of Brittany love so well:—

> "Quand vous étiez, captif, Bertrand, fils de Bretagne,
>   Tous les fuseaux tournaient aussi dans la campagne."

He got no further, for the stanza was finished by a voice that had often joined in the ballad, when Dame Gillian sang it to the children, as she spun:—

> "Chaque femme apporte son écheveau de lin;
>   Ce fut votre rançon, Messire du Guesclin."

Both paused, thinking that some spirit of the wood mocked them; but a loud laugh, and a familiar "Holo! holo!" made Hoël cry, "The forester!" while Gaston dashed headlong into the thicket whence the sound came, there to find the jolly forester, indeed, with a slain deer by his side, waiting to receive them with open arms.

"I taught you to stalk the deer, and spear the boar, not to hunt your fellow-creatures, my lord.

But I forgive you, for it was well done, and I had a hard run to escape," he said, still laughing.

"But how came you here?" cried both the youths, in great excitement; for the good man was supposed to be dead, with his old master.

"A long tale, for which I have a short and happy answer. Come home to supper with me, and I'll show you a sight that will gladden hearts and eyes," he answered, shouldering his load and leading the way to a deserted hermitage, which had served many a fugitive for a shelter. As they went, Gaston poured out his story, and told how Yvonne was waiting for them in the woods.

"Brave lads! and here is your reward," answered the forester, pushing open the door and pointing to the figure of a man, with a pale face and bandaged head, lying asleep beside the fire.

It was the count, sorely wounded, but alive, thanks to his devoted follower, who had saved him when the fight was over; and after weeks of concealment, suffering, and anxiety, had brought him so far toward home.

No need to tell of the happy meeting that night, nor of the glad return; for, though the chateau was in ruins and lives were still in danger, they all were together, and the trials they had passed through only made the ties of love and loyalty between high and low more true and tender. Good Dame Gillian housed them all, and nursed her master back to health. Yvonne and Hoël had a gay wedding in the course of time, and Gaston went to the wars again. A new chateau rose on the ruins of the old, and when the young lord took possession, he replaced the banner that was lost with one of fair linen, spun and woven by the two women who had been so faithful to him and his, but added a white dove above the clasped hands and golden legend, never so true as now, —

"En tout chemin loyauté."

JERSEYS; OR, THE GIRLS' GHOST

"WELL, what do you think of her? She has only been here a day, but it does n't take *us* long to make up our minds," said Nelly Blake, the leader of the school, as a party of girls stood chatting round the register one cold November morning.

"I like her, she looks so fresh and pleasant, and so strong. I just wanted to go and lean up against her, when my back ached yesterday," answered Maud, a pale girl wrapped in a shawl.

"I 'm afraid she 's very energetic, and I do hate to be hurried," sighed plump Cordelia, lounging in an easy chair.

"I know she is, for Biddy says she asked for a pail of cold water at six this morning, and she 's out walking now. Just think how horrid," cried Kitty with a shiver.

"I wonder what she does for her complexion. Never saw such a lovely color. Real roses and cream," said Julia, shutting one eye to survey the freckles on her nose, with a gloomy frown.

"I longed to ask what sort of braces she wears, to keep her so straight. I mean to by and by; she looks as if she would n't snub a body;" and Sally vainly tried to square her own round shoulders, bent with much poring over books, for she was the bright girl of the school.

"She wears French corsets, of course. Nothing else gives one such a fine figure," answered Maud, dropping the shawl to look with pride at her own wasp-like waist and stiff back.

"Could n't move about so easily and gracefully if she wore a strait-jacket like you. She 's not a bit of a fashion plate, but a splendid woman, just natural and hearty and sweet. I feel as if I should n't slouch and poke so much if I had her to brace me up," cried Sally, in her enthusiastic way.

"I know one thing, girls, and that is, *she* can wear a jersey and have it set elegantly, and *we* can't," said Kitty, laboring with her own, which would wrinkle and twist, in spite of many hidden pins.

"Yes, I looked at it all breakfast time, and forgot my second cup of coffee, so my head aches as if it would split. Never saw anything fit so splendidly in my life," answered Nelly, turning to the mirror, which reflected a fine assortment of many colored jerseys; for all the girls were out in their fall suits, and not one of the new jackets set like Miss Orne's, the teacher who had arrived to take Madame's place while that excellent old lady was laid up with a rheumatic fever.

"They are pretty and convenient, but I 'm

afraid they will be a trial to some of us. Maud
and Nelly look the best, but they have to keep
stiff and still, or the wrinkles come. Kit has
no peace in hers, and poor Cordy looks more like
a meal bag than ever, while I am a perfect spectacle, with my round shoulders and long thin
arms. 'A jersey on a bean-pole' describes me;
but let us be in the fashion or die," laughed
Sally, exaggerating her own defects by poking
her head forward and blinking through her
glasses in a funny way.

There was a laugh and then a pause, broken
in a moment by Maud, who said, in a tone of
apprehension:

"I do hope Miss Orne is n't full of the new
notions about clothes and food and exercise and
rights and rubbish of that sort. Mamma hates
such ideas, and so do I."

"I hope she *is* full of good, wise notions about
health and work and study. It is just what we
need in this school. Madame is old and lets
things go, and the other teachers only care to get
through and have an easy time. We ought to be
a great deal better, brisker, and wiser than we
are, and I 'm ready for a good stirring up if
any one will give it to us," declared Sally, who
was a very independent girl and had read as
well as studied much.

"You Massachusetts girls are always raving
about self-culture, and ready for queer new ways.
I 'm contented with the old ones, and want to

be let alone and finished off easily," said Nelly, the pretty New Yorker.

"Well, I go with Sally, and want to get all I can in the way of health, learning, and manners while I'm here; and I'm real glad Miss Orne has come, for Madame's old-fashioned, niminy priminy ways did fret me dreadfully. Miss Orne is more like our folks out West, — spry and strong and smart, see if she is n't," said Julia, with a decided nod of her auburn head.

"There she is now! Girls, she's running! actually trotting up the avenue — not like a hen, but a boy — with her elbows down and her head up. Do come and see!" cried Kitty, dancing about at the window as if she longed to go and do likewise.

All ran in time to see a tall young lady come up the wide path at a good pace, looking as fresh and blithe as the goddess of health, as she smiled and nodded at them, so like a girl that all returned her salute with equal cordiality.

"She gives a new sort of interest to the old treadmill, does n't she?" said Nelly, as they scattered to their places at the stroke of nine, feeling unusually anxious to appear well before the new teacher.

While they pull down their jerseys and take up their books, we will briefly state that Madame Stein's select boarding-school had for many years received six girls at a time, and finished them off

in the old style. Plenty of French, German,
music, painting, dancing, and deportment turned
out well-bred, accomplished, and amiable young
ladies, ready for fashionable society, easy lives,
and entire dependence on other people. Dainty
and delicate creatures usually, for, as in most
schools of this sort, minds and manners were
much cultivated, but bodies rather neglected.
Heads and backs ached, dyspepsia was a common ailment, and poorlies of all sorts affected
the dear girls, who ought not to have known
what " nerves " meant, and should have had no
bottles in their closets holding wine and iron,
cough mixtures, soothing drops and cod-liver oil
for weak lungs. Gymnastics had once flourished,
but the fashion had gone by, and a short walk
each day was all the exercise they took, though
they might have had glorious romps in the old
coach-house and bowling-alley in bad weather,
and lovely rambles about the spacious grounds;
for the house was in the suburbs, and had once
been a fine country mansion. Some of the liveliest girls did race down the avenue now and
then, when Madame was away, and one irrepressible creature had actually slid down the
wide balusters, to the horror of the entire household.

In cold weather all grew lazy and cuddled
under blankets and around registers, like so many
warmth-loving pussies, — poor Madame's rheu-
matism making her enjoy a hot-house tempera-

ture and indulge the girls in luxurious habits.
Now she had been obliged to give up entirely and
take to her bed, saying, with the resignation of
an indolent nature : —

" If Anna Orne takes charge of the school I
shall feel no anxiety. *She* is equal to anything."

She certainly looked so as she came into the
school-room ready for her day's work, with lungs
full of fresh air, brain stimulated by sound sleep,
wholesome exercise, and a simple breakfast, and
a mind much interested in the task before her.
The girls' eyes followed her as she took her place,
involuntarily attracted by the unusual spectacle
of a robust woman. Everything about her
seemed so fresh, harmonious, and happy, that it
was a pleasure to see the brilliant color in her
cheeks, the thick coils of glossy hair on her
spirited head, the flash of white teeth as she
spoke, and the clear, bright glance of eyes both
keen and kind. But the most admiring glances
were on the dark-blue jersey that showed such
fine curves of the broad shoulders, round waist,
and plump arms, without a wrinkle to mar its
smooth perfection.

Girls are quick to see what is genuine, to respect what is strong, and to love what is beautiful; so before that day was over, Miss Orne had
charmed them all; for they felt that she was not
only able to teach but to help and amuse them.

After tea the other teachers went to their
rooms, glad to be free from the chatter of half

a dozen lively tongues; but Miss Orne remained
in the drawing-room, and set the girls to dancing till they were tired, then gathered them
round the long table to do what they liked till
prayer-time. Some had novels, others did fancy-
work or lounged, and all wondered what the new
teacher would do next.

Six pairs of curious eyes were fixed upon her,
as she sat sewing on some queer bits of crash,
and six lively fancies vainly tried to guess what
the articles were, for no one was rude enough
to ask. Presently she tried on a pair of mittens,
and surveyed them with satisfaction, saying as
she caught Kitty staring with uncontrollable
interest: —

"These are my beautifiers, and I never like
to be without them."

"Are they to keep your hands white?" asked
Maud, who spent a good deal of time in caring
for her own. "I wear old kid gloves at night
after cold-creaming mine."

"I wear these for five minutes night and
morning, for a good rub, after dipping them in
cold water. Thanks to these rough friends, I
seldom feel the cold, get a good color, and keep
well," answered Miss Orne, polishing up her
smooth cheek till it looked like a rosy apple.

"I'd like the color, but not the crash. Must
it be so rough, and with *cold* water?" asked
Maud, who often privately rubbed her pale face
with a bit of red flannel, rouge being forbidden
except for theatricals.

"Best so; but there are other ways to get a color. Run up and down the avenue three or four times a day, eat no pastry, and go to bed early," said Miss Orne, whose sharp eye had spied out the little weaknesses of the girls, and whose kind heart longed to help them at once.

"It makes my back ache to run, and Madame says we are too old now."

"Never too old to care for one's health, my dear. Better run now than lie on a sofa by and by, with a back that never stops aching."

"Do you cure your headaches in that way?" asked Nelly, rubbing her forehead wearily.

"I never have them;" and Miss Orne's bright eyes were full of pity for all pain.

"What do you do to help it?" cried Nelly, who firmly believed that it was inevitable.

"I give my brain plenty of rest, air, and good food. I never know I have any nerves, except in the enjoyment they give me, for I have learned how to use them. I was not brought up to believe that I was born an invalid, and was taught to understand the beautiful machinery God gave me, and to keep it religiously in order."

Miss Orne spoke so seriously that there was a brief pause in which the girls were wishing that some one had taught them this lesson and made them as strong and lovely as their new teacher.

"If crash mittens would make my jersey set like yours I'd have a pair at once," said Cordy, sadly eyeing the buttons on her own, which seemed in danger of flying off if their plump wearer moved too quickly.

"Brisk runs are what you want, and less confectionery, sleep, and lounging in easy chairs;" began Miss Orne, all ready to prescribe for these poor girls, the most important part of whose education had been so neglected.

"Why, how did you know?" said Cordy, blushing, as she bounced out of her luxurious seat and whisked into her pocket the paper of chocolate creams she was seldom without.

Her round eyes and artless surprise set the others to laughing, and gave Sally courage to ask what she wanted, then and there.

"Miss Orne, I wish you would show us how to be strong and hearty, for I do think girls are a feeble set now-a-days. We certainly need stirring up, and I hope you will kindly do it. Please begin with me, then the others will see that I mean what I say."

Miss Orne looked up at the tall, overgrown girl who stood before her, with broad forehead, near-sighted eyes, and narrow chest of a student; not at all what a girl of seventeen should be, physically, though a clear mind and a brave spirit shone in her clever face and sounded in her resolute voice.

"I shall very gladly do what I can for you, my dear. It is very simple, and I am sure that a few months of my sort of training will help you much; for you are just the kind of girl who should have a strong body, to keep pace with a very active brain," answered Miss Orne, taking Sally's thin, inky fingers in her own, with a friendly pressure that showed her good will.

"Madame says violent exercise is not good for girls, so we gave up gymnastics long ago," said Maud, in her languid voice, wishing that Sally would not suggest disagreeable things.

"One does not need clubs, dumb bells, and bars for my style of exercise. Let me show you;" and rising, Miss Orne went through a series of energetic but graceful evolutions, which put every muscle in play without great exertion.

"That looks easy enough," began Nelly.

"Try it," answered Miss Orne, with a sparkle of fun in her blue eyes.

They did try, — to the great astonishment of the solemn portraits on the wall, unused to seeing such antics in that dignified apartment. But some of the girls were out of breath in five minutes; others could not lift their arms over their heads; Maud and Nelly broke several bones in their corsets, trying to stoop; and Kitty tumbled down, in her efforts to touch her toes without bending her knees. Sally got on the best of all, being long of limb, easy in her clothes, and full of enthusiasm.

"Pretty well for beginners," said Miss Orne, as they paused at last, flushed and merry. "Do that regularly every day, and you will soon gain

a few inches across the chest and fill out the new
jerseys with firm, elastic figures."

"Like yours," added Sally, with a face full
of such honest admiration that it could not
offend.

Seeing that she had made one convert, and
knowing that girls, like sheep, are sure to follow
a leader, Miss Orne said no more then, but
waited for the leaven to work. The others called
it one of Sally's notions, but were interested to
see how she would get on, and had great fun,
when they went to bed, watching her faithful
efforts to imitate her teacher's rapid and effective
motions.

"The wind-mill is going!" cried Kitty, as
several of them sat on the bed, laughing at the
long arms swinging about.

"That is hygienic elbow-exercise, and that
the Orne Quickstep, a mixture of the grass-
hopper's skip and the water-bug's slide," added
Julia, humming a tune in time to the stamp of
the other's foot.

"We will call these the Jersey Jymnastics,
and spell the last with a J, my dear," said Nelly;
and the name was received with as much applause as the young ladies dared to give it at that
hour.

"Laugh on, but see if you don't all follow
my example sooner or later, when I become a
model of grace, strength, and beauty," retorted
Sally, as she turned them out and went to bed,

tingling all over with a delicious glow that sent the blood from her hot head to warm her cold feet, and bring her the sound, refreshing sleep she so much needed.

This was the beginning of a new order of things, for Miss Orne carried her energy into other matters besides gymnastics, and no one dared oppose her when Madame shut her ears to all complaints, saying, " Obey her in everything, and don't trouble me."

Pitchers of fresh milk took the place of tea and coffee; cake and pie were rarely seen, but better bread, plain puddings, and plenty of fruit.

Rooms were cooled off, feather beds sent up garret, and thick curtains abolished. Sun and air streamed in, and great cans of water appeared suggestively at doors in the morning. Earlier hours were kept, and brisk walks taken by nearly all the girls; for Miss Orne baited her hook cleverly, and always had some pleasant project to make the wintry expeditions inviting. There were games in the parlor instead of novels, and fancy-work in the evening; shorter lessons, and longer talks on the many useful subjects that are best learned from the lips of a true teacher. A cooking class was started, not to make fancy dishes, but the plain, substantial ones all housewives should understand. Several girls swept their own rooms, and liked it after they saw Miss Orne do hers in a becoming dust-cap; and these same pioneers, headed by Sally, boldly coasted on the hill, swung clubs in the coach-house, and played tag in the bowling-alley rainy days.

It took time to work these much-needed changes, but young people like novelty; the old routine had grown tiresome, and Miss Orne made things so lively and pleasant it was impossible to resist her wishes. Sally did begin to straighten up, after a month or two of regular training; Maud outgrew both corsets and back-ache; Nelly got a fresh color; Kitty found her thin arms developing visible muscles; and Julia considered herself a Von Hillern, after walking ten miles without fatigue.

But dear, fat Cordy was the most successful of all; and rejoiced greatly over the loss of a few pounds when she gave up over-eating, long naps, and lazy habits. Exercise became a sort of mania with her, and she was continually trudging off for a constitutional, or trotting up and down the halls when bad weather prevented the daily tramp. It was the desire of her soul to grow thin, and such was her ardor that Miss Orne had to check her sometimes, lest she should overdo the matter.

"All this is easy and pleasant now, because it is new," she said, "and there is no one to criticise our simple, sensible ways; but when you go away I am afraid you will undo the good I have tried to do you. People will ridicule you, fashion will condemn, and frivolous pleasures make our wholesome ones seem hard. Can you be steadfast, and keep on?"

"We will!" cried all the girls; but the older ones looked a little anxious, as they thought of going home to introduce the new ways alone.

Miss Orne shook her head, earnestly wishing that she could impress the important lesson indelibly upon them; and very soon something happened which had that effect.

April came, and the snowdrops and crocuses were up in the garden beds. Madame was able to sit at her window, peering out like a dormouse waking from its winter sleep; and much did the good lady wonder at the blooming faces turned up to nod and smile at her, the lively steps that tripped about the house, and the amazing spectacle of *her* young ladies racing round the lawn as if they liked it. No one knew how Miss Orne reconciled her to this new style of deportment; but she made no complaint, — only shook her impressive cap when the girls came beaming in to pay little visits, full of happy chat about their affairs. They seemed to take a real interest in their studies now, to be very happy; and all looked so well that the wise old lady said to herself : —

"Looks are everything with women, and I have never been able to show such a bouquet of blooming creatures at my breaking up as I shall this year. I will let well enough alone, and if fault is found, dear Anna's shoulders are broad enough to bear it."

Things were in this promising state, and all

were busily preparing for the May fête, at which
time this class of girls would graduate, when the
mysterious events occurred to which we have
alluded.

They were gathered — the girls, not the events
— round the table one night, discussing, with the
deep interest befitting such an important topic,
what they should wear on examination day.

"*I* think white silk jerseys and pink or blue
skirts would be lovely; so pretty and so appro-
priate for the J. J. Club, and so nice for us to
do our exercises in. Miss Orne wants us to show
how well we go together, and of course we want
to please her;" said Nelly, taking the lead as
usual in matters of taste.

"Of course!" cried all the girls, with an
alacrity which plainly showed how entirely the
new friend had won their hearts.

"I would n't have believed that six months
could make such a difference in one's figure and
feelings," said Maud, surveying her waist with
calm satisfaction, though it was no longer slender, but in perfect proportion to the rest of her
youthful shape.

"I've had to let out every dress, and it's a
mercy I'm going home, for I should n't be decent
if I kept on at this rate;" and Julia took a long
breath, proud of her broad chest, expanded by
plenty of exercise, and loose clothing.

"I take mine in, and don't have to worry
about my buttons flying off, *à la* Clara Peggotty.

I'm so pleased I want to be training all the time, for I'm not half thin enough yet," said Cordy, jumping up for a trot round the room, that not a moment might be lost.

"Come, Sally, you ought to join in the jubilee, for you have done wonders, and will be as straight as a ramrod in a little while. Why so sober to-night? Is it because our dear Miss Orne leaves us to sit with Madame?" asked Nelly, missing the gayest voice of the six, and observing her friend's troubled face.

"I'm making up my mind whether I'd better tell you something or not. Don't want to scare the servants, trouble Madame, or vex Miss Orne; for I know *she* would n't believe a word of it, though I saw it with my own eyes," answered Sally, in such a mysterious tone that the girls with one voice cried, —

"Tell us, this minute!"

"I will; and perhaps some of you can explain the matter."

As she spoke, Sally rose and stood on the rug with her hands behind her, looking rather wild and queer; for her short hair was in a toss, her eyes shone large behind her round glasses, and her voice sank to a whisper as she made this startling announcement: —

"I've seen a ghost!"

A general shiver pervaded the listeners, and Cordy poked her head under the sofa pillows with a faint cry, while the rest involuntarily drew nearer to one another.

"Where?" demanded Julia, the bravest of the party.

"On the top of the house."

"Good gracious! When, Sally?" "What did it look like?" "Don't scare us for fun," — cried the girls, undecided whether to take this startling story in jest or earnest.

"Listen, and I'll tell you all about it," answered Sally, holding up her finger impressively.

"Night before last I sat till eleven, studying. Against the rules, I know; but I forgot, and when I was through I opened my window to air the room. It was bright moonlight, so I took a stroll along the top of the piazza, and coming back with my eyes on the sky I naturally saw the roof of the main house from my wing. I couldn't have been asleep, could I? yet, I solemnly declare I saw a white figure with a veil over its head roaming to and fro as quietly as a shadow. I looked and looked, then I called softly, but it never answered, and suddenly it was gone."

"What did you do?" quavered Cordy, in a smothered voice from under the pillow.

"Went straight in, took my lamp and marched up to the cupola. Not a sign of any one, all locked and the floor dusty, for we never go there now, you know. I didn't like it, but just said, 'Sally, go to bed; it's an optical illusion and serves you right for studying against the rule.' That was the first time."

"Mercy on us! Did you see it again?" cried Maud, getting hold of Julia's strong arm for protection.

"Yes, in the bowling-alley at midnight," whispered Sally.

"Do shut the door, Kit, and don't keep clutching at me in that scary way; it's very unpleasant," said Nelly, glancing nervously over her shoulder as the six pairs of wide-opened eyes were fixed on Sally.

"I got up to shut my window last night, and saw a light in the alley. A dim one, but bright enough to show me the same white thing going up and down, with the veil as before. I'll confess I was nervous then, for you know there *is* a story that in old times the man who lived here would n't let his daughter marry the lover she wanted, and she pined away and died, and said she'd haunt the cruel father, and she did. Old Mrs. Foster told me all about it when I first came, and Madame asked me not to repeat it, so I never did. I don't believe in ghosts, mind you, but what on earth is it, trailing about in that ridiculous way?"

Sally spoke nervously and looked excited, for in spite of courage and common sense she *was* worried to account for the apparition.

"How long did it stay?" asked Julia, with her arm round Maud, who was trembling and pale.

"A good fifteen minutes by my watch, then vanished, light and all, as suddenly as before.

I did n't go to look after it that time, but if I see it again I 'll hunt till I find out what it is. Who will go with me?"

No one volunteered, and Cordy emerged long enough to say imploringly: —

"Do tell Miss Orne, or get the police;" then dived out of sight again, and lay quaking like an ostrich with its head in the sand.

"I won't! Miss Orne would think I was a fool, and the police don't arrest ghosts. I 'll do it myself, and Julia will help me, I know. She is the bravest of you, and has n't developed her biceps for nothing," said Sally, bent on keeping all the glory of the capture to themselves if possible.

Flattered by the compliment to her arms, Julia did not decline the invitation, but made a very sensible suggestion, which was a great relief to the timid, till Sally added a new fancy to haunt them.

"Perhaps it is one of the servants moon-struck or love-lorn. Myra looks sentimental, and is always singing: —

> "I 'm waiting, waiting, darling,
> Morning, night, and noon;
> Oh, meet me by the river
> When softly shines the moon."

"It 's not Myra; I asked her, and she turned pale at the mere idea of going anywhere alone after dark, and said cook had seen a banshee gliding down the Lady's Walk one night, when she got up for camphor, having the face-ache. I said no more, not wanting to scare them; ignorant people are so superstitious."

Sally paused, and the girls all tried not to look "scared" or "superstitious," but did not succeed very well.

"What are you going to do?" asked Nelly, in a respectful tone, as Julia and Sally stood side by side, like Horatius and Herminius waiting for a Spurius Lartius to join them.

"Watch, like cats for a mouse, and pounce as soon as possible. All promise to say nothing; then we can't be laughed at if it turns out some silly thing, as it probably will," answered Sally.

"We promise!" solemnly answered the girls, feeling deeply impressed with the thrilling interest of the moment.

"Very well; now don't talk about it or think about it till we report, or no one will sleep a wink," said Sally, walking off with her ally as coolly as if, after frightening them out of their wits, they could forget the matter at word of command.

The oath of silence was well kept, but lessons suffered, and so did sleep, for the excitement was great, especially in the morning, when the watchers reported the events of the night, and in the evening, when they took turns to go on guard. There was much whisking of dressing-gowns up and down the corridor of the west wing, where our six roomed, as the girls flew to ask questions early each day, or scurried to bed, glancing behind them for the banshee as they went.

Miss Orne observed the whispers, nods, and eager confabulations, but said nothing, for Madame had confided to her that the young ladies were planning a farewell gift for her. So she was blind and deaf, and smiled at the important airs of her girlish admirers.

Three or four days passed, and no sign of the ghost appeared. The boldest openly scoffed at the false alarm, and the most timid began to recover from their fright.

Sally and Julia looked rather foolish as they answered, "no news," morning after morning, to the inquiries which were rapidly losing the breathless eagerness so flattering to the watchers.

"You dreamed it, Sally. Go to sleep, and don't do it again," said Nelly, on the fifth day, as she made her evening call and found the girls yawning and cross for want of rest.

"She has exercised too much, and produced a morbid state of the brain," laughed Maud.

"I just wish she would n't scare me out of my senses for nothing," grumbled Cordy; "I used to sleep like a dormouse, and now I dream dreadfully and wake up tired out. Come along, Kit, and let the old ghosts carry off these silly creatures."

"My regards to the Woman in White *when* you see her again, dear," added Kitty, as the four went off to laugh at the whole thing, though they carefully locked their doors and took a peep out of the window before going to sleep.

"We may as well give it up and have a good rest. I'm worn out, and so are you, if you'd own it," said Julia, throwing herself down for a nap before midnight.

"I shall *not* give it up till I'm satisfied. Sleep away, I'll read awhile and call you if anything comes," answered Sally, bound to prove the truth of her story if she waited all summer.

Julia was soon off, and the lonely watcher sat reading till past eleven; then put out her light and went to take a turn on the flat roof of the piazza that ran round the house, for the night was mild and the stars companionable. As she turned to come back, her sharp eye caught sight of something moving on the house-top as before, and soon, clear against the soft gloom of the sky, appeared the white figure flitting to and fro.

A long look, and then Sally made a rush at Julia, shaking her violently as she said in an excited whisper:

"Come! she is there. Quick! upstairs to the cupola; I have the candle and the key."

Carried away by the other's vehemence Julia mutely obeyed, trembling, but afraid to resist; and noiseless as two shadows, they crept up the stairs, arriving just in time to see the ghost vanish over the edge of the roof, as if it had dissolved into thin air. Julia dropped down in a heap, desperately frightened, but Sally pulled her up and led her back to their room, saying, when she got there, with grim satisfaction, "Did I dream it all? Now I hope they will believe me."

"What was it? Oh, what could it be?" whimpered Julia, quite demoralized by the spectacle.

"I begin to believe in ghosts, for no human being could fly off in that way, with nothing to walk on. I shall speak to Miss Orne to-morrow; I've had enough of this sort of fun," said Sally, going to the window, with a strong desire to shut and lock it.

But she paused with her hand raised, as if turned to stone, for as she spoke the white figure went slowly by. Julia dived into the closet, with one spring. Sally, however, was on her mettle now, and, holding her breath, leaned out to watch. With soundless steps the veiled thing went along the roof, and paused at the further end.

Never waiting for her comrade, Sally quietly stepped out and followed, leaving Julia to quake with fear and listen for an alarm.

None came, and in a few minutes, that seemed like hours, Sally returned, looking much excited; but was sternly silent, and, to all the other's eager questions she would only give this mysterious reply: —

"I know all, but cannot tell till morning. Go to sleep."

Believing her friend offended at her base desertion at the crisis of the affair, Julia curbed her curiosity and soon forgot it in sleep. Sally slept also, feeling like a hero reposing after a hard-won battle.

She was up betimes and ready to receive her early visitors with an air of triumph, which silenced every jeer and convinced the most skeptical that she had something sensational to tell at last.

When the girls had perched themselves on any available article of furniture, they waited with respectful eagerness, while Sally retired to the hall for a moment, and Julia rolled her eyes, with her finger on her lips, looking as if she could tell much if she dared.

Sally returned somewhat flushed, but very sober, and in a few dramatic words related the adventures of the night, up to the point where she left Julia quivering ignominiously in the closet, and, like Horatius, faced the foe alone.

"I followed till the ghost entered a window."

"Which?" demanded five awestruck voices at once.

"The last."

"Ours?" whispered Kitty, pale as her collar, while Cordy, her room-mate, sat aghast.

"As it turned to shut the window the veil fell back and I saw the face." Sally spoke in a whisper and added, with a sudden start, "I see it now!"

Every girl sprang or tumbled off her perch as if an electric shock had moved them, and stared about them as Nelly cried wildly, "Where? oh, where?"

"There!" and Sally pointed at the palest face in the room, while her own reddened with the mirth she was vainly trying to suppress.

"Cordy?"

A general shriek of amazement and incredulity followed the question, while Sally laughed till the tears ran down her cheeks at the dumb dismay of the innocent ghost.

As soon as she could be heard she quickly explained: "Yes, it was Cordy, walking in her sleep. She wore her white flannel wrapper, and a cloud round her head, and took her exercise over the roofs at midnight, so that no time might be lost. I don't wonder she is tired in the morning, after such dangerous gymnastics as these."

"But she couldn't vanish in that strange way off the house-top without breaking her neck," said Julia, much relieved, but still mystified.

"She did n't fly nor fall, but went down the ladder left by the painters. Look at the soles of her felt slippers, if you doubt me, and see the red paint from the roof. We could n't open the cupola windows, you remember, but this morning I took a stroll and looked up and saw how she did it asleep, though she never would dare to do it awake. Somnambulists do dreadfully dangerous things, you know," said Sally, as if her experience of those peculiar people had been vast and varied.

"How could I? It's horrid to think of. Why did you let me, Kit?" cried Cordy, uncertain whether to be proud or ashamed of her exploit.

"Never dreamed of *your* doing such a silly thing, and never waked up. Sleep-walkers are always quiet, and if I had seen you I'd have been too scared to know you. I'll tie you to the bedpost after this, and not let you scare the whole house," answered Kitty, regarding it all as a fine joke.

"What did I do when I got in?" asked Cordy, curiously.

"Took off your things and went to bed as if glad to get back. I did n't dare to wake you, and kept the fun all to myself till this morning. Thought I ought to have a good laugh for my pains since I did all the work," answered Sally, in high glee at the success of her efforts.

"I did want to get as thin as I could before I went home, the boys plague me so; and I suppose it wore upon me and set me to walking at night. I'm very sorry, and I never will again if I can help it. Please forgive me, and don't tell any one but Miss Orne; it was so silly," begged poor Cordy, tearfully.

All promised and comforted her, and praised Sally, and plagued Julia, and had a delightfully

noisy and exciting half hour before the breakfast
bell rang.

Miss Orne wondered what made the young
faces so gay and the laughter so frequent, as
mysterious hints and significant nods went on
around the table; but as soon as possible she
was borne into the school-room and told the
thrilling tale.

Her interest and surprise were very flattering,
and when the subject had been well discussed
she promised to prevent any further escapades
of this sort, and advised Cordy to try the Bant-
ing method for the few remaining weeks of her
stay.

"I'll try anything that will keep me from
acting ghost and making every one afraid of
me," said Cordy, secretly wondering why she had
not broken her neck in her nocturnal gymnastics.

"Do you believe in ghosts, Miss Orne?"
asked Maud, — who did, in spite of the comic
explanation of this one.

"Not the old-fashioned sort, but there is a
modern kind that we are all afraid of more or
less," answered Miss Orne, with a half-playful,
half-serious look at the girls around her.

"Do tell about them, please," begged Kitty,
while the rest looked both surprised and interested.

"There is one which I am very anxious to
keep you from fearing. Women are especially
haunted by it, and it prevents them from doing,

being, and thinking all that they might and ought. 'What will people say?' is the name of this formidable ghost; and it does much harm, for few of us have the courage to live up to what we know to be right in all things. You are soon to go away to begin your lives in earnest, and I do hope that whatever I have been able to teach you about the care of minds and bodies will not be forgotten or neglected because it may not be the fashion outside our little world."

"*I* never will forget, or be afraid of that ghost, Miss Orne," cried Sally, quick to understand and accept the warning so opportunely given.

"I have great faith in *you*, dear, because you have proved yourself so brave in facing phantoms more easily laid. But this is a hard one to meet and vanquish; so watch well, stand firm, and let these jerseys that you are so fond of cover not only healthy young bodies but happy hearts, both helping you to be sweet, wise, and useful women in the years to come. Dear girls, promise me this, and I shall feel that our winter has not been wasted, and that our spring is full of lovely promise for a splendid summer."

As she spoke, with her own beautiful face bright with hope and tenderness, Miss Orne opened her arms and gathered them all in, to seal their promise with grateful kisses more eloquent than words.

Long after their school days were over, the

six girls kept the white jerseys they wore at the
breaking-up festival, as relics of the J. J.; and
long after they were scattered far apart, they
remembered the lessons which helped them to be
what their good friend hoped — healthy, happy,
and useful women.

THE LITTLE HOUSE IN THE GARDEN

"I THINK we little ones ought to have a story all to ourselves now," said one of the smaller lads, as they gathered round the fire with unabated interest.

"So do I, and I 've got a little tale that will just suit you, I fancy. The older boys and girls can go and play games if they don't care to hear," answered Aunt Elinor, producing the well-worn portfolio.

"Thanks, we will try a bit, and if it is very namby pamby we can run," said Geoff, catching sight of the name of the first chapter. Aunt Elinor smiled and began to read about

THE LITTLE HOUSE IN THE GARDEN

I. Bears

A BROWN bear was the first tenant; in fact, it was built for him, and this is the way it happened: —

A man and his wife were driving through the woods up among the mountains, and hearing a queer sound looked about them till they spied two baby bears in a tree.

"Those must be the cubs of the old bear that was killed last week," said Mr. Hitchcock, much interested all at once.

"Poor little things! how will they get on without their mother? They look half scared to death, and cry like real babies," said the kind woman.

"They will starve if we don't take care of them. I'll shake them down; you catch them in your shawl and we'll see what we can do for them."

So Mr. Hitchcock climbed up the tree, to the great dismay of the two orphans, who growled funny little growls and crept as far out on the branch as they dared.

"Shake easy, John, or they will fall and be killed," cried the wife, holding out her shawl for this new kind of fruit to fall into.

Down they came, one after the other, and at first were too frightened to fight; so Mr. Hitchcock got them into the wagon safely bundled up, and Mrs. Hitchcock soothed their alarm by gentle pattings and motherly words, till they ceased to struggle, and cuddled down to sleep like two confiding puppies, for they were not much bigger.

Mr. Hitchcock kept the hotel that stood at the foot of the king of the mountains, and in summer the house was full of people; so he was glad of any new attraction, and the little bears were the delight of many children. At first, Tom and

Jerry trotted and tumbled about like frolicsome puppies, and led easy lives, — petted, fed and admired, till they grew so big and bold that, like other young creatures, their pranks made mischief as well as fun.

Tom would steal all the good things he could lay his paws on in kitchen or dining-room, and cook declared she could n't have the rascal loose; for whole pans of milk vanished, sheets of ginger-bread were found in his den under the back steps, and nearly every day he was seen scrambling off with booty of some sort, while the fat cook waddled after, scolding and shaking the poker at him, to the great amusement of the boarders on the piazza. People bore with him a long time; but when he took a lively trot down the middle of the long dinner-table one day, after eating all he liked, and smashing right and left as he scampered off, with a terrible clatter of silver, glass, and china, his angry master declared he would n't have such doings, and chained him to a post on the lawn. Here he tugged and growled dismally, while good little Jerry frisked gayly about, trying to understand what it all meant.

But presently *his* besetting sin got *him* into trouble likewise. He loved to climb, and was never happier than when scrambling up the rough posts of the back piazza to bask in the sun on the roof above, peeping down with his sharp little eyes at the children, who could not follow. He roosted in trees like a fat brown bird, and came tumbling down unexpectedly on lovers who sought quiet nooks to be romantic in. He explored the chimneys and threw into them any trifle he happened to find, — being a rogue, and fond of stealing hats, balls, dolls, or any small article that came in his way. But the fun he liked best was to climb in at the chamber windows and doze on the soft beds; for Jerry was a luxurious fellow and scorned the straw of his own den. This habit annoyed people much, and the poor bear often came bundling out of windows, with old gentlemen whacking him with canes, or ladies throwing water after him.

One evening, when there was a dance and every one was busy down stairs, Jerry took a walk on the roof, and being sleepy, looked about for a cosey bed to take a nap in. Two brothers occupied one of these rooms, and both were Jerry's good friends, especially the younger. Georgie was fast asleep, as his dancing days had not yet begun, and Charlie was waltzing away down stairs; so Jerry crept into bed and nestled down beside his playmate, who was too sleepy to do anything but roll over, thinking the big brother had come to bed.

By and by Charlie did come up, late and tired, and having forgotten a lamp, undressed in the moonlight, observing nothing till about to step into bed; then, finding something rolled up in the clothes, thought it a joke of the other boys, caught up a racket and began to bang away at the suspicious bundle. A scene of wild confusion followed, for Jerry growled and clawed and could n't get out; Georgie woke, and thinking his bed-fellow was his brother being abused by some frolicsome mate, held on to Jerry, defending him bravely, till a rent in the sheet allowed a shaggy head to appear, so close to his own that the poor child was painfully reminded of Red Riding Hood's false grandmother. Charlie was speechless with laughter at this discovery, and while Jerry bounced about the bed snarling and hugging pillows as he tried to get free, terrified Georgie rushed down the hall screaming, " The wolf! the wolf!" till he took refuge in his mother's room.

Out popped night-capped heads, anxious voices cried, " Is it fire?" and in a moment the house was astir. The panic might have been serious if Jerry had not come galloping down stairs, hotly pursued by Charlie in his night-gown, still belaboring the poor beast, and howling, " He was in my bed! He scared George! I 'll thrash him!"

Then the alarmed ladies and gentlemen laughed and grew calm, while the boys all turned out and hunted Jerry up stairs and down, till he was captured and ignominiously lugged away to be tied in the barn.

That prank sealed his fate, and he went to join his brother in captivity. Here they lived for a year, and went to housekeeping in a den in the bank, with a trough for their food, and a high, knotted pole to climb on. They had many visitors, and learned a few tricks, but were not happy bears; for they longed to be free, and the older they grew, the more they sighed for the great forest where they were born.

The second summer something happened that parted them forever. Among the children that year were Fred and Fan Howard, two jolly young persons of twelve and fourteen. Of course the bears were very interesting, and Fred tried their tempers by tormenting them, while Fan won their hearts with cake and nuts, candy and caresses. Tom was Fred's favorite, and Jerry was Fan's. Tom was very intelligent, and covered himself with glory by various exploits. One was taking off the boards which roofed the den, so that the sun should dry the dampness after a rain; and he carefully replaced them at night. Any dog who approached the trough got his ears smartly boxed, and meddlesome boys were hugged till they howled for mercy. He danced in a way to convulse the soberest, and Fred taught him to shoulder arms in such a funny imitation of a stout old soldier of the town that the children rolled on the grass in fits of laughter when the cap was on, and the wooden gun flourished at word of command by the clumsy hero.

Jerry had no accomplishments, but his sweet

temper made many friends. He let the doves eat
with him, the kittens frolic all over his broad
back, and was never rough with the small people
who timidly offered the buns he took so gently
from their little hands. But he pined in captivity, refused his food, and lay in his den all day,
or climbed to the top of the pole and sat there
looking off to the cool, dark forest, with such
a pensive air that Fan said it made her heart
ache to see him. Just before the season ended,
Jerry disappeared. No one could imagine how
the chain broke, but gone he was, and never came
back, to Fan's satisfaction and Tom's great sorrow. He mourned for his brother, and Mr.
Hitchcock began to talk of killing him; for it
would not do to let two bears loose in the neighborhood, as they sometimes killed sheep and did
much harm.

"I wish my father would buy him," said
Fred, "I've always wanted a menagerie, and a
tame bear would be a capital beginning."

"I'll ask him, for I hate to have the poor old
fellow killed," answered Fan. She not only
begged papa to buy Tom, but confessed that she
filed Jerry's chain and helped him to escape.

"I know it was wrong, but I couldn't see him
suffer," she said. "Now if you buy Tom I'll
give you my five dollars to help, and Mr. Hitchcock will forgive me and be glad to get rid of
both the bears."

After some consultation Tom *was* bought, and

orders were sent to have a house built for him
in a sunny corner of the garden, with strong
rings to chain him to, and a good lock on the
door to keep him in. When he was settled in
these new quarters he held daily receptions for
some weeks. Young and old came to see him,
and Fred showed off his menagerie with the
pride of a budding Barnum. A bare spot was
soon worn on the grass where Tom's parade
ground was, and at all hours the poor fellow
might be seen dancing and drilling, or sitting at
his door, thoughtfully surveying the curious
crowd, and privately wishing he never had been
born.

Here he lived for another year, getting so big
that he could hardly turn round in his house,
and so cross that Fred began to be a little afraid
of him after several hugs much too close to be
safe or agreeable. One morning the door of the
house was found broken off, and Tom gone.
Fred was rather relieved; but his father was anxious, and ordered out the boys of the neighborhood to find the runaway, lest he should alarm
people or do some harm. It was an easy matter
to trace him, for more than one terrified woman
had seen the big, brown beast sniffing round her
back premises after food; a whole schoolful of
children had been startled out of their wits
by a bear's head at the window; and one old
farmer was in a towering rage over the damage done to his bee-hives and garden patch by

" the pesky critter, afore he took to the woods."

After a long tramp poor Tom was found rolled up in a sunny nook, resting after a glorious frolic. He went home without much reluctance, but from that time it was hard to keep him. Bolts and bars, chains and ropes were of little use; for when the longing came, off he went, on one occasion carrying the house on his back, like a snail, till he tipped it over and broke loose. Fred was quite worn out with his pranks, and tried to sell or give him away; but nobody would buy or accept such a troublesome pet. Even tender hearted Fan gave him up, when he frightened a little child into a fit and killed some sheep, in his last holiday.

It was decided that he must be killed, and a party of men, armed with guns, set out to carry the sentence into effect. Fred went also to see that all was properly done, and Fanny called after him with tears in her eyes: —

" Say good by for me, and kill him as kindly as you can."

This time Tom had been gone a week and had evidently made up his mind to be a free bear; for he had wandered far into the deepest wood and made a den for himself among the rocks. Here they found him, but could not persuade him to come out, and no bold Putnam was in the troop, to creep in and conquer him there.

" Bullets will reach him if we can't, so blaze away, boys, and finish him off. We have fooled away time enough, and I want to get home to supper," said the leader of the hunt, after many attempts had been made to lure or drive Tom from his shelter.

So they " blazed away," and growls of pain proved that some of the bullets had hit. But Tom would not budge, and having used up their ammunition, the disappointed hunters went home resolving to bring dogs next day and finish the job. They were spared the trouble, however, for when Fred looked from his window in the morning he saw that Tom had returned, and ran down to welcome the rebel back. But one look at the poor beast showed him that he had only come home to die; for he was covered with wounds and lay moaning on his bed of straw, looking as pathetic as a bear could, his shaggy coat full of burrs, his head and breast full of shot, and one paw apparently broken.

Fanny cried over him, and Fred was quite bowed down with remorse; but nothing could be done, and soon, with a vain effort to lick the hands that stroked him, poor Tom lifted his great paw for a farewell shake, and died, with his great head on his master's knee, in token of forgiveness. As if to atone for their seeming cruelty, Fanny hung the little house with black while Tom lay in state, and Fred, resisting all temptations to keep his fine skin, buried him like a warrior " with his martial cloak around him," in the green woods he loved so well.

II. Boys

THE next tenants of the little house were three riotous lads, — for Fred's family moved away, — and the new comers took possession one fine spring day with great rejoicing over this ready-made plaything. They were queer fellows, of eleven, twelve, and fourteen; for, having read the "Boys' Froissart" and other warlike works, they were carried away by these stirring tales, and each boy was a hero. Harry, the eldest, was Henry of Navarre, and wore a white plume on every occasion. Ned was the Black Prince, and clanked in tin armor, while little Billy was William Tell and William Wallace by turns.

.. Tom's deserted mansion underwent astonishing changes about this time. Bows and arrows hung on its walls; battle-axes, lances, and guns stood in the corners; helmets, shields, and all manner of strange weapons adorned the rafters; cannon peeped from its port-holes; a drawbridge swung over the moat that soon surrounded it; the flags of all nations waved from its roof, and the small house was by turns an armory, a fort, a castle, a robber's cave, a warrior's tomb, a wigwam, and the Bastile.

The neighbors were both amused and scandalized by the pranks of these dramatic young persons; for they enacted with much spirit and skill all the historical events which pleased their fancy, and speedily enlisted other boys to join in the new plays. At one time, painted and be-feathered Indians whooped about the garden, tomahawking the unhappy settlers in the most dreadful manner. At another, Achilles, radiant in a tin helmet and boiler-cover shield, dragged Hector at the tail of his chariot (the wheel-bar-row), drawn by two antic and antique steeds, who upset both victor and vanquished before the fun was over. Tell shot bushels of apples off the head of the stuffed suit of clothes that acted his son, Cœur de Leon and Saladin hacked blocks and cut cushions *à la* Walter Scott, and tourna-ments of great splendor were held on the grass, in which knights from all ages, climes, and races, tilted gallantly, while fair dames of tender years sat upon the wood-pile to play Queens of Beauty and award the prize of valor.

Nor were more modern heroes forgotten. Na-poleon crossed the Alps (a muck heap, high fence, and prickly hedge), with intrepid courage. Wellington won many a Waterloo in the melon patch, and Washington glorified every corner of the garden by his heroic exploits. Grant smoked sweet-fern cigars at the fall of Rich-mond; Sherman marched victoriously to Geor-gia through the corn and round the tomato bed, and Phil Sheridan electrified the neighborhood by tearing down the road on a much-enduring donkey, stung to unusual agility by matches tied to his tail.

It grew to be an almost daily question among the young people, "What are the Morton boys at now?" for these interesting youths were much admired by their mates, who eagerly manned the fences to behold the revels, when scouts brought word of a new play going on. Mrs. Morton believed in making boys happy at home, and so allowed them entire liberty in the great garden, as it was safer than river, streets, or ball-ground, where a very mixed crowd was to be found. Here they were under her own eye, and the safe, sweet tie between them still held fast; for she was never too busy to bind up their wounds after a fray, wave her handkerchief when cheers told of victory, rummage her stores for costumes, or join in their eager study of favorite heroes when rain put an end to their out-of-door fun.

So the summer was a lively one, and though the vegetables suffered some damage, a good crop of healthy, happy hours was harvested, and all were satisfied. The little house looked much the worse for the raids made upon it, but still stood firm with the stars and stripes waving over it, and peace seemed to reign one October afternoon as the boys lay under the trees eating apples and planning what to play next.

"Bobby wants to be a knight of the Round Table. We might take him in and have fun with the rites, and make him keep a vigil and all that," proposed William Wallace, anxious to admit his chosen friend to the inner circle of the brotherhood.

"He's such a little chap he'd be scared and howl. I don't vote for that," said the Black Prince, rather scornfully, as he lay with his kingly legs in the air, and his royal mouth full of apple.

"I do!" declared Henry of Navarre, always generous, and amiable. "Bob is a plucky little chap, and will do anything we put him to. He's poor and the other fellows look down on him, so that's another reason why we ought to take him in and stand by him. Let's give him a good trial, and if he's brave, we'll have him."

"So we will! Let's do it now; he's over there waiting to be asked in. *He* doesn't go poking his nose where he isn't wanted, as some folks do," cried Billy, who had often been snubbed by the big boys in his efforts at knightly feats.

A whistle brought Bobby, with a beaming face, for he burned to join the fun, but held back because he was not a gentleman's son. A sturdy, honest little soul was Bobby, true as steel, brave as a lion, and loyal as an old-time vassal to his young lord, kind Billy, who always told him all the plans, explained the mysteries, and shared the goodies when feasts were spread.

Now he stood leaning against one of the posts of the little house whither the boys had adjourned, and listened bashfully while Harry told him what he must do to join the heroes of the Round Table. He did not understand half of it, but was ready for any trial, and took the comical oath administered to him with the utmost solemnity.

" You must stay here locked in for some hours, and watch your armor. That's the vigil young knights had to keep before they could fight. You must n't be scared at any noises you hear, or anything you see, or sing out for help, even if you stay here till dark. You 'll be a coward if you do, and never have a sword."

" I promise truly; hope to die if I don't!" answered Bobby, fixing his blue eyes on the speaker, and holding his curly head erect with the air of one ready to face any peril; for the desire of his soul was to own a sword, like Billy, and clash it on warlike occasions.

Then a suit of armor was piled up on the red box, which was by turns altar, table, tomb, and executioner's block. Banners were hung over it, the place darkened, two candles lighted, and after certain rites which cannot be divulged, the little knight was left to his vigil with the door locked.

The boys howled outside, smote on the roof, fired a cannon, and taunted the prisoner with derisive epithets to stir him to wrath. But no cry answered them, no hint of weariness, fear, or anger betrayed him, and after a half-hour of this sort of fun, they left him to the greater trial of silence, solitude, and uncertainty.

The short afternoon was soon gone, and the

tea bell rang before the vigil had lasted long enough.

"He won't know what time it is; let's leave him till after supper, and then march out with torches and bring him in to a good feed. Mother won't mind, and Hetty likes to stuff fellows," proposed Harry, and all being hungry, the first part of the plan was carried out at once.

But before tea was over, the unusual clang of the fire bells drove all thought of Bobby out of the boys' minds, as they raced away to the exciting scene, to take their share in the shouting, running, and tumbling about in every one's way.

The great hotel was burning, and till midnight the town was in an uproar. No lives were lost, but much property, and nothing else was thought of till dawn. A heavy shower did good service, and about one o'clock, people began to go home tired out. Mrs. Morton and other ladies were too busy giving shelter to the people from the hotel, and making coffee for the firemen, to send their boys to bed. In fact, they could not catch them; for the youngsters were wild with excitement, and pervaded the place like will-o'-the-wisps, running errands, lugging furniture, splashing about with water, and howling till they were as hoarse as crows.

"This is the battle of Beauvais, and we've set the city a-fire by flinging pitch-pots over the walls," croaked Harry to Ned as they bumped against each other, one carrying a great coffee-pot and the other a feather-bed.

"No, it 's the fall of Troy, and I 'm Æneas lugging off the old man," panted Ned, staggering away with the heavy load on his back.

At last the flurry was over, and our three lads, very dirty, wet, and tired, went to bed and to sleep, and never once thought of poor Bobby, till next morning. Then Harry suddenly rose up, with an exclamation that effectually roused both his brothers.

"By St. Dennis, we 've left that boy there all night!"

"He would n't be such a fool as to stay; that old lock 's broken easy enough," said Ned, looking troubled, in spite of his words.

"Yes, he would! He promised, and he 'll keep his word like a true knight. It rained and was cold, and no one knew where he was. Oh dear, I hope he is n't dead," cried Billy, tumbling out of bed and into his clothes as fast as he could.

The others laughed, but dressed with unusual speed and flew to the garden house, to find the lock unbroken, and all as still inside as when they left it. Looking very anxious, Harry opened the door and all peeped in. There, at his post before the altar, lay the little knight fast asleep. Rain had soaked his clothes, the chilly night air made his lips and hands purple with cold, and the trials of those long hours left the round cheeks rather pale. But he still guarded his arms, and at the first sound was awake and ready to defend them, though somewhat shaky with sleep and stiffness.

The penitent boys poured forth apologies, in which fire, remorse, and breakfast were oddly mixed. Bobby forgave them like a gentleman, only saying, with a laugh and a shiver, " Guess I 'd better go home, ma 'll be worried about me. If I 'd known being out all night and getting wet was part of the business, I 'd 'a' left word and brought a blanket. Be I a Round Table now? Shall I have a sword, and train with the rest? I did n't holler once, and was n't much scared, for all the bells, and the dark, and the rain."

" You 've won your spurs, and we 'll knight you just as soon as we get time. You 're a brave fellow, and I 'm proud to have you one of my men. Please don't say much about this; we 'll make it all right, and we 're awfully sorry," answered Harry, while Ned put his own jacket over the wet shoulders, and Billy beamed at him, feeling that his friend's exploit outdid any of his own.

Bobby marched away as proudly as if he already saw the banners waving over him, and felt the accolade that made him a true knight. But that happy moment was delayed for some time, because the cold caught in that shower threatened a fit of sickness; and the boys' play looked as if it might end in sad earnest.

Harry and his brothers confessed all to

mamma, listened with humility to her lecture on true knighthood, and did penance by serving Bobby like real brothers-in-arms, while he was ill. As soon as the hardy boy was all right again, they took solemn counsel together how they should reward him, and atone for their carelessness. Many plans were discussed, but none seemed fine enough for this occasion till Billy had a bright idea.

"Let's buy Bob some hens. He wants some dreadfully, and we ought to do something grand after treating him so badly, and nearly killing him."

"Who's got any money? I haven't; but it's a good idea," responded Ned, vainly groping in all his pockets for a cent to head the subscription with.

"Mamma would lend us some, and we could work to pay for it," began Billy.

"No, I've a better plan," interrupted Harry with authority. "We ought to make a sacrifice and suffer for our sins. We will have an auction and sell our arms. The boys want them, and will pay well. My lords and gentlemen, what say ye?"

"We will!" responded the loyal subjects of King Henry.

"Winter is coming, and we can't use them," said Billy, innocently.

"And by next spring we shall be too old for such games," added Ned.

" 'T is well! Ho! call hither my men. Bring out the suits of mail; sound the trumpets, and set on!" thundered Harry, striking an attitude, and issuing his commands with royal brevity.

A funny scene ensued; for while Billy ran to collect the boys, Ned dismantled the armory, and Hal disposed of the weapons in the most effective manner, on trees, fences, and grass, where the bidders could examine and choose at their ease. Their mates had always admired and coveted these war-like treasures, for some were real, and others ingenious imitations; so they gladly came at sound of the hunter's horn which was blown when Robin Hood wanted his merry men.

Harry was auctioneer, and rattled off the most amazing medley of nonsense in praise of the articles, which he rapidly knocked down to the highest bidder. The competition was lively, for the boys laughed so much they hardly knew what they were doing, and made the rashest offers; but they all knew what the money was to be used for, so they paid their bills handsomely, and marched off with cross-bows, old guns, rusty swords, and tin armor, quite contented with their bargains.

Seven dollars was realized by the sale, and a fine rooster and several hens solemnly presented to Bobby, who was overwhelmed by this unexpected atonement, and immediately established his fowls in the woodshed, where they happily

resided through the winter, and laid eggs with
such gratifying rapidity that he earned quite a
little fortune, and insisted on saying that his vigil
had not only made a knight of him, but a million-
aire.

III. Babies

THE little house stood empty till spring; then
a great stir went on in the garden, getting it
ready for a new occupant. It was mended,
painted red, fitted up with a small table and
chairs, and a swing. Sun-flowers stood sentinel
at the door, vines ran over it, and little beds of
flowers were planted on either side. Paths were
dug all round the lawn, and a baby-carriage was
rolled up and down to harden them. The neighbors wondered what was coming next, and one
June day they found out; for a procession appeared, escorting the new tenant to the red mansion, with great rejoicing among the boys.

First came Billy blowing the horn, then Ned
waving their best banner, then Hal drawing the
baby wagon, in which, as on a throne, sat the
little cousin who had come to spend the summer,
and rule over them like a small, sweet tyrant.
A very sprightly damsel was four-year-old
Queenie, blue-eyed, plump, and rosy, with a
cloud of yellow curls, chubby arms that embraced
every one, and a pair of stout legs that trotted
all day. She surveyed her kingdom with cries

of delight, and took possession of "mine tot-
tage" at once, beginning housekeeping by a
tumble out of the swing, a header into the red
chest, and a pinch in the leaf of the table. But
she won great praise from the boys by making
light of these mishaps, and came up smiling, with
a bump on her brow, a scratch on her pug nose,
and a bruise on one fat finger, and turned out
tea for the gentlemen as if she had done it all
her life; for the table was set, and all manner
of tiny cakes and rolls stood ready to welcome
her.

This was only the beginning of tea parties;
for very soon a flock of lovely little friends came
to play with Queenie, and such pretty revels went
on it seemed as if fairies had taken possession
of the small house. Dolls had picnics, kittens
went a-visiting, tin carts rattled up and down,
gay balloons flew about, pigmy soldiers toddled
round the paths in paper caps, and best of all,
rosy little girls danced on the grass, picked the
flowers, chased butterflies, and sang as blithely
as the birds. Queenie took the lead in these
frolics, and got into no end of scrapes by her
love of exploration, — often leading her small
friends into the strawberry-bed, down the road,
over the wall, or to some neighbor's house, coolly
demanding "a dint a water and dingerbed for
all us ones."

Guards were set, bars and locks put up, orders
given, and punishments inflicted, but all in vain;

the dauntless baby always managed to escape, and after anxious hunts and domestic flurries, would be found up a tree, under the big rhubarb leaves, in a hen house, or calmly strolling to town without her hat. All sorts of people took her to drive at her request, and brought her back just as her agitated relatives were flying to the river in despair. Once she departed with a flock of sheep, and was returned so dirty no one knew her till she was scrubbed. Another time, she passed the morning in the pig-pen, having fallen over the fence; and finding pleasant society in a dozen young piggies, stayed to play with them till discovered among the straw, surrounded by her new friends, one of whom slept sweetly in her arms.

"We must tie her up," said Mrs. Morton, quite worn out with her pranks.

So a strong cord was put round Queenie's waist, and fastened to one of the rings in the little house where Tom used to be chained. At first she raged and tugged, then submitted, and played about as if she did n't care; but she laid plans in her naughty little mind, and carried them out, to the great dismay of Bessie, the maid.

"I want to tut drass," she said in her most persuasive tones.

So Bessie gave her the rusty scissors she was allowed to use, and let her play make hay till her toy wagon was full.

"I want a dint a water, pease," was the next request, and Bessie went in to get it. She was delayed a few moments, and when she came out no sign of Queenie remained but a pile of yellow hair cut off in a hurry, and the end of the cord. Slyboots was gone, scissors and all.

Then there was racing and calling, scolding and wailing, but no Queenie was to be seen anywhere on the premises. Poor Bessie ran one way, Aunt Morton another, and Billy, who happened to be at home, poked into all the nooks and corners for the runaway.

An hour passed, and things began to look serious, when Harry came in much excited, and laughing so he could hardly speak.

"Where *do* you think that dreadful baby has turned up? Over at Pat Floyd's. He found her in the water pipes. You know a lot of those big ones are lying in the back street ready to use as soon as the place is dug. Well, that little rascal crept in, and then could n't turn round, so she went on till she came out by Pat's house, and nearly scared him out of his wits. The pipes were not joined, so she had light and air, but I guess she had a hard road to travel. Such a hot, dirty, tired baby you never saw. Mrs. Floyd is washing her up. You'd better go and get her, Bess."

Bess went and returned with naughty Queenie, looking as if rats had gnawed her curls off, and the sand of the great desert had been ground

into her hands and knees, — not to mention the
iron rust that ruined her pretty pink frock, or
the crown of her hat rubbed to rags.

"I was n't frighted. You said Dod be 'd all
wound, so I goed wite alon, and Mis Foyd gived
me a nice cold tater, and a tootie, and the bid
dord washed my hands wif his wed tun."

That was Queenie's account of the matter,
but she behaved so well after it that her friends
suspected the perilous prank had made a good
impression upon her.

To keep her at home she was set to farming,
and the little house was a barn. In it lived a
rocking horse, several wooden cows, woolly
sheep, cats and dogs, as well as a queer collection of carts and carriages, tools and baskets.
Every day the busy little farmer dug and hoed,
planted and watered her "dardin," made hay,
harvested vegetables, picked fruit, or took care
of animals, — pausing now and then to ride her
horse, drive out in her phaeton, or go to an
imaginary fire with the engine Billy had made
for her.

The little friends came to help her, and the
flower-beds soon looked as if an earthquake had
upheaved them; for things were planted upside
down, holes dug, stones piled, and potatoes laid
about as if expected to dig themselves. But
cheeks bloomed like roses, small hands got
brown, and busy feet trotted firmly about the
paths, while the red barn echoed with the gayest
laughter all day long.

On Queenie's fifth birthday, in September, she had a gipsy party, and all the small neighbors came to it. A tent was pitched, three tall poles held up a kettle over a " truly fire " that made the water really boil, and supper was spread on the grass. The little girls wore red and blue petticoats, gay shawls or cloaks, bright handkerchiefs on their heads, and as many beads and breastpins as they liked. Some had tamborines, and shook them as they danced; one carried a dolly in the hood of her cloak like a true gipsy, and all sung, skipping hand in hand round the fire.

The mammas looked on and helped about supper, and Bess sat in the tent like an old woman, and told pleasant fortunes, as she looked in the palms of the soft little hands the children showed her.

They had a charming time, and all remembered it well; for that night, when the fun was over, every one in bed, and the world asleep, a great storm came on; the wind blew a gale and chimney tops flew off, blinds banged, trees were broken, apples whisked from the boughs by the bushel, and much mischief was done. But worst of all, the dear little house blew away! The roof went in one direction, the boards in another, the poor horse lay heels up, and the rest of the animals were scattered far and wide over the garden.

Great was the lamentation next morning,

when the children saw the ruin. The boys felt that it was past mending, and gave it up; while Queenie consoled herself for the devastation of her farm by the childish belief that a crop of new cats and dogs, cows and horses, would come up in the spring from the seed sowed broadcast by the storm.

So that was the sad end of the little house in the garden.

DAISY'S JEWEL - BOX, AND HOW SHE FILLED IT

"**P**LENTY of time for another. Let the little folks go to bed, now they've had their story, and please go on, auntie," cried Min, when all had listened with more interest than they would confess to the children's tale.

So the small people trotted off, much against their will, and this most obliging of aunts drew forth another manuscript, saying, as she glanced at several of her elder nieces, brave in the new trinkets Santa Claus had sent them: —

"This is a story with a moral to it, which the girls will understand; the boys can take naps while I read, for it won't interest them."

"If it shows up the girls we shall like it," answered Geoff, and composed himself to hear and enjoy

DAISY'S JEWEL - BOX, AND HOW SHE FILLED IT

"IT would be perfectly splendid, and just what I long for, but I don't see how I *can* go with nothing fit to wear," said Daisy, looking up from the letter in her hand, with a face full of girlish eagerness and anxiety.

Mrs. Field set every fear at rest with a reassuring smile, as she quietly made one of the sacrifices mothers think so small, when made for the dear creatures for whom they live.

"You shall go, dear; I have a little sum put by for an emergency. Twenty-five dollars will do a good deal, when tastes are simple and we do our own dress-making."

"But mother, that was for your cloak. You need it so much I can't bear to have you give it up," said sober little Jane, the home-girl, who never cared for visiting like her gay elder sister.

"Hush, dear; I can do very well with a shawl over my old sack. Don't say a word to spoil Daisy's pleasure. She needs a change after this dull autumn, and must be neat and nice."

Janey said no more, and fell to thinking what she had to offer Daisy; for both took great pride in the pretty girl, who was the queen among her young friends.

Daisy heard, but was so busy re-reading the letter that she took no notice then, though she recalled the words later.

"Come and pass the holidays with us. We all want to see you, and Laura begs you will not disappoint her."

This was the invitation that came from Laura's mother; for the two girls had struck up a great friendship during the summer the city family passed in the little country town where Daisy lived. She had ardently hoped that Laura would not forget the charming plan, and now the cordial message came, just when the season would be gayest in town.

"I suppose I must have the everlasting white muslin for a party dress, as that is the cheapest thing a girl can wear. A nun's-veiling is what I long for, but I'm afraid we can't afford it," she said with a sigh, coming back from visions of city delights to the all-important question of dress.

"Yes, you can, and new ribbons, gloves, and slippers as well. You are so small it does n't take much, and we can make it right up ourselves. So run and collect all your finery, while I go and do the shopping at once."

"You dearest of mothers! how you always manage to give me what I want, and smooth all my worries away. I'll be as good as gold, and bring you the best present I can find."

Daisy's grateful kiss warmed the dear woman's heart, and made her forget how shabby the old sack was, as she trudged away to spend the money carefully hoarded for the much needed cloak.

Needles and fingers flew, and two days before Christmas, Daisy set out for the enchanted city, feeling very rich with the pretty new dress in her trunk, and five dollars for pocket money. It seemed a large sum to the country girl, and she

planned to spend it all in gifts for mother and
Janey, whose tired faces rather haunted her after
she had caught the last glimpse of them.

Her reception was a warm one, for all the
Vaughns were interested in the blooming little
creature they had found among the hills, and
did their best to make her visit a pleasant one.
The first day she was in a delightful sort of
maze, things were so splendid, gay and new;
the second she felt awkward and countrified,
and wished she had not come. A letter from
her mother on Christmas morning did her good,
and gave her courage to bear the little trials
that afflicted her.

" My clothes do look dowdy beside Laura's
elegant costumes, though they did seem very
nice at home; but my hair is n't red, and that 's
a comfort," she said to herself, as she dressed
for the party that evening.

She could not help smiling at the bonny figure
she saw in the long mirror, and wishing mother
and Janey could see the work of their hands in
all its glory; for the simple white dress was most
becoming, and her kind host had supplied her
with lovely flowers for bosom and bouquet.

But the smile died as she took up her one
ornament, an antique necklace, given her by
an old aunt. At home it was considered a very
rare and beautiful thing, and Daisy had been
rather proud of her rococo chain till she saw
Laura's collection of trinkets, the variety and

brilliancy of which dazzled her eyes, and woke a burning desire to possess treasures of the same sort. It was some consolation to find that the most striking were not very expensive, and after poring over them with deep interest, Daisy privately resolved to buy as many as her five dollars would compass. These new ornaments could be worn during her visit, and serve as gifts when she went home; so the extravagance would not be so great as it seemed.

This purpose comforted her, as she put on the old necklace, which looked very dingy beside the Rhinestones that flashed, the silver bangles that clashed, and the gilded butterflies, spiders, arrows, flowers, and daggers that shone on the young girls whom she met that evening. Their fine dresses she could not hope to imitate, but a pin and a pair of bracelets were possible, and she resolved to have them, if she had to borrow money to get home with.

Her head was quite turned by this desire for the cheap trinkets which attract all feminine eyes now-a-days, and when, among the pretty things that came to her from the Christmas tree that night, she received a blue plush jewel-box, she felt that it was almost a duty to fill it as soon as possible.

"Isn't it a beauty? I never had one, and it is just what I wanted," said Daisy, delightedly lifting the tray full of satin beds for pretty things, and pulling out the little drawer underneath, where the giver's card lay.

"I told papa a work-box or a fan would be better; but he liked this and would buy it," explained Laura, who knew how useless it was to her friend.

"It was very kind of him, and I prefer it to either of those. I 've nothing but my old chain and a shabby little pin to put in it now, but I 'll fill it in time," answered Daisy, whose eyes seemed to behold the unbought treasures already reposing on the dainty cushion.

"Real jewels are the best, my dear, for their worth and beauty are never lost. The tinsel girls wear now is poor stuff, and money is thrown away in buying it," said Mrs. Vaughn, who overheard them and guessed the temptation which beset the little country girl.

Daisy looked conscious, but answered, with a smile, and a hand on her necklace, "This old thing would n't look well in my pretty box, so I 'll leave it empty till I can afford something better."

"But that antique chain is worth many mock diamonds; for it is genuine, and its age adds to its value. Lovers of such things would pay a good price for that and keep it carefully. So don't be ashamed of it, my dear, — though this pretty throat needs no ornament," added Mrs. Vaughn, hoping the girl would not forget the little lesson she was trying to give her.

Daisy did not, but when she went to bed, set the jewel-box on the table where it would meet

affair, and her face betrayed her in spite of her efforts to be gay.

"I know you were staring at the French diamonds in that corner store. I never can get you by there without a regular tug," cried Laura, when the tale was very briefly told.

"I can't help it; I'm perfectly fascinated by those foolish things, and I know I should have bought some; so it is well that I've lost my money, perhaps," answered Daisy, looking so innocently penitent and so frankly disappointed that Mr. Vaughn said kindly: —

"So it is, for now I have a chance to complete my Christmas present. I was not sure it would suit so I gave it empty. Please use this in buying some of the 'fascinating things' you like so well."

A bright ten-dollar gold piece was slipped into Daisy's hand, and she was obliged to keep it, in spite of all her protestations that she could live without trinkets, and did not need it as her ticket home was already bought. Mrs. Vaughn added a nice little purse, and Laura advised her to keep the lone ten-cent piece for a good-luck penny.

"Now I can do it with a free mind, and fill my box as Mr. Vaughn wishes me to. Won't it be fun?" thought Daisy, as she skipped upstairs after dinner, with a load of care lifted from her spirits.

Laura was taking a music lesson, so her guest

went to the sewing-room to mend the facing of
her dress, which some one had stepped on while
she stood in that fatal crowd. A seamstress was
there, sewing as if for a wager, and while Daisy
stitched her braid she wondered if there was
any need of such haste; for the young woman's
fingers flew, a feverish color was in her cheeks,
and now and then she sighed as if tired or
worried.

"Let me help, if you are in a hurry, Miss
White. I can sew fast, and know something
of dressmaking. Please let me. I'd love to do
anything for Mrs. Vaughn, she is so kind to
me" said Daisy, when her small job was done,
lingering to make the offer, though an interesting book was waiting in her room.

"Thank you, I guess I can get through by
dark. I do want to finish, for my mother is sick,
and needs me as well as the money," answered
the needle-woman, pausing to give the girl a
grateful smile, then stitching away faster than
ever.

"Then I must help. Give me that sleeve to
sew up, and rest a little. You look dreadfully
tired, and you've been working all day," insisted Daisy.

"That's real kind, and it would be a great
help, if you really like it," answered Miss White,
with a sigh of relief as she handed over the
sleeve, and saw how heartily and helpfully Daisy
fell to work.

Of course they talked, for the friendly act opened both hearts, and did both girls good. As the younger listened to the little story of love and labor, the gold piece burned in her pocket, and tinsel trinkets looked very poor beside the sacrifices so sweetly made by this good daughter for the feeble mother whose comfort and support she was.

"Our landlord has raised the rent, but I can't move now, for the cold and the worry would kill ma; so I'm tugging away to pay the extra money, else he will turn us out, I'm afraid."

"Why don't you tell Mrs. Vaughn? She helps every one, and loves to do it."

"So she does, bless her! She has done a deal for us, and that's why I can't ask for more. I won't beg while I can work, but worry wears on me, and if I break down what *will* become of mother?"

Poor Mary shook the tears out of her eyes, for daylight was going, and she had no time to cry; but Daisy stopped to wonder how it would seem to be in her place, "tugging away" day after day to keep a roof over mother. It made her heart ache to think of it, and sent her hand to her pocket with a joyful sense of power; for alms-giving was a new pleasure, and Daisy felt very rich.

"I've had a present to-day, and I'd love dearly to share it with you if you would n't mind. I shall only waste it, so do let me send it to your mother in any shape you like," she said in a timid, but very earnest way.

"Oh, Miss Field! I could n't do it! you are too kind; I never thought of hinting" — began Mary, quite overcome by this unexpected proposal.

Daisy settled the matter by running away to the study, where Mr. Vaughn was napping, to ask him if he would give her two fives for the gold piece.

"Ah! the fascination is at work, I see; and we can't wait till Monday to buy the pretty things. Girls will be girls, and must sow their innocent wild oats I suppose. Here, my dear, beware of pick-pockets, and good luck to the shopping," said the old gentleman, as he put two crisp bills into her hands, with a laugh.

"Pick-pockets won't get this, and I *know* my shopping will prosper now," answered Daisy, in such a happy tone that Mr. Vaughn wondered what plan was in the girl's head to make her look so sweet and glad.

She went slowly up-stairs looking at the two bills, which did not seem half so precious as when in the shape of gold.

"I wonder if it would be very extravagant to give her all of it. I shall do some silly thing if I keep it. Her boots were very thin, and she coughs, and if she is sick it will be dreadful. Suppose I give her five for herself, and five for her mother. I 'd love to feel rich and generous for once in my life, and give real help."

The house was very still, and Daisy paused at the head of the stairs to settle the point, little dreaming that Mrs. Vaughn had heard the talk in the sewing-room, and saw her as she stood thoughtfully staring at the two bits of paper in her hand.

"I should n't feel ashamed if Mrs. Vaughn found me out in this, but I should never dare to let her see my bangles and pins, if I got them. I know she thinks them silly, especially so for me. She said she hoped I 'd set a good example to Laura, in the way of simplicity and industry. I like that, and so will mother. But then, my jewel-box! All empty, and such a pretty thing. Oh dear, I wish I could be wise and silly at the same time."

Daisy sighed, and took a few more steps, then smiled, pulled out her purse, and taking the ten-cent piece tossed it up, saying: "Heads, Mary; tails, myself."

Up flew the bright little coin, and down it came with the goddess of liberty uppermost.

"That settles it; she shall have the ten, and I 'll be content with the old chain for all my jewelry," said Daisy aloud; and looking much relieved she skipped away, leaving the unsuspected observer to smile at her girlish mode of deciding the question, and to rejoice over the generous nature unspoiled as yet.

She watched her young guest with new interest during the next few days; for certain fine plans were in her mind, and every trifle helped the decision for or against.

Mary White went smiling home that night to rejoice with her feeble mother over the help that came so opportunely and so kindly.

Daisy looked as if her shopping *had* prospered wonderfully, though the old necklace was the only ornament she wore; and those who saw her happy face at the merry-making thought that she needed no other. She danced as if her feet were as light as her heart, and enjoyed that party more than the first; for no envy spoiled her pleasure, and a secret content brightened all the world to her.

But the next day she discovered that temptation still had power over her, and she nearly spoiled her first self-conquest by the fall which is very apt to come after a triumph, to show us how hard it is to stand fast, even when small Apollyons get in our way.

She broke the clasp of the necklace, and Mrs. Vaughn directed her to a person who mended such things. The man examined it with interest, and asked its history. Daisy very willingly told all she knew, inquiring if it was really valuable.

"I'd give twenty-five dollars for it any time. I've been trying to get one to go with a pair of earrings I picked up, and this is just what I want. Of course you don't care to sell it, miss?" he asked, glancing at Daisy's simple dress and rather excited face, for his offer almost took her breath away.

She was not sufficiently worldly-wise to see that the jeweller wanted it enough to give more for it, and to make a good bargain for herself. Twenty-five dollars seemed a vast sum, and she only paused to collect her wits, before she answered eagerly:—

"Yes, I *should* like to sell it; I've had it so long I'm tired of it, and it's all out of fashion. Mrs. Vaughn told me some people would be glad to get it, because it is genuine. Do you really think it is worth twenty-five dollars?"

"It's old, and I shall have to tinker it up; but it matches the earrings so well I am willing to pay a good price for it. Will you take the money now, miss, or think it over and call again?" asked the man, more respectfully, after hearing Mrs. Vaughn's name.

"I'll take it now, if you please, sir. I shall leave town in a day or two, and may not have time to call again," said Daisy, taking a half-regretful look at the chain, as the man counted out the money.

Holding it fast, she went away feeling that this unexpected fortune was a reward for the good use she had made of her gold piece.

"Now I can buy some really valuable ornament, and wear it without being ashamed. What shall it be? No tinsel for me this time;" and she walked by the attractive shop window with an air of lofty indifference, for she really was getting over her first craze for that sort of thing.

Feeling as if she possessed the power to buy real diamonds, Daisy turned toward the great jewellers, pausing now and then to look for some pretty gift for Janey, bought with her own money.

"What can I get for mother? She never will own that she needs anything, and goes shabby so I can be nice. I could get some of those fine, thick stockings, hers are all darns, — but they might not fit. Flannel is useful, but it is n't a pretty present. What *does* she need most?"

As Daisy stopped before a great window, full of all manner of comfortable garments, her eye fell on a fur-lined cloak marked "$25." It seemed to answer her question like a voice, and as she looked at it she heard again the words, —

"But, mother, that money was for your cloak, and you need it very much."

"Hush, dear, don't say a word to spoil Daisy's pleasure. I can do very well with a shawl over the old sack."

"How could I forget that! What a selfish girl I am, to be thinking of jewelry, when that dear, good mother has n't a cloak to her back. Daisy Field, I'm ashamed of you! Go in and buy that nice, warm one at once, and don't let me hear of that ridiculous box again."

After this little burst of remorse and self-reproach, Daisy took another look; and prudence suggested asking the advice of some more experienced shopper than herself, before making so important a purchase.   As if the fates were interested in settling the matter at once, while she stood undecided, Mary White came down the street with a parcel of work in her hands.

" Just the person!   The Vaughns need n't know anything about it; and Mary is a good judge."

It was pleasant to see the two faces brighten as the girls met; rather comical to watch the deep interest with which one listened and the other explained; and beautiful to hear the grateful eagerness in Mary's voice, as she answered cordially : —

" Indeed I will!   You 've been so kind to my mother, there 's nothing I would n't be glad to do for yours."

So in they went, and after due consideration, the cloak was bought and ordered home, — both girls feeling that it was a little ceremony full of love and good will; for Mary's time was money, yet she gave it gladly, and Daisy's purse was left empty of all but the good-luck penny, which was to bring still greater happiness in unsuspected ways.

Another secret was put away in the empty jewel-box, and the cloak hidden in Daisy's trunk; for she felt shy of telling her little business transactions, lest the Vaughns should consider her extravagant.   But the thought of mother's surprise and pleasure warmed her heart, and made the last days of her visit the happiest.   Being a mortal girl she did give a sigh as she tied a bit of black velvet round her white throat, instead of the necklace, which seemed really a treasure, now it was gone; and she looked with great disfavor at the shabby little pin, worn where she had fondly hoped to see the golden rose. She put a real one in its place, and never knew that her own fresh, happy face was as lovely; for the thought of the two mothers made comfortable by her was better than all the pearls and diamonds that fell from the lips of the good girl in the fairy tale.

"Let me help you pack your trunk; I love to cram things in, and dance on the lid when it won't shut," said Laura, joining her friend next day, just as she had got the cloak-box well hidden under a layer of clothes.

"Thank you, I'm almost done, and rather like to fuss over my own things in my own way. You won't mind if I give this pretty box of handkerchiefs to mother, will you, dear? I have so many things, I must go halves with some one. The muslin apron and box of bonbons are for Janey, because she can't wear the gloves, and this lovely *jabot* is too old for her," said Daisy, surveying her new possessions with girlish satisfaction.

"Do what you like with your own. Mamma has a box of presents for your people. She is packing it now, but I don't believe you can get it in; your trunk is so much fuller than when you came. This must go in a safe place, or your heart will break," and Laura took up the jewel-box, adding with a laugh, as she opened it, "you have n't filled it, after all! What did you do with papa's gold piece?"

"That's a secret. I'll tell some day, but not yet," said Daisy, diving into her trunk to hide the color in her cheeks.

"Sly thing! I know you've got silver spiders and filagree racquets, and Rhine-stone moons and stars stowed away somewhere and won't confess it. I wanted to fill this box, but mamma said you'd do it better yourself, so I let it alone; but I was afraid you'd think I was a selfish pig, to have a pin for every day in the month and never give you one," said Laura, as she looked at the single tarnished brooch reposing on the satin cushion. "Where's your chain?" she added, before Daisy could speak.

"It is safe enough. I'm tired of it, and don't care if I never see it again." And Daisy packed away, and laughed as she smoothed the white dress in its tray, remembering that it was paid for by the sale of the old necklace.

"Give it to me, then. I like it immensely; it's so odd. I'll exchange for anything of mine you choose. Will you?" asked Laura, who seemed bent on asking inconvenient questions.

"I shall have to tell, or she will think me very ungrateful," — and Daisy felt a pang of regret even then, for Laura's offer was a generous one.

"Like G. W., 'I cannot tell a lie;' so I must 'fess' that I sold the old thing, and spent the money for something I wanted very much, — not jewelry, but something to give away."

Daisy was spared further confessions by the entrance of Mrs. Vaughn, with a box in her hand.

"I have room for something more. Give me that, Laura, it will just fit in;" and taking the little casket, she added, "Mary White wants to try on your dress, dear. Go at once; I will help Daisy."

Laura went, and her mother stood looking down at the kneeling girl with an expression of affectionate satisfaction which would have puzzled Daisy, had she seen it.

"Has the visit been a pleasant one, my dear?"

"Oh, very! I can't thank you enough for the good it has done me. I hope I can pay a little of the debt next summer, if you come our way again," cried Daisy, looking up with a face full of gratitude.

"We shall probably go to Europe for the summer. Laura is a good age for it now, and we shall all enjoy it."

"How splendid! We shall miss you dreadfully, but I'm glad you are going, and I hope Laura will find time to write me now and then. I shall want to know how she likes the 'foreign parts' we've talked about so much."

"You *shall* know. We won't forget you, my

dear," and with a caressing touch on the smiling
yet wistful face upturned to hers, Mrs. Vaughn
went away to pack the empty jewel-box, leaving
Daisy to drop a few irrepressible tears on the
new gown, over the downfall of her summer
hopes, and the longings all girls feel for that
enchanted world that lies beyond the sea.

" We shall see you before we go, so we won't
gush now," said Laura, as she bade her friend
good-by, adding in a whisper, " Some folks can
have secrets as well as other folks, and be as sly.
So don't think you have all the fun to yourself,
you dear, good, generous darling."

Daisy looked bewildered, and Mrs. Vaughn
added to her surprise by kissing her very warmly
as she said:

" I wanted to find a good friend for my
spoiled girl, and I think I have succeeded."

There was no time for explanation, and all
the way home Daisy kept wondering what they
meant. But she forgot everything when she saw
the dear faces beaming at the door, and ran
straight into her mother's arms, while Janey
hugged the trunk till her turn came for something better.

When the first raptures were over, out came
the cloak; and Daisy was well repaid for her
little trials and sacrifices when she was folded
in it as her mother held her close, and thanked
her as mothers only can. Sitting in its soft
shelter, she told all about it, and coming to the

end said, as she took up the jewel-box, unpacked with the other generous gifts: —

"I haven't a thing to put in it, but I shall value it because it taught me a lesson which I hope I never shall forget. See what a pretty thing it is;" and opening it, Daisy gave a cry of surprise and joy, for there lay the golden rose, with Laura's name and "Sub rosa" on a slip of paper.

"The dear thing! she knew I wanted it, and that is what she meant by 'secrets.' I'll write and tell her mine to-morrow."

"Here is something more," said Janey, who had been lifting the tray while her sister examined the long-desired flower.

A pair of real gold bangles shone before her delighted eyes, and a card in Mr. Vaughn's handwriting bore these words: "Handcuffs for the thief who stole the pocketbook."

Daisy hardly had time to laugh gayly at the old gentleman's joke, when Janey cried out, as she opened the little drawer, "Here's another!"

It was a note from Mrs. Vaughn, but all thought it the greatest treasure of the three, for it said briefly, —

"DEAR DAISY, — Mary told me some of your secrets, and I found out the others. Forgive me and go to Europe with Laura, in May. Your visit was a little test. You stood it well, and we want to know more of you. The little box is not quite empty, but the best jewels are the self-denial, sweet charity, and good sense you put in yourself.   Your friend,

"A. V."

Daisy could not speak, and her mother looked into the box with eyes full of tender tears, while Janey danced about them, clashing the bangles like a happy little bayadere, till her sister found her voice again.

Pointing to a great, bright tear that shone on the blue velvet, she said, with her cheek against her mother's: "I always wanted a real diamond, and there's a more precious one than any I could buy. Now I'm sure my jewel-box *is* full."

CORNY'S CATAMOUNT

TWO boys sat on the bars, one whittling, the other whistling, — not for want of thought by any means, for his brow was knit in an anxious frown, and he paused now and then to thump the rail, with an impatient exclamation. The other lad appeared to be absorbed in shaping an arrow from the slender stick in his hand, but he watched his neighbor with a grin, saying a few words occasionally which seemed to add to his irritation, though they were in a sympathizing tone.

"Oh, well, if a chap can't do a thing he can't; and he'd better give up and say, Beat."

"But I won't give up, and I never say 'Beat.' I'm not going to be laughed out of it, and I'll do what I said I would, if it takes all summer, Chris Warner."

"You'll have to be pretty spry, then, for there's only two more days to August," replied the whittler, shutting one eye to look along his arrow and see if it was true.

"I intend to be spry, and if you won't go and blab, I'll tell you a plan I made last night."

"Guess you can trust me. I've heard about a dozen plans now, and never told one of 'em."

"They all failed, so there was nothing to tell. But this one is *not* going to fail, if I die for it. I feel that it's best to tell some one, because it is really dangerous; and if anything *should* happen to me, as is very likely, it would save time and trouble."

"Don't seem to feel anxious a mite. But I'll stand ready to pick up the pieces, if you come to grief."

"Now, Chris, it's mean of you to keep on making fun when I'm in dead earnest; and this may be the last thing you can do for me."

"Wait till I get out my handkerchief; if you're going to be affectin' I may want it. Granite's cheap up here; just mention what you'd like on your tombstone and I'll see that it's done, if it takes my last cent."

The big boy in the blue overalls spoke with such a comical drawl that the slender city lad could not help laughing, and with a slap that nearly sent his neighbor off his perch, Corny said good-naturedly:

"Come now, stop joking and lend a hand, and I'll do anything I can for you. I've set my heart on shooting a wildcat, and I know I can if I once get a good chance. Mother won't let me go off far enough, so of course I don't do it, and then you all jeer at me. To-morrow we are going up the mountain, and I'm set on trying again, for Abner says the big woods are the place to find the 'varmint.' Now you hold your tongue, and let me slip away when I think we've hit the right spot. I'm not a bit afraid, and while the rest go poking to the top, I'll plunge into the woods and see what I can do."

"All right. Better take old Buff; he'll bring you home when you get lost, and keep puss from clawing you. You won't like that part of the fun as much as you expect to, maybe," said Chris, with a sly twinkle of the eye, as he glanced at Corny and then away to the vast forest that stretched far up the mighty mountain's side.

"No, I don't want any help, and Buff will betray me by barking; I prefer to go alone. I shall take some lunch and plenty of shot, and have a glorious time, even if I don't meet that confounded beast. I will keep dashing in and out of the woods as we go; then no one will miss me for a while, and when they do you just say, 'Oh, he's all right; he'll be along directly,' and go ahead, and let me alone."

Corny spoke so confidently, and looked so pleased with his plan, that honest Chris could not bear to tell him how much danger he would run in that pathless forest, where older hunters than he had been lost.

"Don't feel as if I cared to tell any lies about it, and I don't advise your goin'; but if you're mad for catamounts, I s'pose I must humor you and say nothing. Only bear in mind, Abner and I will be along, and if you get into a scrape jest give a yell and we 'll come."

" No fear of that; I 've tramped round all summer, and know my way like an Indian. Keep the girls quiet, and let me have a good lark. I 'll turn up all right by sundown; so don't worry. Not a word to mother, mind, or she won't let me go. I 'll make things straight with her after the fun is over."

" That ain't just square; but it 's not my funeral, so I won't meddle. Hope you 'll have first rate sport, and bag a brace of cats. One thing you mind, don't get too nigh before you fire; and keep out of sight of the critters as much as you can."

Chris spoke in a deep whisper, looking so excited and impressed by the reckless courage of his mate that Corny felt himself a Leather-stocking, and went off to tea with his finger on his lips, full of boyish faith in his own powers. If he had seen Chris dart behind the barn, and there roll upon the grass in convulsions of laughter, he would have been both surprised and hurt.

No deacon could have been more sober, however, than Chris when they met next morning, while the party of summer boarders at the old farm-house were in a pleasant bustle of preparation for the long expected day on the mountain. Three merry girls, a pair of small boys, two amiable mammas, Chris and Corny, made up the party, with Abner to drive the big wagon drawn by Milk and Molasses, the yellow span.

"All aboard!" shouted our young Nimrod, in a hurry to be off, as the lunch-basket was handed up, and the small boys packed in the most uncomfortable corners, regardless of their arms and legs.

Away they rattled with a parting cheer, and peace fell upon the farm-house for a few hours, to the great contentment of the good people left behind. Corny's mother was one of them, and her last words were, — "A pleasant day, dear. I wish you'd leave that gun at home; I'm so afraid you'll get hurt with it."

"No fun without it. Don't worry, mammy; I'm old enough to take care of myself."

"I'll see to him, ma'am," called Chris, as he hung on behind, and waved his old straw hat, with a steady, reliable sort of look, that made the anxious lady feel more comfortable.

"We are going to walk up, and leave the horses to rest; so I can choose my time. See, I've got a bottle of cold tea in this pocket, and a lot of grub in the other. No danger of my starving, is there?" whispered Corny, as he leaned over to Chris, who sat, apparently, on nothing, with his long legs dangling into space.

"Shouldn't wonder if you needed every mite of it. Hunting is mighty hard work on a hot day, and this is going to be a blazer," answered

Chris, pulling his big straw hat lower over his eyes.

As we intend to follow Corny's adventures, we need not pause to describe the drive, which was a merry one; with girls chattering, mammas holding on to excited small boys, in danger of flying out at every jolt, Abner joking till every one roared, Corny's dangerous evolutions with the beloved gun, and the gymnastic feats Chris performed, jumping off to pick flowers for the ladies, and getting on again while Milk and Molasses tore up and down the rough road as if they enjoyed it.

About ten o'clock they reached the foot of the mountain; and after a short rest at the hotel, began the three-mile ascent in high spirits. Abner was to follow later with the wagon, to bring the party down; so Chris was guide, as he knew the way well, and often came with people. The girls and younger boys hurried on, full of eagerness to reach the top. The ladies went more slowly, enjoying the grand beauty of the scene, while Chris carried the lunch-basket, and Corny lingered in the rear, waiting for a good chance to "plunge."

He wanted to be off before Abner came, as he well knew that wise man and mighty hunter would never let him go alone.

"The very next path I see, I'll dive in and run; Chris can't leave the rest to follow, and if I once get a good start, they won't catch me in a hurry," thought the boy, longing to be free and alone in the wild woods that tempted him on either hand.

Just as he was tightening his belt to be ready for the run, Mrs. Barker, the stout lady, called him; and being a well-bred lad, he hastened at once to see what she wanted, feeling that he was the only gentleman in the party.

" Give me your arm, dear; I 'm getting very tired, and fear I can't hold out to the top, without a little help," said the poor lady, red and panting with the heat, and steepness of the road.

" Certainly ma'am," answered Corny, obeying at once, and inwardly resolving to deposit his fair burden on the first fallen log they came to, and make his escape.

But Mrs. Barker got on bravely, with the support of his strong arm, and chatted away so delightfully that Corny would really have enjoyed the walk, if his soul had not been yearning for catamounts. He did his best, but when they passed opening after opening into the green recesses of the wood, and the granite boulders grew more and more plentiful, his patience gave out, and he began to plan what he could say to excuse himself. Chris was behind, apparently deaf and blind to his calls and imploring glances, though he grinned cheerfully when poor Corny looked round and beckoned, as well as he could, with a gun on one arm and a stout lady on the other.

"The hardest part is coming now, and we'd better rest a moment. Here's a nice rock, and the last spring we are likely to see till we get to the top. Come on, Chris, and give us the dipper. Mrs. Barker wants a drink, and so do I," called the young hunter, driven to despair at last.

Up came Chris, and while he rummaged in the well-packed basket, Corny slipped into the wood, leaving the good lady with her thanks half spoken, sitting on a warm stone beside a muddy little pool. A loud laugh followed him, as he scrambled through the tall ferns and went plunging down the steep mountain side, eager to reach the lower woods.

"Let him laugh; it will be my turn when I go home, with a fine cat over my shoulder," thought Corny, tearing along, heedless of falls, scratches, and bruised knees.

At length he paused for breath, and looked about him well satisfied, for the spot was lonely and lovely enough to suit any hunter. The tallest pines he ever saw sighed far overhead; the ground was ankle deep in moss, and gay with scarlet bunch-berries; every fallen log was veiled by sweet-scented Linnea, green vines or nodding brakes; while hidden brooks sang musically, and the air was full of the soft flutter of leaves, the whir of wings, the sound of birds gossiping sweetly in the safe shelter of the forest, where human feet so seldom came.

" I 'll rest a bit, and then go along down, keeping a look out for puss by the way," thought Corny, feeling safe and free, and very happy, for he had his own way, at last, and a whole day to lead the life he loved.

So he bathed his hot face, took a cool drink, and lay on the moss, staring up into the green gloom of the pines, blissfully dreaming of the joys of a hunter's life, — till a peculiar cry startled him to his feet, and sent him creeping warily toward the sound. Whether it was a new kind of bird, or a fox, or a bear, he did not know, but fondly hoped it was a wild cat; though he was well aware that the latter creature sleeps by day, and prowls by night. Abner said they purred and snarled and gave a mewing sort of cry; but which it was now he could not tell, having unfortunately been half asleep.

On he went, looking up into the trees for a furry bunch, behind every log, and in every rocky hole, longing and hoping to discover his heart's desire. But a hawk was all he saw above, an ugly snake was the only living thing he found among the logs, and a fat woodchuck's hind legs vanished down the most attractive hole. He shot at all three and missed them, so pushed on, pretending that he did not care for such small game.

" Now this is what I call fun," he said to himself, tramping gayly along, and at that moment went splash into a mud-hole concealed under the grass. He sunk up to his knees, and with great difficulty got out by clinging to the tussocks that grew near. In his struggles the lunch was lost, for the bottle broke and the pocket where the sandwiches were stored was full of mud. A woful spectacle was the trim lad as he emerged from the slough, black and dripping in front, well spattered behind, hatless, and one shoe gone, having been carelessly left unlaced in the ardor of the chase.

"Here's a mess!" thought poor Corny, surveying himself with great disgust and feeling very helpless, as well as tired, hungry, and mad. "Luckily, my powder is dry and my gun safe; so my fun is n't spoiled, though I do look like a wallowing pig. I've heard of mud baths, but I never took one before, and I'll be shot if I do again."

So he washed as well as he could, hoping the sun would dry him, picked out a few bits of bread unspoiled by the general wreck, and trudged on with less ardor, though by no means discouraged yet.

"I'm too high for any game but birds, and those I don't want. I'll go slap down, and come out in the valley. Abner said any brook would show the way, and this rascal that led me into a scrape shall lead me out," he said, as he followed the little stream that went tumbling over the stones, that increased as the ground sloped toward the deep ravine, where a waterfall shone like silver in the sun.

" I 'll take a bath if the pool is big enough,
and that will set me up. Should n't wonder if
I 'd got poisoned a bit with some of these vines
I 've been tearing through. My hands smart like
fury, and I guess the mosquitoes have about
eaten my face up. Never saw such clouds of
stingers before," said Corny, looking at his
scratched hands, and rubbing his hot face in
great discomfort, — for it was the gnat that
drove the lion mad, you remember.

It was easy to say, " I 'll follow the brook,"
but not so easy to do it; for the frolicsome
stream went headlong over rocks, crept under
fallen logs, and now and then hid itself so cleverly that one had to look and listen carefully to
recover the trail. It was long past noon when
Corny came out near the waterfall, so tired and
hungry that he heartily wished himself back
among the party, who had lunched well and were
now probably driving gayly homeward to a good
supper.

No chance for a bath appeared, so he washed
his burning face and took a rest, enjoying the
splendid view far over valley and intervale
through the gap in the mountain range. He
was desperately tired with these hours of rough
travel, and very hungry; but would not own it,
and sat considering what to do next, for he saw
by the sun that the afternoon was half over.
There was time to go back the way he had come,
and by following the path down the hill he could

reach the hotel and get supper and a bed, or be driven home. That was the wise thing to do, but his pride rebelled against returning empty-handed after all his plans and boasts of great exploits.

" I won't go home, to be laughed at by Chris and Abner. I 'll shoot something, if I stay all night. Who cares for hunger and mosquito bites? Not I. Hunters can bear more than that, I guess. The next live thing I see I 'll shoot it, and make a fire and have a jolly supper. Now which way will I go, — up or down? A pretty hard prospect, either way."

The sight of an eagle soaring above him seemed to answer his question, and fill him with new strength and ardor. To shoot the king of birds and take him home in triumph would cover the hunter with glory. It should be done! And away he went, climbing, tumbling, leaping from rock to rock, toward the place where the eagle had alighted. More cuts and bruises, more vain shots, and all the reward of his eager struggles was a single feather that floated down as the great bird soared serenely away, leaving the boy exhausted and disappointed in a wilderness of granite boulders, with no sign of a path to show the way out.

As he leaned breathless and weary against the crag where he had fondly hoped to find the eagle's nest, he realized for the first time what a fool-hardy thing he had done. Here he was, alone, without a guide, in this wild region where there was neither food nor shelter, and night coming on. Utterly used up, he could not get home now if he had known the way; and suddenly all the tales he had ever heard of men lost in the mountains came into his head. If he had not been weak with hunger he would have felt better able to bear it; but his legs trembled under him, his head ached with the glare of the sun, and a queer faintness came over him now and then; for the city lad was unused to such violent exercise, plucky as he was.

" The only thing to do now is to get down to the valley, if I can, before dark. Abner said there was an old cabin, where the hunters used to sleep, somewhere round that way. I can try for it, and perhaps shoot something on the way. May break my bones, but I can't sit and starve up here, and I was a fool to come. I 'll keep the feather anyway, to prove that I really saw an eagle; that 's better than nothing."

Still bravely trying to affect the indifference to danger and fatigue which hunters are always described as possessing in such a remarkable degree, Corny slung the useless gun on his back and began the steep descent, discovering now the perils he had been too eager to see before. He was a good climber, but was stiff with weariness, and his hands already sore with scratches and poison; so he went slowly, feeling quite unfit for such hard work. Coming to the ravine, he found the only road was down its precipitous side to the valley, that looked so safe and pleasant now. Stunted pines grew in the fissures of the rocks, and their strong roots helped the clinging hands and feet as the boy painfully climbed, slipped, and swung along, fearing every minute to come to some impassable barrier in the dangerous path.

But he got on wonderfully well, and was feeling much encouraged, when his foot slipped, the root he held gave way, and down he went, rolling and bumping to his death on the rocks below, he thought, as a crash came, and he knew no more.

"Wonder if I'm dead?" was the first idea that occurred to him as he opened his eyes and saw a brilliant sky above him, all purple, gold, and red.

He seemed floating in the air, for he swayed to and fro on a soft bed, a pleasant murmur reached his ear, and when he looked down he saw what looked like clouds, misty and white, below him. He lay a few minutes drowsily musing, for the fall had stunned him; then, as he moved his hand something pricked it, and he felt pine-needles in the fingers that closed over them.

"Caught in a tree, by Jupiter!" and all visions of heaven vanished in a breath, as he sat up and stared about him, wide awake now, and conscious of many aching bones.

Yes, there he lay among the branches of one of the sturdy pines, into which he had fallen on his way down the precipice. Blessed little tree! set there to save a life, and teach a lesson to a wilful young heart that never forgot that hour.

Holding fast, lest a rash motion should set him bounding further down, like a living ball, Corny took an observation as rapidly as possible, for the red light was fading, and the mist rising from the valley. All he could see was a narrow ledge where the tree stood, and anxious to reach a safer bed for the night, he climbed cautiously down to drop on the rock, so full of gratitude for safety that he could only lie quite still for a little while, thinking of mother, and trying not to cry.

He was much shaken by the fall, his flesh bruised, his clothes torn, and his spirit cowed; for hunger, weariness, pain, and danger, showed him what a very feeble creature he was, after all. He could do no more till morning, and resigned himself to a night on the mountain side, glad to be there alive, though doubtful what daylight would show him. Too tired to move, he lay watching the western sky, where the sun set gloriously behind the purple hills. All below was wrapped in mist, and not a sound reached him but the sigh of the pine, and the murmur of the waterfall.

"This is a first-class scrape. What a fool I was not to go back when I could, instead of blun-

dering down here where no one can get at me,
and as like as not I can't get out alone! Gun
smashed in that confounded fall, so I can't even
fire a shot to call help. Nothing to eat or drink,
and very likely a day or so to spend here till I 'm
found, if I ever am. Chris said, ' Yell, if you
want us.' Much good that would do now! I 'll
try, though." And getting up on his weary legs,
Corny shouted till he was hoarse; but echo alone
answered him, and after a few efforts he gave
it up, trying to accept the situation like a man.
As if kind Nature took pity on the poor boy, the
little ledge was soft with lichens and thin grass,
and here and there grew a sprig of checkerberry,
sown by the wind, sheltered by the tree, and
nourished by the moisture that trickled down the
rock from some hidden spring. Eagerly Corny
ate the sweet leaves to stay the pangs of hunger
that gnawed him, and finished his meal with grass
and pine-needles, calling himself a calf, and wishing his pasture were wider.

" The fellows we read about always come to
grief in a place where they can shoot a bird, catch
a fish, or knock over some handy beast for supper," he said, talking to himself for company.
" Even the old chap lost in the bush in Australia
had a savage with him who dug a hole in a tree,
and pulled out a nice fat worm to eat. I 'm not
lucky enough even to find a sassafras bush to
chew, or a bird's egg to suck. My poor gun is
broken, or I might bang away at a hawk, and

cook him for supper, if the bog did n't spoil my
matches as it did my lunch. Oh, well! I 'll pull
through, I guess, and when it 's all over, it will
be a jolly good story to tell."

Then, hoping to forget his woes in sleep, he
nestled under the low-growing branches of the
pine, and lay blinking drowsily at the twilight
world outside. A dream came, and he saw the
old farm-house in sad confusion, caused by his
absence, — the women crying, the men sober,
all anxious, and all making ready to come and
look for him. So vivid was it that he woke himself by crying out, "Here I am!" and nearly
went over the ledge, stretching out his arms to
Abner.

The start and the scare made it hard to go to
sleep again, and he sat looking at the solemn sky,
full of stars that seemed watching over him
alone there, like a poor, lost child on the great
mountain's stony breast. He had never seen the
world at that hour before, and it made a deep
impression on him; for it was a vast, wild scene,
full of gloomy shadows below, unknown dangers
around, and a new sense of utter littleness and
helplessness, which taught the boy human dependence upon Heavenly love as no words, even from
his mother's tender lips, could have done.
Thoughts of the suffering his wilfulness had
given her wrung a few penitent tears from him,
which he was not ashamed to shed, since only
the kind stars saw them, and better still, he re-

solved to own the fault, to atone for it, and to learn wisdom from this lesson, which might yet prove to be a very bitter one.

He felt better after this little breakdown, and presently his thoughts were turned from conscience to catamounts again; for sounds in the woods below led him to believe that the much-desired animal was on the prowl. His excited fancy painted dozens of them not far away, waiting to be shot, and there he was, cooped up on that narrow ledge, with a broken gun, unable even to get a look at them. He felt that it was a just punishment, and after the first regret tried to comfort himself with the fact that he was much safer where he was than alone in the forest at that hour, for various nocturnal voices suggested restless and dangerous neighbors.

Presently his wakeful eyes saw lights twinkling far off on the opposite side of the ravine, and he imagined he heard shouts and shots. But the splash of the waterfall, and the rush of the night wind deadened the sound to his ear, and drowned his own reply.

"They are looking for me, and will never think of this strange place. I can't make them hear, and must wait till morning. Poor Chris will get an awful scolding for letting me go. Don't believe he told a word till he had to. I'll make it up to him. Chris is a capital fellow, and I just wish I had him here to make things jolly," thought the lonely lad.

But soon the lights vanished, the sounds died away, and the silence of midnight brooded over the hills, seldom broken except by the soft cry of an owl, the rustle of the pine, or a louder gust of wind as it grew strong and cold. Corny kept awake as long as he could, fearing to dream and fall; but by-and-by he dropped off, and slept soundly till the chill of dawn waked him.

At any other time he would have heartily enjoyed the splendor of the eastern sky, as the red glow spread and brightened, till the sun came dazzling through the gorge, making the wild solitude beautiful and grand.

Now, however, he would have given it all for a hot beefsteak and a cup of coffee, as he wet his lips with a few drops of ice-cold water, and browsed over his small pasture till not a green spire remained. He was stiff, and full of pain, but daylight and the hope of escape cheered him up, and gave him coolness and courage to see how best he could accomplish his end.

The wind soon blew away the mist and let him see that the dry bed of a stream lay just below. To reach it he must leap, at risk of his bones, or find some means to swing down ten or twelve feet. Once there, it was pretty certain that by following the rough road he would come into the valley, from whence he could easily find his way home. Much elated at this unexpected good fortune, he took the strap that had slung his gun, the leathern belt about his waist, and the strong cords of his pouch, and knotting them together, made a rope long enough to let him drop within two or three feet of the stones below. This he fastened firmly round the trunk of the pine, and finished his preparations by tying his handkerchief to one of the branches, that it might serve as a guide for him, a signal for others, and a trophy of his grand fall.

Then putting a little sprig of the evergreen tree in his jacket, with a grateful thought of all it had done for him, he swung himself off and landed safely below, not minding a few extra bumps after his late exploits at tumbling.

Feeling like a prisoner set free, he hurried as fast as bare feet and stiff legs would carry him along the bed of the stream, coming at last into the welcome shelter of the woods, which seemed more beautiful than ever, after the bleak region of granite in which he had been all night.

Anxious to report himself alive, and relieve his mother's anxiety, he pressed on till he struck the path, and soon saw, not far away, the old cabin Abner had spoken of. Just before this happy moment he had heard a shot fired somewhere in the forest, and as he hurried toward the sound he saw an animal dart into the hut, as if for shelter.

Whether it was a rabbit, woodchuck or dog, he had not seen, as a turn in the path prevented a clear view; and hoping it was old Buff looking for him, he ran in, to find himself face to face with a catamount at last.

There she was, the big, fierce cat, crouched in a corner, with fiery eyes, growling and spitting at sight of an enemy, but too badly wounded to fight, as the blood that dripped from her neck, and the tremble of her limbs plainly showed.

"Now 's my chance! Don't care who shot her, I 'll kill her, and have her too, if I pay my last dollar," thought Corny; and catching up a stout bit of timber fallen from the old roof, he struck one quick blow, which finished poor puss, who gave up the ghost with a savage snarl, and a vain effort to pounce on him.

This splendid piece of good luck atoned for all the boy had gone through, and only waiting to be sure the beast was quite dead and past clawing, he flung his prize over his shoulder, and with renewed strength and spirit trudged along the woodland road toward home, proudly imagining his triumphal entry upon the scene of suspense and alarm.

"Wish I did n't look so like a scare-crow; but perhaps my rags will add to the effect. Won't the girls laugh at my swelled face, and scream at the cat. Poor mammy will mourn over me and coddle me up as if I 'd been to the wars. Hope some house is n't very far off, for I don't believe I can lug this brute much farther, I 'm so starved and shaky."

Just as he paused to take breath and shift his burden from one shoulder to the other, a loud shout startled him, and a moment after, several men came bursting through the wood, cheering like lunatics as they approached.

It was Abner, Chris, and some of the neighbors, setting out again on their search, after a night of vain wandering. Corny could have hugged them all and cried like a girl; but pride kept him steady, though his face showed his joy as he nodded his hatless head with a cool —

" Hullo ! "

Chris burst into his ringing laugh, and danced a wild sort of jig round his mate, as the only way in which he could fitly express his relief; for he had been so bowed down with remorse at his imprudence in letting Corny go that no one could find the heart to blame him, and all night the poor lad had rushed up and down seeking, calling, hoping, and fearing, till he was about used up, and looked nearly as dilapidated as Corny.

The tale was soon told, and received with the most flattering signs of interest, wonder, sympathy, and admiration.

" Why in thunder did n't you tell me? — and I 'd a got up a hunt wuth havin', — not go stramashing off alone on a wild goose chase like this. Never did see such a chap as you be for gittin' inter scrapes, — and out of 'em too, I 'm bound to own," growled Abner.

" That is n't a wild goose, is it? " proudly demanded Corny, pointing to the cat, which now lay on the ground, while he leaned against a tree to hide his weariness; for he felt ready to drop, now all the excitement was over.

"No it ain't, and I congratulate you on a good job. Where did you shoot her?" asked Abner, stooping to examine the creature.

"Did n't shoot her; broke my gun when I took that header down the mountain. I hit her a rap with a club, in the cabin where I found her," answered Corny, heartily wishing he need not share the prize with any one. But he was honest, and added at once, "Some one else had put a bullet into her; I only finished her off."

"Chris did it; he fired a spell back and see the critter run, but we was too keen after you to stop for any other game. Guess you 've had enough of catamounts for one spell, hey?" and Abner laughed as he looked at poor Corny, who was a more sorry spectacle than he knew, — ragged and rough, hatless and shoeless, his face red and swelled with the poisoning and bites, his eyes heavy with weariness, and in his mouth a bit of wild-cherry bark which he chewed ravenously.

"No, I have n't! I want this one, and will buy it if Chris will let me. I said I 'd kill one, and I did, and want to keep the skin; for I ought to have something to show after all this knocking about and turning somersaults half a mile long," answered Corny stoutly, as he tried to shoulder his load again.

"Here, give me the varmint, and you hang on to Chris, my boy, or we 'll have to cart you home. You 've done first-rate, and now you want a good meal of vittles to set you up. Right about face, neighbors, and home we go, to the tune of Hail Columby."

As Abner spoke, the procession set forth. The tall, jolly man, with the dead animal at his back, went first; then Corny, trying not to lean on the arm Chris put round him, but very glad of the support; next the good farmers, all talking at once; while old Buff soberly brought up the rear, with his eye on the wildcat, well knowing that he would have a fine feast when the handsome skin was off.

In this order they reached home, and Corny tumbled into his mother's arms, to be no more seen for some hours. What went on in her room, no one knows; but when at last the hero emerged, refreshed by sleep and food, clad in clean clothes, his wounds bound up, and plantain-leaves dipped in cream spread upon his afflicted countenance, he received the praises and congratulations showered upon him very meekly. He made no more boasts of skill and courage that summer, set out on no more wild haunts, and gave up his own wishes so cheerfully that it was evident something had worked a helpful change in wilful Corny.

He liked to tell the story of that day and night when his friends were recounting adventures by sea and land; but he never said much about the hours on the ledge, always owned that Chris shot the beast, and usually ended by sagely ad-

vising his hearers to let their mothers know, when
they went off on a lark of that kind.   Those who
knew and loved him best observed that he was
fonder than ever of nibbling checkerberry leaves,
that he did n't mind being laughed at for liking
to wear a bit of pine in his buttonhole, and that
the skin of the catamount so hardly won lay before his study table till the moths ate it up.

THE COOKING - CLASS

A YOUNG girl in a little cap and a big apron sat poring over a cook-book, with a face full of the deepest anxiety. She had the kitchen to herself, for mamma was out for the day, cook was off duty, and Edith could mess to her heart's content. She belonged to a cooking-class, the members of which were to have a lunch at two P. M. with the girl next door; and now the all absorbing question was, what to make. Turning the pages of the well-used book, she talked to herself as the various receipts met her eye.

"Lobster-salad and chicken-croquettes I've had, and neither were very good. Now I want to distinguish myself by something very nice. I'd try a meat-porcupine or a mutton-duck if there was time; but they are fussy, and ought to be rehearsed before given to the class. Bavarian cream needs berries and whipped cream, and I *won't* tire my arms beating eggs. Apricots *à la* Neige is an easy thing and wholesome, but the girls won't like it, I know, as well as some rich thing that will make them ill, as Carrie's plum-pudding did. A little meat dish is best for lunch. I'd try sweetbreads and bacon, if I didn't hate to burn my face and scent my clothes, frying. Birds are elegant; let me see if I can do larded grouse. No, I don't like to touch that cold, fat stuff. How mortified Ella was, when she had birds on toast and forgot to draw them. I shouldn't make such a blunder as that, I do hope. Potted pigeons — the very thing! Had that in our last lesson, but the girls are all crazy about puff-paste, so they won't try pigeons. Why didn't I think of it at once? — for we've got them in the house, and don't want them to-day, mamma being called away. All ready too; so nice! I do detest to pick and clean birds. 'Simmer from one to three hours.' Plenty of time. I'll do it! I'll do it! La, la, la!"

And away skipped Edith in high spirits, for she did not love to cook, yet wished to stand well with the class, some members of which were very ambitious, and now and then succeeded with an elaborate dish, more by good luck than skill.

Six plump birds were laid out on a platter, with their legs folded in the most pathetic manner; these Edith bore away in triumph to the kitchen, and opening the book before her went to work energetically, resigning herself to frying the pork and cutting up the onion, which she had overlooked when hastily reading the receipt. In time they were stuffed, the legs tied down to the tails, the birds browned in the stew-pan, and put to simmer with a pinch of herbs.

"Now I can clear up, and rest a bit. If I ever have to work for a living I *won't* be a cook," said Edith, with a sigh of weariness as she washed her dishes, wondering how there could be so many; for no careless Irish girl would have made a greater clutter over this small job than the young lady who had not yet learned one of the most important things that a cook should know.

The bell rang just as she got done, and was planning to lie and rest on the dining-room sofa till it was time to take up her pigeons.

"Tell whoever it is that I'm engaged," she whispered, as the maid passed, on her way to the door.

"It's your cousin, miss, from the country, and she has a trunk with her. Of course she's to come in?" asked Maria, coming back in a moment.

"Oh, dear me! I forgot all about Patty. Mamma said any day this week, and this is the most inconvenient one of the seven. Of course, she must come in. Go and tell her I'll be there in a minute," answered Edith, too well bred not to give even an unwelcome guest a kindly greeting.

Whisking off cap and apron, and taking a last look at the birds, just beginning to send forth a savory steam, she went to meet her cousin.

Patty was a rosy, country lass of sixteen, plainly dressed and rather shy, but a sweet, sensible little body, with a fresh, rustic air which marked her for a field-flower at once.

"How do you do, dear? so sorry mamma is away; called to a sick friend in a hurry. But I'm here and glad to see you. I've an engagement at two, and you shall go with me. It's only a lunch close by, just a party of girls; I'll tell you about it up-stairs."

Chatting away, Edith led Patty up to the pretty room ready for her, and soon both were laughing over a lively account of the exploits of the cooking-class. Suddenly, in the midst of the cream-pie which had been her great success, and nearly the death of all who partook thereof, Edith paused, sniffed the air like a hound, and crying tragically, "They are burning! They are burning!" rushed down stairs as if the house was on fire.

Much alarmed, Patty hurried after her, guided to the kitchen by the sound of lamentation. There she found Edith hanging over a stew-pan, with anguish in her face and despair in her voice, as she breathlessly explained the cause of her flight.

"My pigeons! Are they burnt? Do smell and tell me? After all my trouble I shall be heart-broken if they are spoilt."

Both pretty noses sniffed and sniffed again as the girls bent over the pan, regardless of the steam which was ruining their crimps and reddening their noses. Reluctantly, Patty owned that a slight flavor of scorch *did* pervade the air, but suggested that a touch more seasoning would conceal the sad fact.

"I'll try it. Did you ever do any? Do you love to cook? Don't you want to make something to carry? It would please the girls, and make up for my burnt mess," said Edith, as she skimmed the broth and added pepper and salt with a lavish hand: —

"I don't know anything about pigeons, except to feed and pet them. We don't eat ours. I can cook plain dishes, and make all kinds of bread. Would biscuit or tea-cake do?"

Patty looked so pleased at the idea of contributing to the feast, that Edith could not bear to tell her that hot biscuit and tea-cake were not just the thing for a city lunch. She accepted the offer, and Patty fell to work so neatly and skilfully that, by the time the pigeons were done, two pans full of delicious little biscuit were baked, and, folded in a nice napkin, lay ready to carry off in the porcelain plate with a wreath of roses painted on it.

In spite of all her flavoring, the burnt odor and taste still lingered round Edith's dish; but fondly hoping no one would perceive it, she dressed hastily, gave Patty a touch here and there, and set forth at the appointed time to Augusta's lunch.

Six girls belonged to this class, and the rule was for each to bring her contribution and set it on the table prepared to receive them all; then, when the number was complete, the covers were raised, the dishes examined, eaten (if possible), and pronounced upon, the prize being awarded to the best. The girl at whose house the lunch was given provided the prize, and they were often both pretty and valuable.

On this occasion a splendid bouquet of Jaqueminot roses in a lovely vase ornamented the middle of the table, and the eyes of all rested admiringly upon it, as the seven girls gathered round, after depositing their dishes.

Patty had been kindly welcomed, and soon forgot her shyness in wonder at the handsome dresses, graceful manners, and lively gossip of the girls. A pleasant, merry set, all wearing the uniform of the class, dainty white aprons and coquettish caps with many-colored ribbons, like stage maid-servants. At the sound of a silver bell, each took her place before the covered dish which bore her name, and when Augusta said, "Ladies, we will begin," off went napkins, silver covers, white paper, or whatever hid the contribution from longing eyes. A moment of deep silence, while quick glances took in the prospect, and then a unanimous explosion of laughter followed; for six platters of potted pigeons stood upon the board, with nothing but the flowers to break the ludicrous monotony of the scene.

How they laughed! for a time they could do
nothing else, because if one tried to explain she
broke down and joined in the gale of merriment
again quite helplessly. One or two got hyster-
ical and cried as well as laughed, and all made
such a noise that Augusta's mamma peeped in
to see what was the matter. Six agitated hands
pointed to the comical sight on the table, which
looked as if a flight of potted pigeons had
alighted there, and six breathless voices cried in
a chorus: "Isn't it funny? Don't tell!"

Much amused, the good lady retired to enjoy
the joke alone, while the exhausted girls wiped
their eyes and began to talk, all at once. Such
a clatter! but out of it all Patty evolved the fact
that each meant to surprise the rest, — and they
certainly had.

"I tried puff-paste," said Augusta, fanning
her hot face.

"So did I," cried the others.

"And it was a dead failure."

"So was mine," echoed the voices.

"Then I thought I'd do the other dish we
had that day —"

"Just what I did."

"Feeling sure you would all try the pastry,
and perhaps get on better than I."

"Exactly our case," and a fresh laugh ended
this general confession.

"Now we must eat our pigeons, as we have
nothing else, and it is against the rule to add

from outside stores. I propose that we each
pass our dish round; then we can all criticise
it, and so get some good out of this very funny
lunch."

Augusta's plan was carried out; and all being
hungry after their unusual exertions, the girls
fell upon the unfortunate birds like so many
famished creatures. The first one went very
well, but when the dishes were passed again,
each taster looked at it anxiously; for none
were very good, there was nothing to fall back
upon, and variety is the spice of life, as every
one knows.

"Oh, for a slice of bread," sighed one damsel.

"Why did n't we think of it?" asked another.

"I did, but we always have so much cake I
thought it was foolish to lay in rolls," exclaimed
Augusta, rather mortified at the neglect.

"I expected to have to taste six pies, and one
does n't want bread with pastry, you know."

As Edith spoke she suddenly remembered
Patty's biscuit, which had been left on the side-
table by their modest maker, as there seemed to
be no room for them.

Rejoicing now over the rather despised dish,
Edith ran to get it, saying as she set it in the
middle, with a flourish: —

"My cousin's contribution. She came so late
we only had time for that. So glad I took the
liberty of bringing her and them."

A murmur of welcome greeted the much-desired addition to the feast, which would have been a decided failure without it, and the pretty plate went briskly round, till nothing was left but the painted roses in it. With this help the best of the potted pigeons were eaten, while a lively discussion went on about what they would have next time.

"Let us each tell our dish, and not change. We shall never learn if we don't keep to one thing till we do it well. I will choose mince-pie, and bring a good one, if it takes me all the week to do it," said Edith, heroically taking the hardest thing she could think of, to encourage the others.

Fired by this noble example, each girl pledged herself to do or die, and a fine list of rich dishes was made out by these ambitious young cooks. Then a vote of thanks to Patty was passed, her biscuit unanimously pronounced the most successful contribution, and the vase presented to the delighted girl, whose blushes were nearly as deep as the color of the flowers behind which she tried to hide them.

Soon after this ceremony the party broke up, and Edith went home to tell the merry story, proudly adding that the country cousin had won the prize.

"You rash child, to undertake mince-pie. It is one of the hardest things to make, and about the most unwholesome when eaten. Read the receipt and see what you have pledged yourself to do, my dear," said her mother, much amused at the haps and mishaps of the cooking-class.

Edith opened her book and started bravely off at " Puff-paste; " but by the time she had come to the end of the three pages devoted to directions for the making of that indigestible delicacy, her face was very sober, and when she read aloud the following receipt for the mince-meat, despair slowly settled upon her like a cloud.

"One cup chopped meat; 1½ cups raisins; 1½ cups currants; 1½ cups brown sugar; 1⅓ cups molasses; 3 cups chopped apples; 1 cup meat liquor; 2 teaspoonfuls salt; 2 teaspoonfuls cinnamon; ½ teaspoonful mace; ½ teaspoonful powdered cloves; 1 lemon, grated; ¼ piece citron, sliced; ½ cup brandy; ¼ cup wine; 3 teaspoonfuls rose-water.

"Oh me, what a job! I shall have to work at it every day till next Saturday, for the paste alone will take all the wits I 've got. I *was* rash, but I spoke without thinking, and wanted to do something really fine. We can't be shown about things, so I must blunder along as well as I can," groaned Edith.

"I can help about the measuring and weighing, and chopping. I always help mother at Thanksgiving time, and she makes splendid pies. We only have mince then, as she thinks it 's bad for us," said Patty, full of sympathy and good will.

" What are you to take to the lunch? " asked
Edith's mother, smiling at her daughter's
mournful face, bent over the fatal book full of
dainty messes, that tempted the unwary learner
to her doom.

" Only coffee. I can't make fancy things, but
my coffee is always good. They said they
wanted it, so I offered."

" I will have my pills and powders ready, for
if you all go on at this rate you will need a dose
of some sort after your lunch. Give your orders, Edith, and devote your mind to the task.
I wish you good luck and good digestion, my
dears."

With that the mamma left the girls to cheer
one another, and lay plans for a daily lesson
till the perfect pie was made.

They certainly did their best, for they began
on Monday, and each morning through the week
went to the mighty task with daily increasing
courage and skill. They certainly needed the
former, for even good-natured Nancy got tired
of having " the young ladies messing round so
much," and looked cross as the girls appeared in
the kitchen.

Edith's brothers laughed at the various failures which appeared at table, and dear mamma
was tired of tasting pastry and mince-meat in
all stages of progression. But the undaunted
damsels kept on till Saturday came, and a very
superior pie stood ready to be offered for the
inspection of the class.

" I never want to see another," said Edith, as the girls dressed together, weary, but well satisfied with their labor; for the pie had been praised by all beholders, and the fragrance of Patty's coffee filled the house, as it stood ready to be poured, hot and clear, into the best silver pot, at the last moment.

" Well, I feel as if I 'd lived in a spice mill this week, or a pastry-cook's kitchen; and I am glad we are done. Your brothers won't get any pie for a long while I guess, if it depends on you," laughed Patty, putting on the new ribbons her cousin had given her.

" When Florence's brothers were here last night, I heard those rascals making all sorts of fun of us, and Alf said we ought to let them come to lunch. I scorned the idea, and made their mouths water telling about the good things we were going to have," said Edith, exulting over the severe remarks she had made to these gluttonous young men, who adored pie, yet jeered at unfortunate cooks.

Florence, the lunch-giver of the week, had made her table pretty with a posy at each place, put the necessary roll in each artistically folded napkin, and hung the prize from the gas burner, — a large blue satin bag full of the most delicious bonbons money could buy. There was some delay about beginning, as one distracted cook sent word that her potato-puffs *would n't* brown, and begged them to wait for her. So

they adjourned to the parlor, and talked till the
flushed, but triumphant Ella arrived with the
puffs in fine order.

When all was ready, and the covers raised, another surprise awaited them; not a merry one,
like the last, but a very serious affair, which produced domestic warfare in two houses at least.
On each dish lay a card bearing a new name for
these carefully prepared delicacies. The mince-
pie was re-christened " Nightmare," veal cutlets
" Dyspepsia," escalloped lobster " Fits," lemon
sherbet " Colic," coffee " Palpitation," and so
on, even to the pretty sack of confectionery
which was labelled " Toothache."

Great was the indignation of the insulted
cooks, and a general cry of " Who did it? "
arose. The poor maid who waited on them declared with tears that not a soul had been in,
and she herself only absent five minutes getting
the ice-water. Florence felt that her guests had
been outraged, and promised to find out the
wretch, and punish him or her in the most terrible manner. So the irate young ladies ate
their lunch before it cooled, but forgot to criticise the dishes, so full were they of wonder at
this daring deed. They were just beginning to
calm down, when a loud sneeze caused a general
rush toward the sofa that stood in a recess of
the dining room. A small boy, nearly suffo-
cated with suppressed laughter, and dust, was
dragged forth and put on trial without a mo-

ment's delay. Florence was judge, the others jury, and the unhappy youth being penned in a corner, was ordered to tell the truth, the whole truth, and nothing but the truth, on penalty of a sound whipping with the big Japanese war-fan that hung on the wall over his head.

Vainly trying to suppress his giggles, Phil faced the seven ladies like a man, and told as little as possible, delighting to torment them, like a true boy.

"Do you know who put those cards there?"

"Don't you wish *you* did?"

"Phil Gordon, answer at once."

"Yes, I do."

"Was it Alf? He's at home Saturdays, and it's just like a horrid Harvard Soph to plague us so."

"It was — not."

"Did you see it done?"

"I did."

"Man, or woman? Mary fibs, and may have been bribed."

"Man," with a chuckle of great glee.

"Do I know him?"

"Oh, don't you!"

"Edith's brother Rex?"

"No, ma'am."

"Do be a good boy, and tell us. We won't scold, though it was a very, very rude thing to do."

"What will you give me?"

" Do you need to be bribed to do your duty? "

" Well, I guess it 's no fun to hide in that stuffy place, and smell nice grub, and see you tuck away without offering a fellow a taste. Give me a good go at the lunch, and I 'll see what I can do for you."

" Boys are such pigs! Shall we, girls? "

" Yes, we *must* know."

" Then go and stuff, you bad boy, but we shall stand guard over you till you tell us who wrote and put those insulting cards here."

Florence let out the prisoner, and stood by him while he ate, in a surprisingly short time, the best of everything on the table, well knowing that such a rare chance would not soon be his again.

" Now give me some of that candy, and I 'll tell," demanded the young Shylock, bound to make the best of his power while it lasted.

" Did you ever see such a little torment? I can't give the nice bonbons, because we have n't decided who is to have them."

" Never mind. Pick out a few and get rid of him," cried the girls, hovering round their prey, and longing to shake the truth out of him.

A handful of sweeties were reluctantly bestowed, and then all waited for the name of the evil-doer with breathless interest.

" Well," began Phil, with exasperating slowness, " Alf wrote the cards, and gave me half a dollar to put 'em round. Made a nice thing of it, have n't I?" and before one of the girls could catch him he had bolted from the room, with one hand full of candy, the other of mince-pie, and his face shining with the triumphant glee of a small boy who has teased seven big girls, and got the better of them.

What went on just after that is not recorded, though Phil peeped in at the windows, hooted through the slide, and beat a tattoo on the various doors. The opportune arrival of his mother sent him whooping down the street, and the distressed damsels finished their lunch with what appetite they could.

Edith got the prize, for her pie was pronounced a grand success, and partaken of so copiously that several young ladies had reason to think it well named "Nightmare" by the derisive Alfred. Emboldened by her success, Edith invited them all to her house on the next Saturday, and suggested that she and her cousin provide the lunch, as they had some new dishes to offer, not down in the receipt-book they had been studying all winter.

As the ardor of the young cooks was somewhat damped by various failures, and the discovery that good cooking is an art not easily learned, anything in the way of novelty was welcome; and the girls gladly accepted the invitation, feeling a sense of relief at the thought of not having any dish to worry about, though not one of them owned that she was tired of "messing," as the disrespectful boys called it.

It was unanimously decided to wither with silent scorn the audacious Alfred and his ally, Rex, while Phil was to be snubbed by his sister till he had begged pardon for his share of the evil deed. Then, having sweetened their tongues and tempers with the delicious bonbons, the girls departed, feeling that the next lunch would be an event of unusual interest.

The idea of it originated in a dinner which Patty got one day, when Nancy, who wanted a holiday, was unexpectedly called away to the funeral of a cousin, — the fifth relative who had died in a year, such was the mortality in the jovial old creature's family. Edith's mother was very busy with a dressmaker, and gladly accepted the offer the girls made to get dinner alone.

"No fancy dishes, if you please; the boys come in as hungry as hunters, and want a good solid meal; so get something wholesome and plain, and plenty of it," was the much-relieved lady's only suggestion, as she retired to the sewing-room and left the girls to keep house in their own way.

"Now, Edie, you be the mistress and give your orders, and I'll be cook. Only have things that go well together, — not all baked or all boiled, because there is n't room enough on the range, you know;" said Patty, putting on a big apron with an air of great satisfaction; for she loved to cook, and was tired of doing nothing.

"I'll watch all you do, and learn; so that the next time Nancy goes off in a hurry, I can take her place, and not have to give the boys what they hate, — a picked-up dinner," answered Edith, pleased with her part, yet a little mortified to find how few plain things she could make well.

"What do the boys like?" asked Patty, longing to please them, for they all were very kind to her.

"Roast beef, and custard pudding, with two or three kinds of vegetables. Can we do all that?"

"Yes, indeed. I'll make the pudding right away, and have it baked before the meat goes in. I can cook as many vegetables as you please, and soup too."

So the order was given and all went well, if one might judge by the sounds of merriment in the kitchen. Patty made her best gingerbread, and cooked some apples with sugar and spice for tea, and at the stroke of two had a nice dinner smoking on the table, to the great contentment of the hungry boys, who did eat like hunters, and advised mamma to send old Nancy away and keep Patty for cook; which complimentary but rash proposal pleased their cousin very much.

"Now this is useful cookery, and well done,

though it looks so simple. Any girl can learn
how and be independent of servants, if need be.
Drop your class, Edith, and take a few lessons
of Patty. That would suit me better than
French affairs, that are neither economical nor
wholesome."

"I will, mamma, for I'm tired of creaming
butter, larding things, and beating eggs. These
dishes are not so elegant, but we must have
them; so I may as well learn, if Pat will teach
me."

"With pleasure, all I know. Mother thinks
it a very important part of a girl's education;
for if you can't keep servants you can do your
own work well, and if you are rich you are not
so dependent as an ignorant lady is. All kinds
of useful sewing and housework come first with
us, and the accomplishments afterward, as time
and money allow."

"That sort of thing turns out the kind of
girl I like, and so does every sensible fellow.
Good luck to you, cousin, and my best thanks
for a capital dinner and a wise little lecture for
dessert."

Rex made his best bow as he left the table,
and Patty colored high with pleasure at the
praise of the tall collegian.

Out of this, and the talk the ladies had afterward, grew the lunch which Edith proposed,
and to the preparation of which went much
thought and care; for the girls meant to have

many samples of country fare, so that various tastes might be pleased. The plan gradually grew as they worked, and a little surprise was added, which was a great success.

When Saturday came the younger boys were all packed off for a holiday in the country, that the coast might be clear.

" No hiding under sofas in my house, no meddling with my dinner, if you please, gentlemen," said Edith, as she saw the small brothers safely off, and fell to work with Patty and the maid to arrange the dining-room to suit the feast about to be spread there.

As antique furniture is the fashion now-a-days, it was easy to collect all the old tables, chairs, china, and ornaments in the house, and make a pleasant place of the sunny room where a tall clock always stood; and damask hangings a century old added much to the effect. A massive mahogany table was set forth with ancient silver, glass, china, and all sorts of queer old salt-cellars, pepper-pots, pickel-dishes, knives, and spoons. High-backed chairs stood round it, and the guests were received by a very pretty old lady in plum-colored satin, with a muslin pelerine, and a large lace cap most becoming to the rosy face it surrounded. A fat watch ticked in the wide belt, mitts covered the plump hands, and a reticule hung at the side. Madam's daughter, in a very short-waisted pink silk gown, muslin apron, and frill, was even prettier

than her mother, for her dark, curly hair hung
on her shoulders, and a little cap was stuck on
the top, with long pink streamers. Her mitts
went to the elbow, and a pink sash was tied in
a large bow behind. Black satin shoes covered
her feet, and a necklace of gold beads was round
her throat.

Great was the pleasure this little surprise gave
the girls, and gay was the chatter that went on
as they were welcomed by the hostesses, who
constantly forgot their parts. Madam frisked
now and then, and "Pretty Peggy" was so
anxious about dinner that she was not as devoted to her company as a well-bred young lady
should be. But no one minded, and when the
bell rang, all gathered about the table eager to
see what the feast was to be.

"Ladies, we have endeavored to give you a
taste of some of the good old dishes rather out
of fashion now," said Madam, standing at her
place, with a napkin pinned over the purple
dress, and a twinkle in the blue eyes under the
wide cap-frills. "We thought it would be well
to introduce some of them to the class and to
our family cooks, who either scorn the plain
dishes, or don't know how to cook them *well*.
There is a variety, and we hope all will find
something to enjoy. Peggy, uncover, and let us
begin."

At first the girls looked a little disappointed,
for the dishes were not very new to them; but

when they tasted a real "boiled dinner," and found how good it was; also baked beans, neither hard, greasy, nor burnt; beefsteak, tender, juicy, and well flavored; potatoes, mealy in spite of the season; Indian pudding, made as few modern cooks know how to do it; brown bread, with home-made butter; and pumpkin pie that cut like wedges of vegetable gold, — they changed their minds, and began to eat with appetites that would have destroyed their reputations as delicate young ladies, if they had been seen. Tea in egg-shell cups, election-cake and cream-cheese with fruit ended the dinner; and as they sat admiring the tiny old spoons, the crisp cake, and the little cheeses like snow-balls, Edith said, in reply to various compliments paid her: —

"Let us give honor where honor is due. Patty suggested this, and did most of the cooking; so thank her, and borrow her receipt-book. It's very funny, ever so old, copied and tried by her grandmother, and full of directions for making quantities of nice things, from pie like this to a safe, sure wash for the complexion. May-dew, rose-leaves, and lavender, — does n't that sound lovely?"

"Let me copy it," cried several girls afflicted with freckles, or sallow with too much coffee and confectionery.

"Yes, indeed. But I was going to say, as we have no prize to-day, we have prepared a little souvenir of our old-fashioned dinner for

each of you. Bring them, daughter; I hope the
ladies will pardon the homeliness of the offering, and make use of the hint that accompanies
each."

As Edith spoke, with a comical mingling of
the merry girl and the stately old lady she was
trying to personate, Patty brought from the
side-board, where it had stood covered up, a
silver salver on which lay five dainty little loaves
of bread; on the top of each appeared a receipt
for making the same, nicely written on colored
cards, and held in place by a silver scarf-pin.

"How cunning!" "What lovely pins!"
"I'll take the hint and learn to make good
bread at once." "It smells as sweet as a nut,
and is n't hard or heavy a bit." "Such a pretty
idea, and so clever of you to carry it out so
well."

These remarks went on as the little loaves
went round, each girl finding her pin well suited
to her pet fancy or foible; for all were different,
and all very pretty, whether the design was a
palette, a skate, a pen, a racquet, a fan, a feather,
a bar of music, or a daisy.

Seeing that her dinner was a success in spite
of its homeliness, Edith added the last surprise,
which had also been one to Patty and herself
when it arrived, just in time to be carried out.
She forgot to be Madam now, and said with a
face full of mingled merriment and satisfaction,
as she pushed her cap askew and pulled off her
mitts: —

"Girls, the best joke of all is, that Rex and Alf sent the pins, and made Phil bring them with a most humble apology for their impertinence last week. A meeker boy I never saw, and for that we may thank Floy; but I think the dinner Pat and I got the other day won Rex's heart, so that he made Alf eat humble pie in this agreeable manner. We won't say anything about it, but all wear our pins and show the boys that we can forgive and forget as 'sweet girls' should, though we do cook and have ideas of our own beyond looking pretty and minding our older brothers."

"We will!" cried the chorus with one voice, and Florence added: —

"I also propose that when we have learned to make something besides 'kickshaws,' as the boys call our fancy dishes, we have a dinner like this, and invite those rascals to it; which will be heaping coals of fire on their heads, and stopping their mouths forevermore from making jokes about our cooking-class."

THE HARE AND THE TORTOISE

TRAMP, tramp, tramp! that was the boys going down stairs in a hurry.

Bump, bump! that was the bicycle being zigzagged through the hall.

Bang! that was the front door slamming behind both boys and bicycle, leaving the house quiet for a time, though the sound of voices outside suggested that a lively discussion was going on.

The bicycle fever had reached Perryville, and raged all summer. Now the town was very like a once tranquil pool infested with the long-legged water bugs that go skating over its surface in all directions; for wheels of every kind darted to and fro, startling horses, running over small children, and pitching their riders headlong in the liveliest manner. Men left their business to see the lads try new wheels, women grew skilful in the binding of wounds and the mending of sorely rent garments, gay girls begged for rides, standing on the little step behind, and boys clamored for bicycles that they might join the army of martyrs to the last craze.

Sidney West was the proud possessor of the

best wheel in town, and displayed his treasure with immense satisfaction before the admiring eyes of his mates. He had learned to ride in a city rink, and flattered himself that he knew all there was to learn, except those feats which only professional gymnasts acquire. He mounted with skilful agility, rode with as much grace as the tread-mill movements of the legs permit, and managed to guide his tall steed without much danger to himself or others. The occasional headers he took, and the bruises which kept his manly limbs in a chronic state of mourning he did not mention; but concealed his stiffness heroically, and bound his younger brother to eternal silence by the bribe of occasional rides on the old wheel.

Hugh was a loyal lad, and regarded his big brother as the most remarkable fellow in the world; so he forgave Sid's domineering ways, was a willing slave, a devoted admirer, and a faithful imitator of all the masculine virtues, airs, and graces of this elder brother. On one point only did they disagree, and that was Sid's refusal to give Hugh the old wheel when the new one came. Hugh had fondly hoped it would be his, hints to that effect having been dropped when Sid wanted an errand done, and for weeks the younger boy had waited and labored patiently, sure that his reward would be the small bicycle on which he could proudly take his place as a member of the newly formed club;

with them to set forth, in the blue uniform, with horns blowing, badges glittering, and legs flying, for a long spin, — to return after dark, a mysterious line of tall shadows, "with lanterns dimly burning," and warning whistles sounding as they went.

Great, therefore, was his disappointment and wrath when he discovered that Sid had agreed to sell the wheel to another fellow, if it suited him, leaving poor Hugh the only boy of his set without a machine. Much as he loved Sid, he could not forgive this underhand and mercenary transaction. It seemed so unbrotherly to requite such long and willing service, to dash such ardent hopes, to betray such blind confidence, for filthy lucre; and when the deed was done, to laugh, and ride gayly away on the splendid British Challenge, the desire of all hearts and eyes.

This morning Hugh had freely vented his outraged feelings, and Sid had tried to make light of the affair, though quite conscious that he had been both unkind and unfair. A bicycle tournament was to take place in the city, twenty miles away, and the members of the club were going. Sid, wishing to distinguish himself, intended to ride thither, and was preparing for the long trip with great care. Hugh was wild to go, but having spent his pocket-money and been forbidden to borrow, he could not take the cars as the others had done; no horse was to be had, and their own stud consisted of an old donkey, who would have been hopeless even with the inducement offered in the immortal ditty, —

> " If I had a donkey that would n't go,
> Do you think I 'd whip him ? Oh, no, no !
> I 'd take him to Jarley's Wax-work Show."

Therefore poor Hugh was in a desperate state of mind as he sat on the gate-post watching Sid make his pet's toilet, till every plated handle, rod, screw, and axle shone like silver.

"I know I could have ridden the Star if you had n't let Joe have it. I do think it was right down mean of you; so does Aunt Ruth, and father too, — only he won't say so, because men always stand by one another, and snub boys."

This was strong language for gentle Hugh, but he felt that he must vent his anguish in some way or cry like a girl; and that disgrace must be avoided, even if he failed in respect to his elders.

Sid was whistling softly as he oiled and rubbed, but he was not feeling as easy as he looked, and heartily wished that he had not committed himself to Joe, for it would have been pleasant to take "the little chap," as he called the fourteen-year-older, along with him, and do the honors of the rink on this great occasion. Now it was too late; so he affected a careless air, and added insult to injury by answering his brother's reproaches in the joking spirit which is peculiarly exasperating at such moments.

"Children should n't play with matches, nor small boys with bicycles. I don't want to commit murder, and I certainly should if I let you try to ride twenty miles when you can't go one without nearly breaking your neck, or your knees," and Sid glanced with a smile at the neat darns which ornamented his brother's trousers over those portions of his long legs.

"How 's a fellow going to learn if he is n't allowed to try? Might as well tell me to keep away from the water till I can swim. You give me a chance and see if I can't ride as well as some older fellows who have been pitched round pretty lively before *they* dared to try a twenty-mile spin," answered Hugh, clapping both hands on his knees to hide the tell-tale darns.

"If Joe does n't want it, you can use the old wheel till I decide what to do with it. I suppose a man has a right to sell his own property if he likes," said Sid, rather nettled at the allusion to his own tribulations in times past.

"Of course he has; but if he 's promised to give a thing he ought to do it, and not sneak out of the bargain after he 's got lots of work done to pay for it. That 's what makes me mad; for I believed you and depended on it, and it hurts me more to have you deceive me than it would to lose ten bicycles;" and Hugh choked a little at the thought, in spite of his attempt to look sternly indignant.

"You are welcome to your opinion, but I would n't cry about it. Play with chaps of your own size and don't hanker after men's property. Take the cars, if you want to go so much, and stop bothering me," retorted Sid, getting cross because he was in the wrong and would n't own it.

"You know I can't! No money, and must n't borrow. What's the use of twitting a fellow like that?" and Hugh with great difficulty refrained from knocking off the new helmet-hat which was close to his foot as Sid bent to inspect the shining hub of the cherished wheel.

"Take Sancho, then; you might arrive before the fun was all over, if you carried whips and pins and crackers enough to keep the old boy going; you'd be a nice span."

This allusion to the useless donkey was cruel, but Hugh held on to the last remnant of his temper, and made a wild proposal in the despair of the moment.

"Don't be a donkey yourself. See here, why can't we ride and tie? I've tried this wheel, and got on tip-top. You'd be along to see to me, and we'd take turns. Do, Sid! I want to go awfully, and if you only will I won't say another word about Joe."

But Sid only burst out laughing at the plan, in the most heartless manner.

"No, thank you. I don't mean to walk a step when I can ride; or lend my new wheel to a chap who can hardly keep right side up on the old one. It looks like a jolly plan to you, I dare say, but *I* don't see it, young man."

" I hope *I* sha'n't be a selfish brute when I 'm seventeen. I 'll have a bicycle yet, — A, No. 1, — and then you 'll see how I 'll lend it, like a gentleman, and not insult other fellows because they happen to be two or three years younger."

" Keep cool, my son, and don't call names. If you are such a smart lad, why don't you walk, since wheels and horses and donkeys fail. It 's *only* twenty miles — nothing to speak of, you know."

" Well, I could do it if I liked. I 've walked eighteen, and was n't half so tired as you were. Any one can get over the ground on a bicycle, but it takes strength and courage to keep it up on foot."

" Better try it."

" I will, some day."

" Don't crow too loud, my little rooster; you are not cock of the walk yet."

" If I was, I would n't hit a fellow when he 's down; " and fearing he should kick over the tall bicycle that stood so temptingly near him, Hugh walked away, trying to whistle, though his lips were more inclined to tremble than to pucker.

" Just bring my lunch, will you? Auntie is putting it up; I must be off," called Sid, so used to giving orders that he did so even at this un-propitious moment.

" Get it yourself. I'm not going to slave for you any longer, old tyrant," growled Hugh; for the trodden worm turned at last, as worms will.

This was open revolt, and Sid felt that things were in a bad way, but would not stop to mend them then.

" Whew! here's a tempest in a teapot. Well, it is too bad; but I can't help it now. I'll make it all right to-morrow, and bring him round with a nice account of the fun. Hullo, Bemis! going to town?" he called, as a neighbor came spinning noiselessly by.

" Part way, and take the cars at Lawton. It's hard riding over the hills, and a bother to steer a wheel through the streets. Come on, if you're ready."

" All right; " and springing up, Sid was off, forgetting all about the lunch.

Hugh, dodging behind the lilac-bushes, heard what passed, and the moment they were gone ran to the gate to watch them out of sight with longing eyes, then turned away, listlessly wondering how he should spend the holiday his brother was going to enjoy so much.

At that moment Aunt Ruth hurried to the door, waving the leathern pouch well stored with cake and sandwiches, cold coffee and pie.

" Sid's forgotten his bag. Run, call, stop him!" she cried, trotting down the walk with her cap-strings waving wildly in the fresh October wind.

For an instant Hugh hesitated, thinking sullenly, " Serves him right. I won't run after him; " then his kind heart got the better of his bad humor, and catching up the bag he raced down the road at his best pace, eager to heap coals of fire on Sid's proud head, — to say nothing of his own desire to see more of the riders.

" They will have to go slowly up the long hill, and I 'll catch them then," he thought as he tore over the ground, for he was a good runner and prided himself on his strong legs.

Unfortunately for his amiable intentions, the boys had taken a short cut to avoid the hill, and were out of sight down a lane where Hugh never dreamed they would dare to go, so mounted.

" Well, they have done well to get over the hill at this rate. Guess they won't keep it up long," panted Hugh, stopping short when he saw no signs of the riders.

The road stretched invitingly before him, the race had restored his spirits, and curiosity to see what had become of his friends lured him to the hill-top, where temptation sat waiting for him. Up he trudged, finding the fresh air, the sunny sky, the path strewn with red and yellow leaves, and the sense of freedom so pleasant that when he reached the highest point and saw the world all before him, as it were, a daring project seemed to flash upon him, nearly taking his breath away with its manifold delights.

" Sid said, ' Walk,' and why not? — at least
to Lawton, and take the cars from there, as
Bemis means to do. Would n't the old fellows
be surprised to see me turn up at the rink? It 's
quarter past eight now, and the fun begins at
three; I could get there easy enough, and by
Jupiter, I will! Got lunch all here, and money
enough to pay this car-fare, I guess. If I
have n't, I 'll go a little further and take a horse-
car. What a lark! here goes," — and with a
whoop of boyish delight at breaking bounds,
away went Hugh down the long hill, like a colt
escaped from its pasture.

The others were just ahead, but the windings
of the road hid them from him; so all went on,
unconscious of each other's proximity. Hugh's
run gave him a good start, and he got over the
ground famously for five or six miles; then he
went more slowly, thinking he had plenty of
time to catch a certain train. But he had no
watch, and when he reached Lawton he had the
pleasure of seeing the cars go out at one end of
the station as he hurried in at the other.

" I won't give it up, but just go on and do
it afoot. That will be something to brag of
when the other chaps tell big stories. I 'll see
how fast I can go, for I 'm not tired, and can eat
on the way. Much obliged to Sid for a nice
lunch."

And chuckling over this piece of good luck,
Hugh set out again, only pausing for a good

drink at the town-pump. The thirteen miles
did not seem very long when he thought of
them, but as he walked them they appeared to
grow longer and longer, till he felt as if he must
have travelled about fifty. He was in good
practice, and fortunately had on easy shoes; but
he was in such a hurry to make good time that
he allowed himself no rest, and jogged on, up
hill and down, with the resolute air of one walking for a wager. There we will leave him, and
see what had befallen Sid; for his adventures
were more exciting than Hugh's, though all
seemed plain sailing when he started.

At Lawton he had parted from his friend and
gone on alone, having laid in a store of ginger-
bread from a baker's cart, and paused to eat,
drink, and rest by a wayside brook. A few
miles further he passed a party of girls playing
lawn tennis, and as he slowly rolled along regarding them from his lofty perch, one suddenly
exclaimed : —

"Why, it's our neighbor, Sidney West!
How did *he* come here?" and waving her racquet, Alice ran across the lawn to find out.

Very willing to stop and display his new uniform, which was extremely becoming, Sid dis-
mounted, doffed his helmet, and smiled upon
the damsels, leaning over the hedge like a knight
of old.

"Come in and play a game, and have some
lunch. You will have plenty of time, and some

of us are going to the rink by and by. Do, we want a boy to help us, for Maurice is too lazy, and Jack has hurt his hand with that stupid base ball," said Alice, beckoning persuasively, while the other girls nodded and smiled hopefully.

Thus allured, the youthful Ulysses hearkened to the voice of the little Circe in a round hat, and entered the enchanted grove, to forget the passage of time as he disported himself among the nymphs. He was not changed to a beast, as in the immortal story, though the three young gentlemen did lie about the lawn in somewhat grovelling attitudes; and Alice waved her racquet as if it were a wand, while her friends handed glasses of lemonade to the recumbent heroes during pauses in the game.

While thus blissfully engaged, time slipped away, and Hugh passed him in the race, quite unconscious that his brother was reposing in the tent that looked so inviting as the dusty, tired boy plodded by, counting every mile-stone with increasing satisfaction.

"If I get to Uncle Tim's by one o'clock, I shall have done very well. Four miles an hour is a fair pace, and only one stop. I 'll telegraph to auntie as soon as I arrive; but she won't worry, she 's used to having us turn up all right when we get ready," thought Hugh, grateful that no over-anxious mamma was fretting about his long absence. The boys had no mother, and Aunt Ruth was an easy old lady who let them do as they liked, to their great contentment.

As he neared his journey's end our traveller's spirits rose, and the blisters on his heels were forgotten in the dramatic scene his fancy painted, when Sid should discover him at Uncle Tim's, or calmly seated at the rink. Whistling gayly, he was passing through a wooded bit of road when the sound of voices made him look back to see a carriage full of girls approaching, escorted by a bicycle rider, whose long blue legs looked strangely familiar.

Anxious to keep his secret till the last moment, also conscious that he was not in company trim, Hugh dived into the wood, out of sight, while the gay party went by, returning to the road as soon as they were hidden by a bend.

"If Sid had n't been so mean, I should have been with him, and had some of the fun. I don't feel like forgiving him in a hurry for making me foot it, like a tramp, while he is having such a splendid time."

If Hugh could have known what was to happen very soon after he had muttered these words to himself, as he wiped his hot face, and took the last sip of the coffee to quench his thirst, he would have been sorry he uttered them, and have forgiven his brother everything.

While he was slowly toiling up the last long hill, Sid was coasting down on the other side, eager to display his courage and skill before the girls, — being of an age when boys begin to wish to please and astonish the gentler creatures whom they have hitherto treated with indifference or contempt. It was a foolish thing to do, for the road was rough, with steep banks on either side, and a sharp turn at the end; but Sid rolled gayly along, with an occasional bump, till a snake ran across the road, making the horse shy, the girls scream, the rider turn to see what was the matter, and in doing so lose his balance just when a large stone needed to be avoided. Over went Sid, down rattled the wheel, up rose a cloud of dust, and sudden silence fell upon the girls at sight of this disaster. They expected their gallant escort would spring up and laugh over his accident; but when he remained flat upon his back, where he had alighted after a somersault, with the bicycle spread over him like a pall, they were alarmed, and flew to the rescue.

A cut on the forehead was bleeding, and the blow had evidently stunned him for a moment. Luckily, a house was near, and a man seeing the accident hastened to offer more efficient help than any the girls had wit enough to give in the first flurry, as all four only flapped wildly at Sid with their handkerchiefs, and exclaimed excitedly: —

"What shall we do? Is he dead? Run for water. Call somebody, quick."

"Don't be scat, gals; it takes a sight of thumpin' to break a boy's head. He ain't hurt much; kinder dazed for a minute. I'll hist up this pesky *mas*hine and set him on his legs, if he hain't damaged 'em."

With these cheering words, the farmer cleared away the ruins, and propped the fallen rider against a tree; which treatment had such a good effect that Sid was himself in a moment, and much disgusted to find what a scrape he was in.

" This is nothing, a mere bump; quite right, thanks. Let us go on at once; so sorry to alarm you, ladies." He began his polite speech bravely, but ended with a feeble smile and a clutch at the tree, suddenly turning sick and dizzy again.

" You come along a me. I 'll tinker you and your whirligig up, young man. No use sayin' go ahead, for the thing is broke, and you want to keep quiet for a spell. Drive along, gals, I 'll see to him; and my old woman can nuss him better 'n a dozen flutterin' young things scat half to death."

Taking matters into his own hands, the farmer had boy and bicycle under his roof in five minutes; and with vain offers of help, many regrets, and promises to let his Uncle Tim know where he was, in case he did not arrive, the girls reluctantly drove away, leaving no sign of the catastrophe except the trampled road, and a dead snake.

Peace was hardly restored when Hugh came down the hill, little dreaming what had happened, and for the second time passed his brother, who just then was lying on a sofa in the farm-house, while a kind old woman adorned his brow with a large black plaster, suggesting brown paper steeped in vinegar, for the various bruises on his arms and legs.

"Some one killed the snake and made a great fuss about it, I should say," thought Hugh, observing the signs of disorder in the dust; but, resisting a boy's interest in such affairs, he stoutly tramped on, sniffing the whiffs of sea air that now and then saluted his nose, telling him that he was nearing his much-desired goal.

Presently the spires of the city came in sight, to his great satisfaction, and only the long bridge and a street or two lay between him and Uncle Tim's easy chair, into which he soon hoped to cast himself.

Half-way across the bridge a farm-wagon passed, with a bicycle laid carefully on the barrels of vegetables going to market. Hugh gazed affectionately at it, longing to borrow it for one brief, delicious spin to the bridge end. Had he known that it was Sid's broken wheel, going to be repaired without loss of time, thanks to the good farmer's trip to town, he would have paused to have a hearty laugh, in spite of his vow not to stop till his journey was over.

Just as Hugh turned into the side street where Uncle Tim lived, a horse-car went by, in one corner of which sat a pale youth, with a battered hat drawn low over his eyes, who handed out his ticket with the left hand, and frowned when the car jolted, as if the jar hurt him. Had he looked out of the window, he would have seen a very dusty boy, with a pouch over his shoulder, walking smartly down the street where his relation lived. But Sid carefully turned his head aside, fearing to be recognized; for he was on his way to a certain club to which Bemis belonged, preferring his sympathy and hospitality to the humiliation of having his mishap told at home by Uncle Tim, who would be sure to take Hugh's part, and exult over the downfall of the proud. Well for him that he avoided that comfortable mansion; for on the door-steps stood Hugh, beaming with satisfaction as the clock struck one, proclaiming that he had done his twenty miles in a little less than five hours.

"Not bad for a 'little chap,' even though he is 'a donkey,'" chuckled the boy, dusting his shoes, wiping his red face, and touching himself up as well as he could, in order to present as fresh and unwearied an aspect as possible, when he burst upon his astonished brother's sight.

In he marched when the door opened, to find his uncle and two rosy cousins just sitting down to dinner. Always glad to see the lads, they gave him a cordial welcome, and asked for his brother.

"Hasn't he come yet?" cried Hugh, surprised, yet glad to be the first on the field.

Nothing had been seen of him, and Hugh at once told his tale, to the great delight of his jolly uncle, and the admiring wonder of Meg and May, the rosy young cousins. They all enjoyed the exploit immensely, and at once insisted that the pedestrian should be refreshed by a bath, a copious meal, and a good rest in the big chair, where he repeated his story by particular request.

"You deserve a bicycle, and you shall have one, as sure as my name is Timothy West. I like pluck and perseverance, and you've got both; so come on, my boy, and name the wheel you like best. Sid needs a little taking down, as you lads say, and this will give it to him, I fancy. I'm a younger brother myself, and I know what their trials are."

As his uncle made these agreeable remarks, Hugh looked as if *his* trials were all over; for his face shone with soap and satisfaction, his hunger was quenched by a splendid dinner, his tired feet luxuriated in a pair of vast slippers, and the blissful certainty of owning a first-class bicycle filled his cup to overflowing. Words could hardly express his gratitude, and nothing but the hope of meeting Sid with this glorious news would have torn him from the reposeful Paradise where he longed to linger. Pluck and perseverance, with cold cream on the blistered heels, got him into his shoes again, and he rode away in a horse-car, as in a triumphal chariot, to find his brother.

"I won't brag, but I do feel immensely tickled at this day's work. Wonder how he got on. Did it in two or three hours, I suppose, and is parading round with those swell club fellows at the rink. I 'll slip in and let him find me, as if I was n't a bit proud of what I 've done, and did n't care two pins for anybody's praise."

With this plan in his head, Hugh enjoyed the afternoon very much; keeping a sharp lookout for Sid, even while astonishing feats were being performed before his admiring eyes. But no-where did he see his brother; for he was search-ing for a blue uniform and a helmet with a cer-tain badge on it, while Sid in a borrowed hat and coat sat in a corner looking on, whenever a splitting headache and the pain in his bones allowed him to see and enjoy the exploits in which he had hoped to join.

Not until it was over did the brothers meet, as they went out, and then the expression on Sid's face was so comical that Hugh laughed till the crowd about them stared, wondering what the joke could be.

" How in the world did *you* get here?" asked the elder boy, giving his hat a sudden pull to hide the plaster.

" Walked, as you advised me to."

Words cannot express the pleasure that an-swer gave Hugh, or the exultation he vainly tried to repress, as his eyes twinkled and a grin of real boyish fun shone upon his sunburnt coun-tenance.

" You expect me to believe that, do you?"

" Just as you please. I started to catch you with your bag, and when I missed you, thought

I might as well keep on. Got in about one, had dinner at uncle's, and been enjoying these high jinks ever since."

"Very well, for a beginning. Keep it up and you'll be a Rowell by and by. What do you suppose father will say to you, small boy?"

"Not much. Uncle will make that all right. *He* thought it was a plucky thing to do, and so did the girls. When did you get in?" asked Hugh, rather nettled at Sid's want of enthusiasm, though it was evident he was much impressed by the "small boy's" prank.

"I took it easy after Bemis left me. Had a game of tennis at the Blanchards' as I came along, dinner at the club, and strolled up here with the fellows. Got a headache, and don't feel up to much."

As Sid spoke and Hugh's keen eye took in the various signs of distress which betrayed a hint of the truth, the grin changed to a hearty " Ha! ha!" as he smote his knees exclaiming gleefully, "You've come to grief! I know it, I see it. Own up, and don't shirk, for I'll find it out somehow, as sure as you live."

"Don't make such a row in the street. Get aboard this car and I'll tell you, for you'll give me no peace till I do," answered Sid, well knowing that Alice would never keep the secret.

To say that it was "nuts" to Hugh faintly expresses the interest he took in the story which was extracted bit by bit from the reluctant suf-

ferer; but after a very pardonable crow over
the mishaps of his oppressor, he yielded to the
sympathy he felt for his brother, and was very
good to him.

This touched Sid, and filled him with remorse
for past unkindness; for one sees one's faults
very plainly, and is not ashamed to own it, when
one is walking through the Valley of Humiliation.

"Look here, I'll tell you what I'll do," he
said, as they left the car, and Hugh offered an
arm, with a friendly air pleasant to see. "I'll
give you the old wheel, and let Joe get another
where he can. It's small for him, and I doubt
if he wants it, any way. I do think you were
a plucky fellow to tramp your twenty miles in
good time, and not bear malice either, so let's
say 'Done,' and forgive and forget."

"Much obliged, but uncle is going to give
me a new one; so Joe need n't be disappointed.
I know how hard that is, and am glad to keep
him from it, for he's poor and can't afford a
new one."

That answer was Hugh's only revenge for his
own trials, and Sid felt it, though he merely
said, with a hearty slap on the shoulder, —

"Glad to hear it. Uncle is a trump, and so
are you. We'll take the last train home, and
I'll pay your fare."

"Thank you. Poor old man, you did get a
bump, did n't you?" exclaimed Hugh, as they

took off their hats in the hall, and the patch appeared in all its gloomy length and breadth.

"Head will be all right in a day or two, but I stove in my helmet, and ground a hole in both knees of my new shorts. Had to borrow a fitout of Bemis, and leave my rags behind. We need n't mention any more than is necessary to the girls; I hate to be fussed over," answered Sid, trying to speak carelessly.

Hugh had to stop and have another laugh, remembering the taunts his own mishaps had called forth; but he did not retaliate, and Sid never forgot it. Their stay was a short one, and Hugh was the hero of the hour, quite eclipsing his brother, who usually took the first place, but now very meekly played second fiddle, conscious that he was not an imposing figure, in a coat much too big for him, with a patch on his forehead, a purple bruise on one cheek, and a general air of dilapidation very trying to the usually spruce youth.

When they left, Uncle Tim patted Hugh on the head, — a liberty the boy would have resented if the delightful old gentleman had not followed it up by saying, with a reckless generosity worthy of record, —

"Choose your bicycle, my boy, and send the bill to me." Then turning to Sid he added, in a tone that made the pale face redden suddenly, "And do you remember that the tortoise beat the hare in the old fable we all know."

"That is the last of the stories, for our holiday is over, and to-morrow we must go home. We have had a splendid time, and thank you and aunties so much, dear grandma," said Min, expressing the feeling of all the children, as they stood about the fire when the bicycle tale ended.

"I'm so glad, my darlings, and please God we'll all meet here again next year, well and happy and ready for more fun," answered the old lady, with arms and lap full of loving little people.

"Auntie deserves a vote of thanks, and I rise to propose it," said Geoff; and it was passed with great applause.

"Many thanks. If the odds and ends in my portfolio have given you pleasure or done you any good, my fondest wishes are gratified," answered Aunt Elinor, laughing, yet well pleased. "I tucked a moral in, as we hide pills in jelly, and I hope you did n't find them hard to swallow."

"Very easy and nice. I intend to look after little things faithfully, and tell the girls how to make their jerseys fit," said Min.

"I'm going to fill my jewel-box as Daisy did, and learn to cook," added Lotty.

"Eli is the boy for me, and I won't forget to be kind to *my* small chap," said Walt, stroking his younger brother's head with unusual kindness.

"Well, I'm rather mixed in my heroes, but

I 'll take the best of Corny, Onawandah, and the banner fellow for my share," cried Geoff.

The little people proclaimed their favorites; but as all spoke together, only a comical mixture of doves, bears, babies, table-cloths and blue hose reached the ear. Then came the good-night kisses, the patter of departing feet, and silence fell upon the room. The little wheel was still, the chairs stood empty, the old portraits looked sadly down, the fire died out, and the Spinning-Wheel Stories were done.

THE END.